SCREAMING BONES

A CRIME CLUB BOOK

PUBLISHED BY DOUBLEDAY
a division of Bantam Doubleday Dell Publishing Group, Inc.
666 Fifth Avenue, New York, New York 10103

DOUBLEDAY and the portrayal of a man
with a gun are trademarks of Doubleday,
a division of Bantam Doubleday Dell
Publishing Group, Inc.

Library of Congress Cataloging-in-Publication Data
Burden, Pat.
    Screaming bones / Pat Burden.
        p.   cm.
    "A Crime Club book."
    I. Title.
    PR6052.U614S37   1990
    823'.914—dc20   90-3622
                                                          CIP
ISBN 0-385-41522-2
Copyright © 1989 by Pat Burden
All Rights Reserved

Printed in the United States of America
December 1990
First Edition in the United States of America

SCREAMING BONES

PAT BURDEN

A Crime Club Book

DOUBLEDAY

New York   London   Toronto   Sydney   Auckland

The Bronsil Castle legend is on record; so too the fact of the Civil War and the battle that took place on Jack the Poacher's territory; but whether the unfortunate Gurney ever existed has yet to be proved.

SCREAMING BONES

CHAPTER 1

It was a crisp sunny November morning, perfect for walking, so Helen Geeson parked her Suzuki jeep on the first wide stretch of grass verge she came to in Long Lane and went the remaining half-mile to Keeper's Cottage on foot. Keeper's Cottage stood on one side of the lane, its garage, outbuildings, and a restored pigsty on the other. She reached the pigsty first, attracted to that side of the lane by sounds of a human voice and chuckles and not-so-human grunts, snuffles, and squeals of delight. She went right up to the wall, stood on tiptoe and peered over. Three fat faces gazed back at her. "Oh—" She smiled. "I'm looking for Mr. Bassett."

One of the faces spoke. "I'm Bassett, the one with the hat."

It was an appropriate remark, since Bassett was crouching, on a level with his pigs. He stood up and straightened the hat, a battered old bush hat, slightly less grubby than the khaki smock worn over a thick polo-necked sweater, baggy corduroys, and wellington boots. Helen half grinned and looked away.

"What healthy-looking pigs—" she began admiringly.

"Want to be introduced?" Bassett slapped the nearest pig, a gilt, affectionately on its plump pink back. "This one's Miss Piggy. You can maybe see the resemblance?" He had automatically reached for the yard broom leaning against the inner gate: Miss Piggy promptly transferred her attention to the bristles and began eating them; he pushed her gently off. "And this is Barrington-Smythe. One brown eye, one blue, and snowy white eyelashes, see? Reminds me of a chap, a lawyer, I once knew . . ."

"Your lawyer friend has odd eyes?"

"No. But the rest of him fits." He grinned towards Helen Geeson's laughing gaze.

○

She liked him, liked the absence of self-importance; and understood why he and his wife had been accepted so readily into the village community.

Helen had met his wife, Mary, but not until now the man himself. Ex–Detective Chief Superintendent Henry Bassett. Mary had described him endearingly: "He hates being called Henry, doesn't mind Harry, prefers to be called Bassett, even by me. And if that conjures up a picture of a floppy-eared, soft-jowled, lovable hound with a deliciously mournful face and expressive eyes he can produce on cue—that's as near as darn it my husband."

From Mary, Helen had learnt how the Bassetts had fallen in love with the Cotswolds and the Malverns while on a touring holiday, how they had "found" this area of unspoilt countryside where the counties of Worcestershire, Herefordshire and Gloucestershire meet, and how lucky they considered themselves when they acquired Keeper's Cottage, their retirement haven. Its very name bespoke a situation among ancient woodland; and with half the land around them safeguarded by the Malvern Hills Trust and the other half owned by a landowner mindful of conservation there was scant likelihood, in their lifetime at any rate, of their being uprooted by motorways and office blocks. "Of course the very fact that little seems to have changed here for decades led us to wonder . . ." Mary had confided. "Not everyone appreciates a policeman living in the neighbourhood, retired or not."

But the Bassetts were such friendly souls—"No side on her" was the consensus regarding Mary; and the ex-policeman about whom Tod Arkwright, local gloom and doom merchant, had rumbled darkly, "Once a copper allus a copper . . ." was soon being referred to as a "decent bloke." It wasn't long before the Bassetts were swapping bean plants for tomatoes, cabbages for lettuces, had received advice on how to get eighty-five per cent egg production from their hens, and Bassett had developed the habit of making regular trips to the front gate to do his country yokel bit. No offence intended, he merely donned his tatty hat, stuck a match in his mouth like a straw, and chatted to passers-by. Some days there was none, they lived so isolated; then Bassett would return to wherever Mary was working, shaking his head and telling her, "Like Piccadilly Circus out there, all rush . . ." And after being in towns and cities all their working lives they loved it, the peace and the quiet.

A year of untold happiness and all the time in the world to spend with each other were all Bassett and Mary were allowed: before Bassett got round to clearing their second summer's crop of nettles Mary had been taken ill; and died.

"I'm sorry about your wife," Helen began now.

Bassett looked at her with interest. Who was she? How did she know?

She answered the unspoken question: "I'm Helen. Helen Geeson?"

Bassett stared a moment, then jabbed the air between them with a mittened hand. "Labradors! We've spoken on the phone!"

Helen nodded, gave a small self-conscious laugh. "Yes." When Mary Bassett was alive, when they had both wanted a dog. Their "order" had been cancelled when Mary's condition had worsened. Afterwards there had been some doubt as to whether Bassett would stay.

"You don't look like a dog-breeder," he said impulsively. Most breeders he'd met were inclined to be horsey, or at least had been short on youth and beauty, whereas this was one attractive lady. Silky blonde hair arranged in a bun; healthy skin that required no make-up; chunky cream and tan sweater that gleamed fresh and clean and sweet-smelling under the sun. Worn with a belt, model-girl style, he guessed.

"You don't look like a police officer!" she countered, laughing.

"Ah! That's probably because I'm not. I'm a countryman now. Trying to be." Bassett patted the rump of the pig now using his legs as a rubbing-board. "Tame as tame, this one. Rolls on to her back to have her belly tickled, just like a dog. But you can't share your fireside with a pig, can you? Good grief!" The reason for Helen Geeson's visit suddenly dawned on Bassett. "I'm a mite slow this morning. Someone's told you I've been talking again about a pup!"

A nod. "Jack Carter."

"And you've come to vet me—if you'll pardon the expression."

"Well . . ." Helen couldn't help but grin.

"Quite right too! Got to be sure I'll make a suitable pet-owner." Bassett made a token sweep with the broom, uttered a cheerful promise to the pigs to return, left the sty, bolted the inner gate behind him, and came round to his visitor. He was right about the sweater, it was belted in at the waist, over a full smooth tweed skirt that flowed with the movements of her body as she walked. "What shoes are you wearing?" He glanced down. "Sensible ones. Want to come with me while I check these two's dinner? Then I'll brew us some coffee and produce me credentials."

They crossed the lane to Keeper's Cottage. He took her in the back way through a heavy gate which creaked under its own weight when swung open, along a covered walk lined with climbing roses, and up to where a huge boiler, the kind great-grandmother cooked her washing in, stood on the edge of what was otherwise an immaculate lawn. A fire glowed red at the base; steam escaped from around the lid; pleasant odours emanated.

"Potatoes, milled barley, and corn," Bassett said shyly. "Best way to get old-fashioned crackling, they tell me. Not sure I'll ever find out, though. Seems cannibalistic, eating pigs you've known by name . . ."

"Especially a Barrington-Smythe."

Bassett smiled into Helen's laughing eyes. "I feel guilty eating their eggs—" meaning Gert and Daisy, two busy brown hens who had come in search of pickings. He raised the lid of the boiler, tested the contents. "Ten minutes will do it. Mind if I stoke up? Then I can leave it to finish off on its own."

Helen Geeson not only didn't mind, to Bassett's mild amazement she rolled up her sleeves and fed wood chips into the fire as he chopped them.

"Do you ever miss your detective work?" she inquired.

"I did, after Mary died. I was all set to pack my bags and return whence I came. Used to daydream about reunions with old colleagues, popping into the office for a chinwag, joining the lads for a beer, and of course, poking my nose in—solving their cases for them. Fortunately common sense prevailed. I'd soon have worn out the welcome. Retired personnel who refuse to let go are a pain in the neck . . . Besides, they're a good crowd here, the people—too good to lose. In fact I sometimes feel I'm living in a different world. If it weren't for newspapers and television I could easily believe there was no such thing as crime."

"Nothing much happens here, you mean," Helen said, reaching for a handful of sticks.

They smiled at each other.

"Yet wasn't it Sherlock Holmes who said that crime was easier in the country?"

Bassett paused from chipping with his axe. "Easier to conceal, certainly."

"Conceal. Yes, of course. It's ages since I read Sherlock."

"If I remember correctly," Bassett said conversationally, "the example Holmes gave was of someone held prisoner in the attic of a lonely country house."

"Yes . . ." Helen smiled up from her stooping position. "Who —he asked Watson—would hear a prisoner's cries for help?"

A few more sticks went into the flames.

"I was never without a dog when I was a nipper," Bassett said, when they were drinking the coffee Helen had made while he washed and made himself presentable. "Grew up with them. Thought they came as part of the family. You know, when you were born there they were—mother, father, and a dog or two . . . Had a collie when I married Mary. Named Ruff. When he died we postponed having another. Towns and cities are no places for dogs, not big dogs; and I'm a big-dog man. But now— here's the countryside, acres of unfenced romping land. Plus a garden for a playground. And I'm not garden proud."

Which went without saying, Helen thought, casting an amused mind's-eye glance at the boiler on his back lawn.

He couldn't bring himself to speak of the looked-forward-to pleasure of having a warm little body to snuggle up against his on cold winter nights, of eternal companionship, of a friend ever there to love and be loved . . . So he quietly sold himself as worthy; and it did not occur to either of them to think there was anything odd about a one-time Detective Chief Superintendent of police doing this.

But if Helen Geeson let him carry on longer than was necessary, it was because she enjoyed listening to him. For his voice had that confident and soothing quality known to comfort fretful babies, calm restless animals, and restore order where disorder might reign.

"Do I pass muster?" he said at last.

"You always did. You had my approval before I came. I confess I was curious to know if you planned to stay; if not I was going to warn you that labradors need loads of exercise and space—but you obviously know already. What I really came for," said Helen, wide-eyed, "was to tell you I have a litter, only four weeks old, not ready yet, but dying to make your acquaintance. If you'd like to come and choose one . . . ?"

"Or better still have one choose me . . . ?" Eyebrows arched.

"You *do* know dogs." Helen nodded, warmed by the way Bassett's face lit up. "Only one problem—all the males are earmarked for gun dogs."

"A bitch will suit me admirably. When can I come?"

"This afternoon?"

A time was agreed. Helen Geeson prepared to leave. "I'd better go. Your pigfood—"

"Oh, I have to cool it down anyway. Too hot and they whittle at me."

"You spoil them," Helen said, laughing.

"I'm glad you're friends with Jack Carter, by the way," Helen said as Bassett escorted her to the front gate. "I haven't seen nearly enough of him myself since he came back."

"Came back?" Bassett queried.

"Yes . . ." She looked sidelong at Bassett, prompted by something in his voice.

"I didn't know Jack had ever been away," he said. "I was under the impression that, war years apart, he'd lived in these parts all his life."

"No. Far from it. He spent his childhood here; and his teens. Then came the war—and Jack joined up as soon as he was old enough, half way through. He came back for a year, maybe less, then went off again. For good, everybody thought—until he turned up out of the blue three or four years ago." Another sidelong look towards Bassett. "You seem surprised."

"I am. He's so knowledgeable about this area. So well-informed he seems to be a part of the scenery. I quite thought he'd made a lifetime study . . ."

Helen nodded. "I think he did. When he was young. He knew every inch of these hills and woods. And not a great deal has changed, as you can perhaps see." She waved a hand to encompass the views: everywhere green or shades of autumn gold. "Some of the woods are smaller, a few hedges have disappeared, but no major alterations have taken place. No brand-new houses. No street lighting. Half the cottages still have no mains for water and sewerage. This lane—I can remember when it was a dirt track. Even the people are basically the same. Same families, I mean. Jessie, Tod Arkwright, Charlie Allsop, and his mother, to name but four, were all here when Jack left. They have simply grown older, like him."

They both smiled. "I for one never expected to see him again," Helen said. "He had little to thank anyone for. If he ever did come back, I used to think, it would be as the stinkingly rich 'local boy makes good' arrived to thumb his nose at old adversaries. Or as my father was accustomed to say: He'll turn up in his Rolls-Royce on a filthy wet day to splash us peasants with mud."

Once more a smile. Bassett noticed the hint of a dimple this time. And now a faint flush as she realized he was staring at her. "Forgive me," he said, "but the war ended forty years ago. You hardly look old enough—"

"To have known Jack in those days? I was only a little girl, yes," she confessed. "But I was what my mother used to call old-headed, and a little Miss Big-Ears to boot. I liked to know what was going on." She lowered her tone to an almost childlike whisper. "To be truthful, I had a soft spot for Jack. I secretly admired him tremendously in spite of what he was.

"And now I really must dash. I'm so pleased we've met at last . . ."

CHAPTER 2

Helen Geeson's "I secretly admired Jack in spite of what he was" had fired Bassett's curiosity. For no particular reason, except that Jack was a friend, and as a friend interested him. On the force he would have put out feelers and quickly got a potted history. But he was no longer on the force, and since retirement had curbed his natural inclination to ask questions; his new friends had been accepted at face value. This was really how he wanted to keep it, yet the fact remained he was curious.

Since he was with his pigs, serving them the food he and Helen had prepared, and had no one else to talk to, he talked to them. "Who shall I ask, eh? Without proclaiming 'copper' as soon as I open my mouth. Helen Geeson, when I go this afternoon? Or Sally?"

Sally was his cleaning lady, a round jolly woman in her sixties, who gave him Tuesdays and Fridays and the benefit of her reputation. "Everyone'll tell you, Mr. Bassett—I'm clean: when you bring up a brood the size of mine in a two-up-two-down you 'ave to be clean or go under. I'm reliable. And I don't gossip. Can't afford to. I'm in and out of so many houses it wouldn't do . . ."

But she wasn't averse to passing on the odd tidbit. Her "You know I never gossip, *but* . . ." had become a standing private joke between her and Mary Bassett. "Quite harmless titbits," Bassett told his pigs. "So I think our Sally, don't you?"

Today was Friday, but Sally had warned Bassett not to expect her on time for once. "They're coming for a water sample," she'd said. He had thought she was poorly and had begun to voice concern, but it was her tap water the district council wanted tested. EEC guidelines, apparently: all private water supplies were to be checked regularly for impurities. Sally's water source was a spring.

"Bit late in the day," she grouched, bustling in just after eleven o'clock. "To test my water, I mean, seeing as I've been drinking it every day for the past twenty years. And what they think I can do about it if they do find bugs I'm sure I don't know. They quoted me eight thousand pounds for mains last time I inquired, and that was ten years ago." She was hot and bothered and suddenly minus her usual rubber-ball bounce.

"Sally," Bassett said consolingly, "people *sell* spring water. They bottle it, slap on a pretty label, and sell it at fancy prices. It's people with wells who may have something to worry about. Come and sit down, have a cuppa with me. It's ages since we had a proper chat . . ."

"Had a visitor earlier," Bassett said, when the two of them were sipping tea in his cosy kitchen. "Helen Geeson. First time we've met. Can't recall ever meeting her husband either."

"You wouldn't like it if you did. She's a widow."

"Oh." He looked briefly into Sally's twinkling eyes. Good; her sense of humour was returning. "She's got some pups. I'm going this afternoon to line meself up for their inspection."

"Breeds horses too. Mind you don't bring one of them back with you."

"Years since I rode a horse," Bassett murmured, smiling reminiscently. "She mentioned Jack—Jack Carter. Said he'd only recently come back."

"That's right. Home to his origins."

"He was born here, then?" Bassett probed gently.

"Born and raised. And here he might have stayed if it hadn't been for the war. The war made a difference to a lot of lives. Upset some, improved others. Made a world of difference to

Jack. He went out a nobody, came back an officer, smart as smart. So they say."

So they say? "You didn't know him? I thought you and he were much of an age."

"I can give him a few years if the truth be told. But no, I didn't know him. I lived five miles away, and before the war, Mr. Bassett, that might as well have been fifty. Only the rich had cars then, and the lucky ones bikes . . . I'd heard of Jack, though. Nearly everybody for miles around had heard of him, I should think; word always got round even if people didn't. And we'd all meet up once or twice a year at each other's village fêtes. High spots of our lives, village fêtes were. Jack sometimes turned up, won many a prize . . ." Sally shook her head, a twinkle in her eyes again. "Poor Jack. Many a girl worshipped him from afar, and many a lad—and grown man!—envied him his looks and physical strength; but hardly anybody *knew* him, if you understand me. You didn't mix with the likes of Jack, not unless you wanted to be led astray."

"Bad lad, was he?" Bassett asked whimsically.

"Some said he was, some said he wasn't," Sally began. Suddenly she was laughing. "Whether he was or not, he got blamed for everything. Scores of youngsters got away with blue murder thanks to Jack. They'd scrump apples or damsons or such, or poach a wild rabbit for Sunday dinner, and swear blind it wasn't them as did it, it was Jack. Good job his back was broad. Although—and he won't mind me telling you, it was all so long ago, he's probably had many a laugh about it himself since— ninety-nine occasions out of a hundred Jack *was* the culprit. Where do you think he got his nickname from: the Poacher?"

"Ah!" Bassett felt slightly foolish. "Meet Jack the lad. Otherwise known as the Poacher." They hadn't told him why and he hadn't asked, at the time his head had been full of Mary.

"Good poacher, was he?"

"The best, Mr. Bassett. If there'd ever been such a contest he'd have been champion in *The Guinness Book of Records.*"

"And a champion would know his territory, every nook and cranny." Hence Jack's knowledge of the area. "Why did he leave, Sally? To do with the war, you said."

"Oh, it wasn't the war made him leave altogether. At least I don't think so. No," she said awkwardly. "I think he went finally because of a woman."

But who the woman was Sally wasn't divulging: that information did come under the heading "gossip."

And indicated, Bassett thought, that the woman in question still lived hereabouts.

It was an hour later when he went in with a basket of eggs for Sally to take home with her that he received the message. Sally called to him, "Mr. Bassett? I nearly forgot. Message from Tod Arkwright. I've scribbled a note, it's on the kitchen table."

"I've got it." He read: "Be sure to go to the Pheasant tonight." "What's it about?" he asked, going into the room he called a parlour. His favourite room, this, furnished in subtle colours by Mary to reflect the countryside seen from their windows. The room smelt pleasantly of Sally's cleanliness, apple-wood smoke, and polish. "I always do go to the Pheasant on Fridays."

Sally flicked her duster. "He wanted to make certain you went tonight, that's all I know."

So Bassett, who had oddly enough been thinking of playing truant in favour of a programme he wanted to see on television, filed the message in his head and later acted upon it.

No regrets either, for the evening was to be a kind of beginning. A beginning for him, that is: the actual story—or stories—had their roots way back.

"Just the bloke we want to solve a mystery!" The cry went up as Bassett entered the steamy warmth of the Golden Pheasant.

They were all there, the stanchions, the faithful who supported the village pub when the tourists who walked the Malverns had put away boots and maps until daffodil time. For on winter Friday nights—traditional pay nights and most pensioners' favourite for socializing—landlord Archie Wood, an exdrayman with a brewers' goitre to prove it, provided a huge log fire for his regulars and laid on a full keg of Special Bitter, the better to keep them all happy.

"Come on, Harry!" A welcome and no mistake. Bassett raised

both gloved hands in greeting to the merry band hogging the fire. A cry now from Jessie, the only woman present: "Hurry up and come and hear what Tod has to say, Mr. B., before he blows a gasket!"

"Daft lot . . ." landlord Archie scoffed jovially, drawing Bassett's pint. A moment later Bassett was setting his pewter retirement tankard on the table and taking possession of the seat the daft lot had reserved for him.

There was Jan Podwojski: "Once a Polish wartime RAF pilot, now a cowman," was how happy-go-lucky Jan had introduced himself; Jessie, his wife and village milk lady, knitter of hats— tonight a red one perched cheekily atop a mop of greying curls . . . ; Charlie Allsop, egg producer, although Charlie swore his blind old mother ruled the roost in their establishment; Reverend William Brewerton, a man of the cloth Bassett could get on with, for Willy only spoke down to people on Sundays when the bulk of his tiny congregation not only expected but wanted him to do so—the rest of the time he was as normal (as Tod would insist upon putting it) as everybody else; Tod Arkwright, retired estate worker, who now called himself somewhat grandly gamekeeper, although they hadn't had shoots at the Hall for decades; and last but not least Jack Carter, also known as the Poacher. Bassett regarded Jack with renewed interest. He had liked the grey-haired, bearded giant instinctively on their first meeting. Now, after his chats with Helen Geeson and Sally, he knew why.

"What's to do?" he said to no one in particular.

"Spooks," said Charlie.

"Spooks?"

"Ghosts," said Jan.

"Ghosts?"

"Ar. Ghosts," Tod Arkwright rumbled portentously.

It seemed that gloom and doom merchant Tod was the purveyor of bad news; queer goings-on at any rate.

"With wheels." Jessie touched Bassett's sleeve and nodded at him with big round eyes. Meaning: Tod's serious; ignore the stifled laughter in my voice.

"Wheels, ar," rumbled Tod. "Old-fashioned 'uns. A-creaking

and a-groaning, a-trundling through the night. No tyres on 'em to deaden the noise. A cart it'll be. An old-fashioned cart." He picked up his beer mug and drank thirstily.

Bassett drank too, eyeing Tod, the only man he knew who could be doubled up with laughter, so to speak, and still look a picture of misery. "Who else has heard them?"

No one.

Jessie sprouted a frown. "When do you hear this—er—horse and cart, Tod? In the *middle* of the night?"

"Midnight, anyroad. I mebbe can't swear to a horse. Never hear horses' hooves, only wheels."

"A barn door swinging in the breeze," Jack said, his massive shoulders rising an inch. "Or something wearing loose on one of the derelict cottages."

"Wheels," Tod said stubbornly.

"A creaky tree branch," Charlie suggested lazily.

"Sheet of corrugated iron flapping loose." This from Jan.

"Rusty hinges," Reverend Willy drawled mildly. "Could be anywhere—"

"*Wheels,*" Tod persisted.

"Sounds travel, and they get exaggerated in the quiet of the night, Tod," Jessie said tentatively.

"That's true," Bassett agreed. "I've a mouse in the rafters who stomps about in hobnail boots."

"Wheels!" Tod said doggedly. "And not noises carried miles on the air. Anybody'd think I hadn't lived in the country all me life! Wheels, I heard. A-creaking through the woods. Top Woods, Harry—them back o' you."

"Thanks a bundle," Bassett murmured. "No, I can't say I've heard anything unusual." Only foxes and owls and the cries and screams of a thousand and one nocturnal creatures living and dying all around him. "But I sleep at the front."

They had been joined by Fred Ansen, a man of about forty, the latest newcomer to the village and chauffeur to Sir Marcus Clarkson at the Hall for the past several months. Fred must have been listening in while ostensibly conversing with Archie and others at the bar because he promptly asked: "Whose ghost do you think it is, Tod?"

The reply was equally prompt: "Old Gurney's."

"Sixteen hundred and forty-something it was, time of the Civil War, ar. Gloucester was held by the Roundheads under General Massey, and t'others—Cavaliers from Hereford and Worcester— were a-mustering to go and attack Massey's troops. Well, there was a cock-up of some sort. Fighting broke out where it shouldn't've, and a battle took place in cornfields and where some blokes was a-working. Old Gurney got hisself caught up in it, an innocent bystander you might say, didn't even believe in warring. So, well, he upped and spake a curse when he lay a-dying . . ."

I'm being wound up, was Bassett's thought; Tod has rehearsed this, he's word-perfect, the old devil.

Tod himself drank beer lugubriously, licked froth off his lips, and continued, "Mebbe got the idea from t'old Bronsil Castle legend—"

"In the time of Peter the Hermit and the Crusades four to five centuries earlier," said Willy, airing his knowledge of history, albeit he wasn't sure of his dates.

"Ar." Tod nodded solemnly. "The Lord of Bronsil as was then went off to the Holy Land. Afore he went he hid the family treasure in a secret part of the moat. But don't you worry none! he told his missus; if I get killed the treasure'll be found as long as my bones get brung home for Christian burial. Well, his bones did get brung home—but some must've got lost on the way, because they say the treasure never was found."

Bassett was familiar with the Bronsil legend. He had read it in a guide book. "Wasn't there a tame raven involved?"

"Lord Bronsil's tame raven." Reverend Willy again. "It was put to guard the treasure."

"And to this day," Tod said darkly, "they say that on the stroke of midnight the croak of a raven can be heard where the moat used to be."

Everyone fell silent.

"What's that got to do with Gurney?" Charlie Allsop inquired after a while. "He didn't have no raven—"

"Didn't have no treasure either," Tod retorted impatiently. " 'Cept mebbe a bit o' wages poor sod never had a chance to collect—beg pardon, Jessie. But old Gurney didn't need no treasure to lay a curse, he just cursed the devils as'd sworded him through. Cursed 'em long and loud, he did. Get my bones home afore I die! he warned—or else!"

"What went wrong?" Bassett asked innocently.

"Died too soon. They tried to get 'im back but he snuffed it on the way." Tod paused to pull tragically on his beer. "Planted him in the woods, so it's told. Folk remembered hearing the cart in the woods—the silence—then the cart a-trundling for dear life back the way it had come." Tod's jaw dropped, his eyes drooped into ovals. "Never did get as far as his hovel."

Bassett played the game. "I'll buy it. Where was Gurney's hovel?" Was this the punchline? No.

"In Dickie Debbs's Wood," Tod replied; and nobody laughed.

"Where's that?"

"Up by the Hall," Tod informed him. "Starts at your place though, Keeper's Cottage. Stands to reason there'd be woods all round there once upon a time. Thick woods. Good hunting land this used to be . . . Where was I? Yes, the woods—"

Bassett grinned. "Them back o' me."

"Bluebell Wood you call that one nearest you. If you was to follow it up the back hill you'd come to what we call Top Wood. Cottage up there that's haunted, nothing to do with Gurney though, so leave that for now . . . Follow the woods round—" Tod described directions with a raised arm—"cross country to the Hall boundary and East Drive. Been there? For blackberries, chestnuts—?" For blackberries, with Mary; not since. "That's it, you've got it." Tod lowered his arm with a sigh of satisfaction. "Among them brambles is where Gurney's hovel used to be."

They all busied themselves with the tray of beers landlord Archie brought to the table as if on cue.

"This cart—" chauffeur Fred said.

"Gurney's bones trying to get home!" Jessie told him.

"But the East Drive—the woods there run right the way down to the stables—"

"That's right. Most of Dickie Debbs's was cut down when they built the Hall. Not much older than two hundred years, the Hall, no history attached . . . Another for Fred, please, Archie—" Tod said.

"He'll need it," Jessie said playfully. "Tod's about to tell him the stables were probably built on the site of Gurney's hovel— and his flat's above the stables."

Fred looked sick. "Make that beer a half," he said when he was called to the telephone . . . "His Nibs," he explained, returning to the table. "Trip to Cheltenham tomorrow. We'll be up and off at first light, so I'll say good night . . ."

"His Nibs my foot," Jessie muttered after the chauffeur had gone. "His wife more like. I think it's her night off. She works at that new nursing home, Rosemead. Honestly, she's a torment to Fred. Nag, nag, nag. That's where he'll have gone. He'll have had his orders."

"Ducking-stool for her in the old days," Charlie said happily. He was on his third pint and getting merry.

"In the old days he could have sold her at market," observed Reverend Willy. "In 1802 a butcher auctioned his wife at Hereford market. Got one pound, four shillings and a bowl of punch for her."

"Nobody'd have that'un as a gift," Tod growled unkindly.

"On the other hand"—a subtle reprimand from Jan—"Fred might just have wanted an excuse to get home, doors bolted, before the witching hour. All this talk of ghosts . . . Didn't you notice he was getting green around the gills? He seemed to take it seriously."

"So he should. Anyroad—" Tod addressed Bassett. "There's a job for you, Harry, you being nearest we've got to a village bobby."

"And you living closest to where Gurney was bedded down," Jack added devilishly.

Bassett shook his head. "I'm retired."

"So's Gurney in a manner of speaking," said Charlie. "But if Tod's right he's come out of retirement."

"Ar. And today's Friday. 'Twas on a Friday Gurney got brung off that battlefield. Two Fridays running I've heard that cart. Mark my words, if he comes again tonight there'll be a death soon. You mark my words—"

But this was venturing on dangerous ground; ghosts were one thing, anything further was superstitious nonsense, warned Reverend Willy. Conversation reverted, with the help of other Pheasant customers, to customary topics: fatstock prices, the Common Market, failing farms and the new rural poor, the latest dumping of nuclear waste, and village inter-pub darts matches.

For all that, Tod managed to have the final word. To Bassett and Bassett alone, a peculiar gleam in Tod's eyes. "If you was a good'un, a good copper, Henry Bassett, I say curiosity'll get you in the end. I reckon you'll be giving it a go afore long."

CHAPTER 3

Bassett took the short cut home through Bluebell Wood. He trod lightly as he picked his way along a meandering pathway, and he kept the beam of his torch low so as not to frighten the timid creatures of the night. There was a frost now, which seemed to sharpen by the minute; the sky seen through the trees was full of stars. A good night for walking . . . He and Mary had often gone for a midnight stroll when they were town dwellers. There was something both exciting and restful about streets that were sleeping. They would walk, window shop, whisper, laugh, dream; and all the dreams would be possible because they were the only two people left in the world . . . God, he missed her.

Suddenly he was blinded by tears. He stopped, used his handkerchief; then carried on.

He reflected on the evening he'd just spent, with friends who had been his salvation when Mary died. He pictured the fire-warmed faces, the good-humoured ribbing, the smell of ancient timbers and cider and old-fashioned genuine beer. You're a lucky man, Bassett! he told himself.

A mystery to solve, they'd said; but they hadn't told him what they wanted him to do. Lay a ghost? They'd been half-serious, Tod on the face of it totally serious, but you could never really tell with Tod . . . Ghosts! he thought with a smile. Or was Tod trying to tell him something about sheep rustling? He'd heard the odd whisper, hadn't mentioned it himself; hadn't remembered it till now, to tell the truth . . . Cartwheels on the move in the middle of the night? Rustlers shifting a sheep or two? Small scale, from what he'd overheard: one here, two there, not like a Christmas turkey raid.

Why hadn't they mentioned it? Someone there in the Pheasant they weren't sure of? Who?

Anyhow . . . strange sounds. If there was anything in it others must have heard them too. The farmers whose sheep had been stolen—wouldn't they have been up and out investigating?

He gave a thought to Fred Ansen: it wasn't altogether surprising that the chauffeur had gone knock-kneed at the turn the conversation took. The country could be a pretty frightening place at night for people accustomed only to city lights and bustle: Mary had had her moments, but she had at least liked the country; from little things Fred had let slip occasionally it was obvious he and his wife did not. They were from the North, Newcastle apparently, here solely to escape the noose of unemployment.

The path narrowed, winding its way through clumps of fallen branches and tangles of twigs and foliage. Bassett concentrated on where he was walking. A large bird, a pheasant perhaps, taking sudden noisy flight, startled him momentarily. "Sorry," he whispered. Sorry for disturbing you. If indeed he was responsible for the disturbing. He wondered how many tiny eyes were watching his progress . . . Not to mention old Gurney, he told himself with a chuckle. He peered into the darkness: I can't go investigating a ghost, now can I? Give me a body, I might raise enthusiasm.

But only if it didn't interfere with the pup he'd be bringing home in a fortnight's time. He'd chosen the plumpest, cuddliest little one imaginable. Belle, he was going to call her; Belle for beautiful. He planned to take her everywhere with him, even to the Pheasant: he would carry her sort of papoose fashion tucked inside his belted jacket, as he'd done when he was a lad and had a puppy named Jo . . . The path widened, he no longer needed to concentrate, and so he daydreamed. His feet grew lighter. It might almost be said he skipped a few steps. Why not? But it was then, when his mind was filled with colour and promised joy, that an unearthly scream tore across the silence, terrifying him half out of his wits.

God in heaven! what was that?

A vixen's scream. He knew it. Hadn't he caught the musty scent of a passing fox earlier? Yet he'd still been taken unawares, his neck hair standing on end, his spine tingling, his foot pumping air. Switching his torch light to full beam, he swung it round, almost afraid of what he might see. Damn and blast Tod Arkwright and his talk of ghosts! All his primeval fears had surfaced, and in spite of himself he was straining to hear sounds of cartwheels.

He was glad when he spotted the pinpoint of light that was his porch lamp.

Later, hands round a generous brandy, he wondered. Those farmers, who, if they had heard the sounds Tod had described, had done nothing about them—were they *scared?*

Jessie set out on her milk round earlier than usual next morning, Saturday: 4:30 A.M. to be precise. She wasn't sleeping well lately, had several times lain awake until nearly dawn and then bump!—she had dropped off and overslept. So when she was awake at three o'clock she had got up, made herself a pot of tea, and finished the matinée coat she was knitting for the baby her daughter was expecting. At four o'clock she heard the day's milk crates being delivered by the dairy and so, restless, she decided to start work.

Her round straggled. She delivered to two villages: her own, Oakleigh, and Lymock five miles away, plus farms and houses in the area. The easiest section of her round was the main road between the two villages: some big houses, two homes for the elderly, a school, a row of six council houses, and the vicarage, with reasonable intervals between stops. The remainder was a pleasure in summer, a menace in winter—a labyrinth of country lanes where dwellings had grown up haphazardly, and frequently were tucked out of sight on dirt roads and tracks. It was her custom to deliver to Lymock and surrounding area first and gradually work her way homewards. Today, because of the hour and a heavy mist, she started on home ground, familiar terrain she could negotiate with her eyes shut.

First stop, the top, high end of the lane in which Bassett lived. A pretty little spot with five well-spaced cottages and a green. A century ago a stonemason, a blacksmith, a coffin-maker, a bailiff, and a miller had resided here. Now two of the cottages were holiday homes, two had been restored by retired couples. The fifth had stood empty, derelict, for two decades. But this, too, was now being rebuilt. Its name: Wyndham Cottage.

The mist, which had been patchy this far, thickened. Jessie didn't like it. Some people hate the wind, some the rain, snow, ice—Jessie hated fog and mist. Seldom was the foul stuff allowed to upset her routine, at worst it merely slowed her down, but for some inexplicable reason this morning she was loath to leave her Land-Rover. So why do so? She was ahead of herself: she stayed where she was and lit a cigarette.

But you cannot sit for long surrounded by mist and ignore the stuff; the thicker the murk, the more you want to see into it or through it. At any rate you do if you are Jessie. Gurney's ghost? She would have laughed in your face . . . But there was *something*. Something sensed rather than seen . . .

And then she did see it, or thought she did. A movement, a slight change in direction of floating particles a short distance away on her left.

Practical down-to-earth Jessie took over. It was a fox. A bird. A sheep. Was it in these conditions that sheep were stolen? An opportunist thief comes across a lone animal in a dark or misty lane and answers an impulse to steal, whisks the animal into his van, and—? No. One, maybe. But too many had gone missing lately: three or four at a time. And that last batch of four included ewes in lamb.

Ewes in lamb! Indignation dispelled fear. Anyhow, the quicker the milk was delivered, the sooner she could get to daughter Christine's.

Two pints, half of cream, and six eggs for The Birches . . . Skip Cherry Trees, they're away for the weekend . . . Next one up, Wyndham. Yes—Saturday—Mr. Wilson would be there. Two pints to last him. Last weekend's to pay for. And the weekend before that. Must leave a bill soon; or else ask Davey . . . Tiny little box, this. A doll's house. Must have had plans in, though: look at the scaffolding . . . And they do say he's excavating into the back rise. Must be making the cottage longer, rebuilding the front to please the Planning Department, the back to suit himself. Very nice . . .

Access to the front step being blocked by sand and gravel and a job lot of paving stones, Jessie made her way with the aid of a flashlamp round the scaffolding towards the rear. She fancied she saw a halo of light, a glow in the mist . . . He's here, then. Doesn't normally arrive till ten-ish. Probably stayed the night now the new roof is on. Good, he can pay what he owes me.

As she rounded the end of the cottage she saw that the light wasn't coming from a window as she had supposed, but from a storm lantern on the ground near scaffolding in the far corner. And—oh! my God!—Mr. Wilson! Dumping the milk crate by the back steps, she stumbled over bricks, concrete, and a plank of wood to where the shape was lying: "Are you all right? Mr. Wilson . . . ?" He was still. Too still. "Mr. Wilson . . ." Jessie repeated, edging closer. Curse this mist! She stooped down, put a hand forward to touch him, focused her lamp on his face . . .

It wasn't Mr. Wilson. It wasn't anybody . . . It was teeth drawn back in a deadly grin, skin tightly stretched across prominent cheekbones, eye sockets filled with . . . clay. It was—oh God!—her feet had her running before her mind caught up with her: it was a mummified face.

Bassett watched her hand flutter in her lap. She had arrived mid-morning with his milk and a request for an ear. Naturally he had invited her in, and over coffee she had begun to recount what had happened. But honestly . . . He just wished she didn't look so peaky . . .

"Sounds ridiculous, doesn't it?" she said with a nervous little laugh.

"Jessie—" Bassett was about to voice a denial but Jessie was slowly shaking her head.

"I don't blame you," she said brightly, perhaps a shade over-brightly. "Or Jan—" She shrugged.

"You've told Jan, of course."

"Oh yes. Raced home. You can imagine."

Jan had said she was overtired. "We're neither of us as young as we were, yet you rush about as if you had yet to see sixteen." He was forever telling her. "Come and sit by the stove. Then breakfast and bed for you, my girl. I'll finish the round."

But Jessie wasn't having that. She would finish the round herself, Jan had his own work to go to. He could do her one favour, though: ring in late and go with her to Wyndham Cottage to see . . . It was daylight when they got there. Not full light, but light enough to see without a torch.

There was no body, mummified or otherwise. No storm lantern. All they found was the milk crate where Jessie had left it. To please her, Jan scoured outside and looked through the downstairs windows for a sight of an overcoat or storm lantern. No sign of either.

"The only thing I could think of was last night in the Pheasant. Rotten lot. This was somebody's idea of a joke. We laughed it off. Although Jan was annoyed deep down. Until he remembered I'd seen the thing at ten to five in the morning. Who," she said wryly, "would play a joke at that hour?"

Bassett's lips moved sympathetically.

"Precisely," Jessie continued. "I asked Jan not to say anything to anybody, they'd think I'd gone barmy, and he's promised not to breathe a word. Now"—her head tilted self-consciously, her smile was weary—"if he'd had the faintest suspicion that someone was bent on frightening—even teasing—me he'd have stayed hopping mad."

"And you?"

"I thought at first he might be right. No sleep. Worrying about the baby—which is silly, I know. In our day we expected our babies to be perfect and they usually were. Today's expectant mothers seem to live in fear of *im*perfect babies—so we *all* worry for nine months. So, yes, I did think I might be more tired than I realized."

"But you had second thoughts."

"I did. Which is why I deliberately left you until last. You don't *imagine* a *mummified* body in *modern* clothing, do you?" She searched Bassett's eyes for his reaction; and must have approved of what she saw, for she went on, "If I'd *imagined* a body it would have been Gurney's—and his remains would have been wearing sixteen-hundred-and-something clothes, rags most likely. He might have been wrapped in a coat, which might have been a greatcoat, but not a *khaki* . . . Do you *see?*"

Bassett was beginning to, yes. "A modern army overcoat . . ."

"I don't know how modern," Jessie said, "but I did recognize it for what it was. I wouldn't imagine a modern coat on ancient bones. And anyway I hadn't let Tod's tale prey on my nerves. That's what Jan thought, bless him. You know Jan—easygoing, went as good as gold with me to Wyndham, but I know he was humouring me really."

Bassett took care not to smile, remembering the assault on his own nerves in Bluebell Wood. "What time did you say this was, Jessie?"

"About ten to five when I saw the thing. Getting on for half past seven when Jan and I went together."

"Nearly three hours had elapsed."

"Jan couldn't see the need to hurry," Jessie said sheepishly. "If I'd said 'body'—meaning a real live body, if you understand me, he'd have gone in his pyjamas. But a skeleton . . ."

"I was thinking more of the weather," Bassett said. "A thick mist and pitch black the first time—"

"There was a lamp there," Jessie reminded him. "Also I had a torch."

"Which you shone on the face. Did you see any other part of the body? A hand? A leg?"

"I didn't stop to look. It seemed to be—not whole, not fleshy, but all there. The right size, right shape for a man."

"Jessie," Bassett said kindly, "I'm going to suggest a fake—like a scarecrow, or a Guy Fawkes—"

"Or something left over from Hallowe'en?" Jessie shook her head, said adamantly, "No."

"A turnip and some skill with a knife? Isn't it just possible?"

Again the headshake. "I went to touch him. I would never have done that if the thing hadn't looked near enough human."

Bassett noted the slight emphasis on *human*. It suggested something to him; he wasn't sure what so he let it pass.

"Besides," Jessie went on, "if it was a joke why put it there? If they'd placed it on my own garden path the effect would have been the same. I don't think it was a joke, Bassett."

"Or if it was, it wasn't aimed at you." Bassett stood up. "Come on. Let's go look." He donned an old jacket, pulled on wellingtons, plonked his bush hat on his head, and went with Jessie in her Land-Rover.

As they crested the rise at the top of the lane, and the green and cluster of cottages came into view, they saw a white Rover saloon car moving away from Wyndham Cottage in the opposite direction.

CHAPTER 4

"That's Sir Marcus's car, isn't it?" Bassett remarked.

"It was Fred Ansen driving it, anyway." So much for Fred having to go to Cheltenham.

"He's making a lovely job of it . . ." Referring to the cottage and its new owner now.

"Mm. Central heating, the lot, he's having," Jessie said. "And now the undergrowth's been cleared away can't you see how it catches the sun. Proper little suntrap." For the sun was now shining brightly, that early morning mist only a haze brushing the hilltops.

A few weeks earlier Wyndham had been an eyesore: windows drooping open to the elements, crumbling brick and stone, swaybacked roof, and a garden that appeared to be swallowing the tumbledown whole. Today: new roof, new windows, a solid front door, the entire front wall had been refaced with stone, other walls started upon, and the cottage stood proudly on a large expanse of flat ground roughly gravelled to keep down the mud.

As they climbed out of the Land-Rover Jessie spoke the obvious. "We'll have to keep to the right, everywhere else is blocked. This is the way I came this morning . . . It looks different in daylight."

They followed the scaffolding round and halted at the back step. Jessie pointed. "That's where it was. By the far corner. Lying crosswise. The lamp was to the left of it, by the scaffolding."

"Show me exactly."

Jessie demonstrated. "I was here at the step—saw the light—

had to stumble over rubble—" She darted puzzled glances around. "There's hardly any here now. And there was a plank—"

"This?" Bassett touched it with a foot: a piece of wooden pallet which could have come with the bricks.

"Yes. Could be . . . The body was here."

Hard ground, Bassett noted. A scattering of leaves, soggy under the sun after a night of frost, but drying patchily. "Shut your eyes, Jessie, and describe what you saw. Slowly. Every detail."

She closed her eyes, opened them almost immediately. "It was lying on a sheet of plastic!"

"Black? Like a dustbin liner?"

"No, transparent—"

"Heavy duty?" Bassett indicated a stacked pile of empty plastic sacks, which he guessed were to be utilized to cover wet concrete. Most were vivid blue and Telecom yellow, but there were also a few transparent ones. He pulled one out. "Like this?"

"Not sacks," Jessie said. "I don't have that impression . . ." A small shake of the head, then thoughtfully: "You know what it might have been? The stuff they use for damp-proof courses. You buy it in sheets off a roll."

Bassett nodded. "I get the picture. Now, how was the body lying?"

"On its back, head to one side."

"Sure? How were the legs and arms positioned?"

"I didn't stay around to—" Jessie broke off and stared at where the body had lain. "Yes, I see what you mean. Was an arm flung out or a leg twisted underneath him, or something like that. No. The impression I have is that he was flat on his back, arms at his sides, legs straight." She looked up at Bassett with a weary smile. "I'm sure I'd have noticed if it had looked crumpled or in a heap." She closed her eyes once more. "Yes. Flat on its back . . . not wrapped in the coat—wearing it . . . and I'm sure there were legs—feet—boots . . . Oh dear—" Her eyelids fluttered open. "The only face I get is the one I saw. It insists on getting in the way."

Nightmare material.

Bassett drew her attention to where she said a lamp had been standing. "You said a storm lantern, Jessie. What shape?" He gazed fixedly at the ground.

"It was a Tilley's."

"Then come and look at this." Bassett stooped down, began examining the ground. "Look." A faint impression of a circle, made possible because the ground in this spot contained small amounts of sand. "It's about the right size. And"—using a sharp-edged flat stone he carefully removed a centimetre of damp sand, rubbed it in the palm of a hand, and sniffed—"paraffin. Here—smell."

A sniff and a humourless laugh. "Proves I'm not completely bonkers. So what's it about, Bassett? Have you any ideas?"

He did have an idea, which for the time being he wanted to keep to himself. So he sidestepped. "You were right about the lamp, anyhow. As for the rest—perhaps when Mr. Wilson arrives he'll have an explanation."

"He's late," Jessie said. "So's Davey." She frowned and went quiet.

"Davey?"

"My cousin's boy. He's been giving Mr. Wilson a hand."

"Wilson only comes here at weekends, I believe—"

Jessie nodded. "Mainly. He's doing the bulk of the work himself. Knows what he's doing, Davey says. Family connections with the building trade." She looked at her watch. "Eleven o'clock. They should have been here by now. Fred Ansen puts in a few hours as well when he's not required at the Hall." She tugged at her woolly hat—Norfolk Green today—adjusting it over her ears. "I'd best get off before I start imagining something else."

"Such as what?" Bassett inquired with a smile.

"Oh, I don't know," Jessie groaned. "It's just that . . . It's funny. Funny peculiar. Fred turning up when he should be in Cheltenham. A lovely sunny day—ideal for building work—but no Derek Wilson, and no Davey—"

"Ah! Stop right there, Jessie." Bassett tapped her comfortingly on the arm. "You may have hit the nail on the head, if you'll pardon the expression. Lovely day. Perhaps the last chance to do a spot of concreting before the *real* frosts hit us—" He waved a hand towards where extension foundations were pegged out. "Could be they've gone shopping for sand and cement. And Fred? Dropped Sir Marcus off in Cheltenham and came back here. Found a note saying back in an hour. Which he pocketed," he added hastily when Jessie threw a look at the back door; "and he's popped home to change into work clothes . . . Make sense?"

"Makes sense. Although it doesn't explain . . ." She faltered. Then looked at him with arched eyebrows. "I feel heaps better for coming to you. You'll let me know if you hear anything about the other thing? Still keep it a secret, though," she said, shamefaced.

He declined a lift home but walked with her to the Land-Rover, where she asked sidelong, "You don't suppose they *could* have dug up Gurney . . . ?"

Dug up Gurney? Dug up by Tod out of his brain, more likely. A dress rehearsal for the tourists next season. Good for many a free pint.

He watched Jessie's Land-Rover move out of sight, then returned to Wyndham's backyard. He had a further search to make.

Previously he had noticed that the ground near the scaffolding across from where Jessie had seen what he, for simplicity's sake, was going to call a skeleton, had been recently disturbed: leaves mixed in with a top layer of what looked like clinker instead of lying on the surface where they had been blown. He had also noticed that the ties which should have been securing the scaffold at that point were missing. He wondered about subsidence. Had the scaffolding slipped? Had it been untied while the ground underneath had been stabilized? In short, had the new owner come last night to work by lamplight—and had he fallen off the scaffold?

And had Jessie found him, his face disfigured by the effects of exposure . . . ?

He hadn't voiced the possibility because of Jessie's feelings. She had run away, leaving the man to his suffering. Who might subsequently have found him? Not Davey. Too early: the body had vanished before seven-thirty . . . A man and his dog, then. The dog sniffs out Wilson and the man may automatically have contacted the Hall, a residual impulse from the days when Sir Marcus's family owned the entire village and required to be informed of everything that happened. That could explain the presence of the Rover: Fred had been sent to clean up after Wilson.

A check confirmed that this particular section of scaffolding was loose; some poking and lifting with his penknife blade established that the ground underneath had been dug deeply very recently. He noted the presence of clay. He gave the scaffolding another tug; it wobbled. Wouldn't any builder, professional or amateur, have done the same, tested the stability of the scaffolding before attempting to climb it? And in any case wouldn't Wilson have taken a light up with him? Nobody with common sense would mount even cottage-height scaffolding in darkness. If he had taken the lamp, and was holding it when he fell, the lamp would have gone down with him. If he hadn't been holding the lamp, it should have been up there on a ledge . . .

Nevertheless assume he did climb the scaffolding. To re-secure the ties. Which would have been where—in his pockets? Which would explain why there was no sign of them now: assume they were in the pockets of his khaki working greatcoat.

But why in the pockets? He has to loosen the scaffolding in order to get to the ground underneath. He undoes the ties . . . Wouldn't the obvious place to put them be on the ledge? However, we do not always do the most sensible. So: he pockets the ties, climbs down, completes the earthworks, climbs back up the scaffold to replace the ties—leaving the lamp on the ground where all it does is cast useless shadows—the scaffolding wobbles, he topples off, hurting himself so badly he's still unconscious when Jessie arrives . . .

There Bassett metaphorically scratched his head. It *could* have been what happened, but it was unsatisfactory. For one thing, why mess about with earthworks and scaffolding at night? For another—it was too quiet here. By rights somebody should have been here before now to view the scene of the accident: morbid curiosity. Besides—an ambulance? Jessie would have been apprised of this phenomenon during her milk round.

Derek Wilson having had an accident and then being mistaken for a skeleton seemed improbable after all.

He was half way home when it occurred to him: suppose Wilson did go to his cottage last night, where did he park his car? Jessie hadn't mentioned it . . . Perhaps because he'd parked on the green; first time round, in the murk, Jessie wouldn't have seen it. Second time?

Second time it wasn't there to be seen.

"Know why the car wasn't there?" he said to his pigs, tossing them the acorns he'd gathered along the lane. "He'd cleared off, scarpered. Remember when I knocked myself out in the orchard and Mary knew nothing about it until I suddenly stood up? What if Wilson did the same? He was out cold when Jessie arrived, recovered consciousness later, staggered to his car to sit and gather his wits. Decided he felt too groggy to carry on working, phoned Davey to tell him not to come in. Fred wasn't at home to receive the message; he turned up and went away again . . . What do you think? Eh, Barrington-Smythe?"

B.S. gave Bassett his blue eye, Miss Piggy a trembling bottom lip before snorting and galloping frantically around the pen.

"It wasn't that bad a theory," Bassett complained. "Try this, then. Why was Wilson messing about in the middle of the night? Answer, good weather is forecast for the weekend. He decides to get cracking on the extension foundations. But the scaffolding begs attention, work he can do on his own by lamplight. He works on through the night to get the scaffold job done and so leave a whole weekend of fine weather for concreting. Exertion makes him sweat. He removes his overcoat, lays it on the ground rolled up lengthwise along a strip of plastic sheet to protect it from damp. Jessie arrives while he's round a corner answering the call of nature . . . He probably heard her asking his overcoat, and maybe his hat and scarf squatting on a lump of rock, if it was all right . . .

"What's the matter? What are you laughing at?" he said with a deep-throated chuckle. The pigs were grunting friskily, a not unusual response to Bassett's tone of voice. "It makes sense. After all, it *was* five o'clock in the morning, and foggy and creepy, and Jessie hasn't been sleeping well. All that on top of Gurney's dead-of-night chariot wheels . . ."

And yet, less than an hour later he found himself speculating all over again, on his face the look of a dog who has buried his bone and can't for the life of him remember where. He scolded himself for it. First gather facts, then speculate, Bassett old lad. The trouble was he couldn't help the feeling that he had gathered some facts. And answers . . . But they were answers to questions that hadn't been asked yet.

This was the reason why, after a snack lunch, Bassett set off on a walk; and why, when he was invited to a farmers' meeting, he agreed to attend against what was really his better judgement.

CHAPTER 5

In good weather Bassett enjoyed a daily jaunt anyway, a continuation of daily outings with Mary during which they had discovered new places of beauty and wild flowers, birds and butterflies not seen since childhood—some, wild flowers in particular, extremely rare. Recall the momma pheasant trooping her chicks? No chicks about in November, of course, but the memory of that delightful scene had come to him because today, in his mind, he had his pup with him; a pup who would be discouraged from chasing wildlife. Oh, how she was going to love all this, though!—the space and the freedom to romp for miles on land where the only restriction signs begged walkers to refrain from picking wild flowers, please.

But Wyndham Cottage was also with him.

From a vantage point on a dogs' favourite romping hill he had looked down upon the cottage to see no sign of activity, no change whatsoever since he had left. Nor were any of Wilson's neighbours about, so no excuse for him to go down and chat, indulge in a spot of gentle probing. Instead he descended the hill in another direction, and set off along the lanes by a round-about route in order to meet as many people as possible. The woodman, a nature buff, and the owner of a cherry orchard all passed the time of day. People waved from field and garden. But no one rushed to impart information. A visit to the village shop produced not a whisper.

He crossed a meadow, skirted a blackcurrant plantation, climbed up and over the bottom end of the chase, and was on the homeward trek. There Jack Carter and a man Bassett knew only by sight, afterwards introduced as John Stokes, small farmer, found him contemplating a fallen branch blocking the downward path.

"Looking at it won't shift it," Jack said unhelpfully.

"If that's an offer of muscle," Bassett said with a grin, "offer accepted. Ash, isn't it? Burns wet or dry?" He rubbed his nose with a knuckle, feigning self-consciousness. "Seems a shame to waste it . . ." He might have been gazing with empty stomach at mouthwatering hot pies. John Stokes giggled. Jack laughed. "Is that what you came out for, firewood?"

"No . . ." Although he wasn't above wood-gathering. "Matter of fact I was going to have a chat with the chap at Wyndham, see how he was getting on . . ."

"Wyndham?" Farmer John looked puzzled.

"Wyndham Cottage, at the top of the lane above me. Chap by the name of Wilson bought it—"

"The Bentleys' old place," Jack informed the farmer, who nodded absently and muttered "Oh, aye—" until the penny dropped, when his voice rose and brightened. "I know it! 'Course I know it, aye. Making a fair job of restoring it, they say."

"He was," Bassett said drily. "Seems to have come to a stand-still. I expected to see him working flat out, this weather, but nobody's there."

"Aye, well, he won't be having so many Saturdays off from now on." The farmer spoke as one who knows. "He's the manager of that new supermarket, Mayberry's, opened last Tuesday in Glevebourne. I know who you mean now—comes from Manchester. Couldn't recall the name of the cottage, never called it Wyndham. Same as yours—when you've been here a bit longer nobody'll remember its old name, it'll be Bassett's. Bassett's Cottage. But that's who he is. Wife recognized him, gave her half a pound of free sausages."

"They've been getting that shop ready for weeks," Bassett said. "Presumably he was involved with the setting-up. Know if he commutes, or is he in digs?" He made it sound casual.

"Caravan," was the reply. "At the Prince William on the Gloucester Road. They've a small site behind the pub. I think that's why he's been rushing the work on his cottage, he wants to move in before winter. Don't blame him. A decent roof and a fireplace has got to be better than a caravan when there's snow about."

"Anyway—" Jack the Poacher spat on the palm of each hand, rubbed them together, and flexed his shoulders preparatory to attacking the fallen branch. "Let's get rid of this . . . Just as well we were on our way to see you," he said as he took the weight.

They marched the log single file down the path and along the lane to Bassett's woodshed.

"What did you want to see me about?" Bassett asked, when they were drinking beers to replace the sweat they had lost.

"Sheep rustling," Jack said. "There's a meeting of part-time farmers and smallholders like John here in the Pheasant tonight, the club room, to discuss the problem. We wondered if you'd like to come. I'll rephrase that. We are inviting you to come."

"What's the object of the meeting?"

"Prevention," Jack said, looking Bassett straight in the eye.

Bassett pondered on the word and the implication. "All right," he said. "Fill me in."

There was nothing new about sheep losses, apparently; the

odd animal or two went missing every year; but larger-scale rustling was sporadic, and a fresh spate of thefts appeared to have begun. "We've warned the big farms," Jack told Bassett. "They've had trouble in the past. But these latest thieves seem to be concentrating on isolated spots, where houses are few and far between and traffic virtually non-existent."

Farmer John took up the tale. He ripped off names of farmers whose sheep grazed common lands. "All hit, two or three animals a week going, till they formed a posse a week or two back. We think the thieves were warned off and they're moving in on us, this area."

Tim Parker, a mate of the farmer's, had lost four animals a week ago, his brother Tony was four down last week, three in lamb.

According to the commonlanders the thieves struck at weekends, usually Fridays, but Tony had only been certain of his losses yesterday. He had made a few inquiries, had learnt about Tim, had put two and two together and, well, they wanted to stop the buggers . . .

"Meeting's to decide what's best to do," Jack said.

"Last night—Friday. Anything happen?" Bassett said.

Not as far as they knew.

"You said there'd been trouble in the past . . . ?"

"Aye," the farmer replied. "Five or six years ago. It fizzled out. Put down to hippies, rightly or wrongly, in the end. Couple of sheepskins were found in a ruin Lymock way—oh, twelve months after. Looked as if they'd killed and skinned the sheep there and just carted away the meat."

"This latest. Police been informed?"

No point, they said; the local force hadn't the manpower. This was a large area to patrol.

Bassett acknowledged this with a nod. "I should add it to the agenda anyway . . . What will your suggestion be at the meeting, Jack?"

"To do the same as the commonlanders—foot patrols, with plenty of lights and dogs. Frighten them off."

And so it was. Any fears Bassett might have had about lynch mob ideas were quickly dispelled. As Jack pointed out to the assembly, there wasn't a hope in hell of catching the thieves: their best chance of stopping the rustling was simply to let themselves be seen.

Starting tonight.

Meeting over, Bassett and his companions resumed their seats in the pub proper, where Tod kicked off a light-hearted discussion on the non-appearance of Jan and Jessie Podwojski, Fred Ansen, and Reverend Brewerton. They settled on Jan and Jessie having gone to daughter Christine's; aired the rumour that Fred had been spotted drinking in the Prince William; and proposed that Reverend Willy was working on his sermon for tomorrow, Sunday. Tod rumbled an opinion that vicar'd had all week to compose a sermon, why spoil a perfectly good Saturday night . . .

And Bassett's attention wandered. It had wavered a few minutes earlier when a smartly dressed middle-aged couple had entered. They had been unsmiling, backward with their good evenings, and were now sitting stiffly, apart from the main body of customers. It was obvious from the reception they received that they weren't strangers, yet no one had bothered with them after they sat down; which was extraordinary for this public house . . . They were vaguely disturbing.

He thought: Such people exist, who seem to whisper, think malice; who look secretive, sly, and by their very presence cause others to feel downright uncomfortable. He looked away . . . and back again. And he had it: they were listening. Listening, watching, deliberately—while at the same time contriving non-interest in what was going on around them.

In the periphery of his vision Bassett saw Jack turn and look in their direction, saw Jack's nod and, moving slightly, the man's silent response, the woman's half-smile; thought he saw a certain look in her eye as she gazed rather too long at the Poacher. A second, and Jack turned back again. In passing he flicked an eyebrow at Bassett. "Molly and I were at school together."

Willy Brewerton arrived. "A pint for the Reverend, Archie!" Followed by a group of young people in fancy dress, the Roaring

Twenties predominating. They turned out to be with Davey, Jessie's young relative, and were headed for a twenty-first birthday party in Tewkesbury. "Soft drinks only!" landlord Archie called.

"Bit late to start a party," farmer John muttered as the group gravitated to the other end of the bar. It was nine-fifteen.

"Them?" Charlie Allsop said lazily. "Dressed in that gear? Never!"

"Could be what they want us to think."

"Not Davey," rumbled Tod.

"Not Davey what?"

"Not Davey a-thieving. Underneath that rubbish he's a-wearing is a good lad."

The Pheasant was filling up. Bassett's table was drawn into neighbourly conversations. If Bassett was saying less than most this was because he was more accustomed to listen, frequently on two levels. This wasn't consciously done, nor mischievously: it was habit more than anything else: a copper's habit. And tonight it paid results. "Was it you who played that joke on the milk lady, Davey?" he heard above the hubbub.

He couldn't see the speaker, there was a crowd around Davey, but he was able to hear, barely, Davey's reply. "Joke? What joke? Has someone been upsetting my Aunt Jess?" Then came garbled voices, a titter or two, and, "A what? A skeleton!" the remainder muffled by a soft explosion of laughter and a different voice choking on, "Oh, I say . . . !"

Bassett glanced swiftly round his table. All were immersed in private conversations. All except Tod, who reared his head to see into the crowd and asked no one specifically, "What are they on about?" For no special reason but perhaps a reluctance to let Tod catch his eye Bassett looked in the direction of the middle-aged couple . . . They were staring at each other and mouthing "Ske—le—ton." But then Charlie was leaning over, blocking his view: "It sounds as if somebody's pinched Tod's Gurney tale."

Bassett nodded and smiled and forbore disabusing him.

The young people's voices rose. "Come on, own up. Peter! Was it you?" "Your Hallowe'en costume . . . skeleton in luminous paint . . ." "Not guilty, I tell you!" Then Davey again: "You're all wrong! I saw Aunt Jess not two hours ago. She said nothing about it to me . . ."

The voices and laughter reached a near crescendo; and broke up at the announcement that their transport had just arrived. Bassett fell in with his companions, following the youngsters out to a Dormobile already packed with revellers; watched them drive away to the raw sound of Heavy Metal. No rustler there.

And the night patrol was uneventful. Shortly before dawn Bassett went home. He fed his pigs and chickens, had a bath, and went to bed, timing his alarm for one o'clock. It was coming up to midday when he was woken by the telephone . . .

Derek Wilson, the new owner of Wyndham Cottage, had turned up. He was in the church graveyard sitting on a tombstone.

And he was dead.

CHAPTER 6

A pretty little church, Oakleigh. A twelfth-century building with a lovely old oak porch, a timbered clock tower and oak-shingled spire, and stained glass rescued from a long-gone priory, it stands picturesquely in rich farming land. Its Parish Records, dated from 1630, were enthralling, said Willy Brewerton; they provided a vivid account of what life was like here in bygone days. Pleasant living, apparently.

There had been a heavy spring-like shower of rain during the hours Bassett was sleeping: by the time he got to the church the sun was shining, the sky was blue, and the entire autumn countryside looked freshly washed and sparkling clean. At first glance the scene seemed no different from any other Sunday. Reverend Brewerton was seeing off his congregation, all twelve of them leaving in cars, those who didn't own cars being given lifts by those who did. Only the informed would have known that the figures wandering about by the far hedged boundary of the churchyard were police and police photographer and not visitors interested in ancient tombstones. The police surgeon was there too; Bassett recognized the sports coat and snowy white hair. Their cars had been parked out of view behind the church; it was all being handled discreetly.

As the last of the parishioners drove reverently away, an even paler than usual William came to meet Bassett. "You've heard? Sad business," he said in his Sunday voice. They shook hands, a mechanical gesture on the part of the curate: Bassett was congregator thirteen. "Is it Derek Wilson?" Bassett inquired.

"So Jack told me. I never met the man myself. Was it Jack who passed the news on to you? I know he went to use the phone. His parents are buried here, you know. He tends their graves every Sunday—but alas never sets foot in church. Which makes two of you," William remonstrated mildly.

"Jack found the body?"

"No. The Barnett children. Their mother packed them off to church—between showers, she thought—miles too soon, with instructions to sit quietly in their pews. When it didn't rain again, and it was nowhere near service time, they did what most children would have done, they went out to play. Hide-and-seek, naturally . . ."

"And stumbled on the body."

"Yes," the curate said solemnly. "They didn't realize the man was dead. Sensible little mites. Came to me all serious-faced. 'There's a man sitting in your churchyard, Vicar. We think he's poorly.' They hadn't touched him, you see. Just watched from a distance, spoke to him, and got no reply. They directed me to where he was, I asked Jack to go with me while my house-keeper looked after the children—"

"What time was this, Willy?"

"About ten-thirty—? It was ten to eleven when I phoned the police . . . I told them I had an eleven o'clock service—which didn't start until eleven-fifteen in the finish—and was advised to carry on as normal, they were not sure how long it would take them to gather their team." He gazed thoughtfully towards the scene of police activity. "I suppose it would take a while to round up all concerned on a Sunday morning . . ." And turning back to Bassett: "I hadn't appreciated that what appears to be a natural death would attract the same attention as foul play."

"Any unexpected death has to be investigated, Willy," Bassett said easily. "Just in case."

"I see." A wan smile. "That's all I know. The children stayed with my housekeeper, Jack agreed to mind the body till the police arrived, and I went ahead with the service. I had to agree with the police that to have told my parishioners the service was cancelled would have been to invite a deal of unwanted curiosity. Far better to have them closeted in church." He pulled a face. "I'm afraid they still know something is afoot. I warrant that by this evening they will know more than we do."

"Not if we steal a march on 'em," Bassett said. He glanced towards the police, then to William: "Coming?" And he started walking.

William walked with him. A plainclothes policeman was strolling in the well-maintained top, modern portion of the graveyard, a solitary figure among a profusion of chrysanthemums. "Why?" William whispered.

"To ward off spectators. Why do you think I wanted you with me? You're wearing your cassock."

The curate laughed lightly. "Not necessary. One of the officers is a friend of yours. Inspector Greenaway. Your name was mentioned."

"Ah. Bob's here, is he?"

It was several months after the Bassetts moved to Oakleigh that Bassett located the nearest police station, six miles away in the small market town of Glevebourne. He had called in one day for a look-see, and to satisfy himself that there was a force, it had been so long since he had seen a familiar uniform. At the station he had found an old colleague. Bob Greenaway, one of his sergeants from the past, was an inspector here.

The police were on the verge of leaving. Bob Greenaway detached himself from the others and came to them. More handshakes, then to William, "It was you who phoned the station? We know how busy you are on Sundays, but if you could spare a few minutes to give my sergeant a statement? Purely routine. We've already spoken to the children. One of my men has run them home." He signalled. Amiable, outgoing Sergeant Miller came running.

"This is Reverend Brewerton, Sergeant, who reported the finding of the body . . . All right if I hand you over to Sergeant Miller, Reverend? If there's anything further we'll be in touch tomorrow."

"Where shall we go, Sergeant? Would you like a cup of tea? My housekeeper . . ."

As they moved out of earshot, Inspector Greenaway addressed Bassett. "You could be of help, Bassett, you being a neighbour. What do you know about him?"

"Who are we talking about, Bob? All I have is hearsay—"

"OK, OK. Want to see the body?"

"Thought you'd never ask."

Age: late twenties. Average height. Well-nourished. Clean-shaven. Dark hair cut short. Wearing a thick grey polo-necked sweater under a black gabardine (or modern imitation) anorak, dark grey corduroy trousers, black footwear of the type called sneakers.

Bassett made mental notes of what he saw.

Found in a sitting position in an old graveyard, a crumbling headstone for a backrest. Legs outstretched. Arms in lap. Head bent forward and slightly to one side. No obvious signs of injury or violence. Facial expression—he tilted the head—peaceful.

Greenaway read from his notebook: "Derek James Wilson. Aged twenty-nine. Late of Salford, Manchester, temporarily residing at The Caravan, Prince William public house, Gloucester Road, Glevebourne." He shut the notebook. "We got those details from his driving licence and papers in his wallet. Provided it is his wallet."

Bassett nodded. "It's him. We've spoken once or twice . . ."

He regarded the body thoughtfully. "Derek Wilson, the man from Wyndham Cottage—he's been found dead in Oakleigh churchyard; thought you might care to know," was Jack's message over the telephone. Bassett's mind had instantly linked Wilson's death with Jessie's find at the dead man's cottage. Which was why he was here: he had thought to see Wilson wearing a khaki overcoat.

"Not telling us much, is he?" he growled.

"Nothing much to tell." Jim McPherson, the police surgeon, joined them. "Hello, Bassett, nice to see you. Didn't expect to see us when you stepped out of church, eh?" Bassett didn't put him right. Doc had completed his initial cursory examination of the body minutes before and had been chatting to the photographer, they were both keen naturalists. "Did you know our friend here?"

"Hardly," Bassett said. "Bob says it looks like a natural death."

"Seems like it," said Doc. "Looks as if the man felt ill, came into the churchyard to consult his Maker—and collapsed. The autopsy will show."

"How long has he been dead?" Bassett inquired.

"At least twenty-four hours."

"And was he in that position when he was found?"

"That was how the children found him," Inspector Bob Greenaway affirmed. "Sitting on a tombstone. What can you tell us about him?"

"Not a lot. Nothing first hand," Bassett replied. "He's a newcomer, as you know from his previous address. Manager of Mayberry's new superstore, I understand. He started rebuilding Wyndham Cottage about seven weeks ago. Doing most of the work himself."

"Could have overtaxed himself," Doc said. "History of illness, Bassett? No, no, you wouldn't know."

"There's the van," Greenaway observed. A blue van came to collect the body. The three men began walking to the churchyard gates. "Sunday, the shop will be shut. We'll try the Prince William—first job, next of kin for formal identification."

"Mind if I tag along?" Bassett begged.

"Wouldn't dream of stopping you," his erstwhile sergeant said. "As long as you buy first round."

Margaret Gulliver, the barlady at the Prince William, was blonde, buxom, generous-hearted, the epitome of the drinking man's favourite barlady. That women liked her too was due to some extent to Margaret's reputation for never being without a smile. Today was no exception, but underneath the smile was a touch of secret venom. The first man she had really fancied in ages had been going to take her out last night, her first free Saturday in weeks. She had bought a new outfit, paid a fortune at the hairdresser's; and the rotter hadn't shown up.

She was slicing beef for cold lunches, each cut tantamount to a wring of Derek Wilson's neck, when her brother Ben, owner of the Prince William, came into the kitchen.

"Some people to see you, sis. Police."

Ben had one of those rosy-apple complexions that bespeak healthiness though their owners might feel half dead. He felt sick but didn't show it: his voice was the giveaway.

"What's wrong?" Margaret dropped the carving knife on to the table, wiped her hands, and began removing her frilly pink apron. "Ben—come on—what is it?" she said anxiously.

"Derek Wilson. He's been found dead. At Oakleigh. In the churchyard."

Brother and sister stared at each other. It took a few seconds to penetrate, then: "Oh no," Margaret groaned. She sank down on to a stool by the table. "How? What on earth happened?" Ben Gulliver shrugged with feeling. "They think natural causes. It looks as if he walked into the churchyard, sat down—and died."

"Must have had a heart attack or something . . ." Margaret murmured. "Poor Derek. He never mentioned being ill. But you don't always know it yourself, do you? Think of Maisie. Right as rain one day, dead in the bath the next. And she was only twenty-four."

"The police are waiting," Ben prodded gently. "They want a word with you."

Margaret's violet eyes widened. "With me? Whatever for?"

"My fault, sorry," Ben apologized. "I told them you and he were pally."

"Not in *that* way," she reproached.

"Pally, I said. Meaning you know more about Derek than I do." Ben spoke softly, with emphasized patience. "They are upstairs."

Upstairs in the Gullivers' private sitting-room. Three of them. "Come in, Miss Gulliver." Introductions were brief and friendly. Inspector Greenaway—the tall, lean one. Sergeant Miller—stocky, cheeky-faced, she'd seen him before somewhere. And a peculiar-looking man named Bassett; who, after introduction, moved to a window and stood studiously looking out.

"Please sit down," Greenaway said. "It's good of you to spare us the time. We won't keep you long. Your brother has told you about Mr. Wilson? Good . . . He has probably given us all we need to know, but if you can add anything . . . He says Mr. Wilson was last seen here two days ago—on Friday. It was late-night opening at the shop where Mr. Wilson was manager. The shop closed at eight, he arrived here at around half past. He had a beer in the bar, then went to his caravan to wash and change . . . returning to the bar for his evening meal." He consulted his notes. "Cottage pie and chips, apple pie and cream, coffee and another beer. You agree with that?"

"Yes. He liked his food. But why do you want to know what Derek ate, Inspector?"

"It could help to establish time of death—"

Behind him Bassett winced. Soften your tone, Bob! Always were an unfeeling so-and-so.

"Did he eat alone?"

"We have a separate room where knife and fork meals are served. It's not actually a dining-room, more a bar with tables. He was the only one in there . . . But I was with him for a while. At the beginning of his meal, and at the end."

"Can you recollect what he was wearing?"

"Yes. A black anorak, grey pullover, and dark grey trousers."

"You're very observant."

"Not really." Bashful.

"I see. Mr. Wilson had his meal between nine and nine-thirty, then he went out. Have you any idea where to?"

Bassett altered his position a trifle so that he could see Margaret Gulliver's expression . . . No fluster. Perfectly innocent. "You know about his little cottage? I think he went there."

"And you haven't seen him since. Why would he go to the churchyard, do you think?"

"I don't know."

"Had he said anything about being ill?"

"No. Never."

"Do you know anything about his family?"

"His parents live in Manchester. And I believe he has a brother in Gloucester or Hereford. I've an idea it was this brother who put him on to the cottage, but I couldn't swear to it. But I don't know any addresses, I'm afraid."

"Not to worry. There's probably something in his caravan. I think that's all we need bother you with, Miss Gulliver." Bassett sensed Greenaway's smile; it was often worth the waiting when it came. "Just the matter of the key."

From the corner of an eye Bassett watched Greenaway upend the envelope containing the contents of Wilson's pockets. "Which is the caravan key?" Margaret leaned forward to look, extended a forefinger: "That one." A pause, then: "Are these . . . ?" Detecting a note of perplexity in the woman's tone, Bassett moved to look too. Wallet, penknife, a variety of keys, handkerchief, coins, half a tube of Extra Strong mints . . . "He had a roll of notes when he left here on Friday night . . ." She lifted her shoulders and held them there for a moment before lowering them with a sigh. "I suppose he could have paid out for building materials. He bought a lot of second-hand stuff, and they are usually cash transactions, aren't they?"

Greenaway nodded non-committally. "We'll take a peek at the caravan now. Thank you, Miss Gulliver, for your cooperation."

Bassett opened the door for her. "Miss Gulliver . . ." He smiled. He's nice, she thought. Nice and gentlemanly, not peculiar at all. It's only his hat.

It was a fairly new two-berth caravan containing all the comforts of home; an ideal temporary pad for a single man. Very clean and tidy, Wilson was no slob. And tidy-minded people are normally careful people; you would not expect them, say, to leave scaffolding ties undone . . . Thus ran Bassett's musings while Bob Greenaway went through drawers and cupboards, Andy Miller having stopped off at the Gents. Automatically, as though from habit, Bassett opened and shut a few doors himself: no overcoat of any description, no paraffin lamp.

"No address here," Greenaway said. He had found letters in a bedside table drawer but none carried an address at the top. "Just a quick note . . . from Mum"—and why should Mum write her address when her son already knew it?

"Try the blanket stores . . ." Bassett stripped one bunk, Greenaway another. They found a metal box file.

Inside the file, methodically indexed, were Wilson's personal papers: car records, insurance policies, receipts, documents pertaining to Wyndham, bank statements, et cetera; and letters. Among the letters was one from his parents: addressed. Greenaway's search was over. "Next of kin, father. I'll take this lot with me and start the ball rolling."

Bassett handed him a letter he had been reading. "Seems Wilson was the apple of his gran's eye. She left him several thousand in her will, his sister and brothers a paltry five hundred apiece. Now we know where he got the money to buy the cottage. What we don't know is what the rest of the family thought about it."

Greenaway fed him a look, folded the letter in half, dropped it in the appropriate folder in the file, closed the file, tucked it awkwardly under an armpit, and stood facing Bassett almost defiantly. "I've got what I came for. How about you?"

Bassett spread his hands. "I am simply a spectator. Here, give me the key, I'll lock up."

He waited until Greenaway's back was turned and he was descending the steps, then quick as a flash he reached up for the big old-fashioned key hanging on a hook at ceiling level behind the door, and slid this into a pocket. Then he left the caravan, locked up, and gave Greenaway the caravan key.

"Something's bugging you," Greenaway grouched.

"Sheep rustling."

His one-time sergeant was unconcerned. "That started again?" He sighed. "OK, what thoughts have you got?"

"Give you two to be going on with. One—Oakleigh church is never locked, Bob. If I felt off-colour and wanted somewhere to sit down, and was in the vicinity of the church, I'd choose the church itself. If I hadn't the strength to lift the latch—it's a heavy cumbersome thing—I would sit on the bench in the porch, or failing that on the seat by the tap in the modern graveyard. I certainly wouldn't pass them by—and the vicarage —to go and squat among decaying tombstones and knee-high grass."

"But you are assuming Wilson was on the road side of the church when he fell ill," Greenaway argued mildly. "What if he was on the other?"

"I'd go to the farm that backs on."

"Second thought?"

"It's three miles by road from here to the church, a similar distance to his cottage. Where is his car?"

Greenaway considered for a moment, then: "You are suggesting he could have spotted rustlers, and took off after them on foot?"

"Now you are assuming," Bassett said. "Pre-supposing any-how—that he died during the hours of darkness. We don't know when he died. All I'm saying, Bob, is find his car. It may supply a clue to what he's been doing since Friday. It may even provide evidence of a crime."

Greenaway scowled at him. "Hope you realize you've just ruined the rest of my Sunday."

CHAPTER 7

It being Sunday and Bassett having no Mary to cook lunch, the appetizing roast beef smells emanating from the Prince William kitchen decided him to lunch there.

"Miss Gulliver . . ." Raising his hat and one almost comical eyebrow, he said, "May I beg a favour? May I have one of your delicious beef lunches, and will you join me, be my guest—?"

Margaret Gulliver flushed with shy pleasure. "The lunch, yes, of course . . . but I'm working, I . . ."

"Oh, I'm sure your brother and the other staff can cope without you for half an hour." He waved a hand—towards a bar that was far from crowded, and a dining-room not exactly busy.

She gave a little laugh. "Yes, we're not rushed off our feet, are we? Is it just you? Your friends—they've gone." Then in a different voice, low, curious, "Who are you? Not a policeman?"

"I'm an old man, all on his own, asking a young woman to lunch with him."

"Not so old," she said coyly. "I'll see what I can do."

In the event she joined him at the coffee stage. "You don't mind, do you? Only I'm not used to eating at this hour," she said when she brought him his meal. "And there's nothing worse than someone who's eating being watched by someone who isn't . . ."

He understood.

"I'm rather glad you're here," were her opening words when she did sit down with him. "The Inspector didn't say much about Derek. There are all sorts of questions I'd have liked to ask . . ."

"Such as?"

"Such as, when did Derek die?"

"I'm afraid we won't know until the post-mortem."

"You make it sound as if it could have been yesterday."

"It's possible," Bassett said.

"Or even Friday night?" she said tentatively.

"Why do you say that?"

"The Inspector. Saying Derek hadn't been seen since Friday night."

Bassett, of course, had the advantage of knowing a shade more than Greenaway. For example, he knew that someone, or something, had been at Wilson's cottage early on Saturday morning.

Margaret Gulliver's expression was troubled, questioning. "Why don't you tell me what's worrying you," Bassett said gently.

"It's just me . . . being silly." A small impatient shrug of her shoulders. "It's just that—" She looked down at her coffee and up again. "It's just that before you came I'd been condemning the man. He was supposed to take me out last night, but hadn't turned up . . . If I had known he was missing, ill . . . if we'd got to him in time, we might have saved him . . . Do you think?"

"No." Bassett answered unhesitatingly; but tempered abruptness with a smile. "Suppose we talk about it. Talking helps, they say. Let's start with Friday night. You said when Derek left here you thought he was going to his cottage. Did he actually say so?"

"No, but until Mayberry's opened for business he went there most evenings and every Saturday and Sunday. He wanted to get it habitable before winter set in. And that's the point, you see; he'd done that. Most mornings I'd see the lights on in his caravan before he left for the shop. When there was no light on yesterday morning I assumed he'd left early. His first Saturday —he was bound to be extra busy. Later I thought perhaps he had spent the night at the cottage. He'd told us that at a pinch he could live in it now and we weren't to worry if he didn't come home any night; we could take it he'd bedded down there."

"Where did he breakfast, Miss Gulliver?"

"He didn't. Never ate breakfast."

"So he wasn't here on boarding terms, didn't have to cancel meals or anything."

"No. We don't have boarders. And we don't, strictly speaking, cater for caravanners. We only do hot meals at weekends, the rest of the week it's snacks and ploughmans'. Derek was a special arrangement. I—we—cooked his evening meal with ours."

"Last night, Saturday, what did you think when Derek failed to show? I mean what did you think was a reason?"

"I don't know." She brushed that aside. "I *do* know. I thought it had to do with his girlfriend."

"You weren't his girlfriend?" Bassett affected mild surprise.

She shook her head. "No, I wasn't." But would have liked to be, Bassett thought. "We were friends, that's all. Derek was unhappy and lonely. He was engaged to a girl who seemed to be changing her mind about him. Only a few days ago he said, 'Perhaps she's growing up and I'm not.' She smiled sadly. "His cottage—he bought it for her. It was her ambition to own a country cottage. And he had such plans! It was going to be a little palace. He was going to have it ready for her to walk into —a surprise wedding present—but she came to see it unbeknowns to him, and blew her top. *That* wasn't her idea of a dream home. She wanted an acre or two of parkland and a four-bedroomed executive house with roses round the door and a thatch . . . He was choked."

"Did he speak of breaking off the engagement?"

"Oh no. Men as soft as Derek take a long time to learn."

"His fiancée lives where?"

"Manchester. Where he comes from."

"If I remember correctly you said he had a brother in this area. Would you know what he does for a living?"

"Sorry. I don't think he ever said."

"What about pals—drinking pals?"

"There was one, a man called Fred. Derek left a message for him on Friday night, as a matter of fact. If Fred comes or phones, he said, tell him I've gone on ahead and I'll see to the bucket and spade. I took that to be a joke—the bucket and spade bit. You know."

Bassett regarded Margaret in silence for a moment, then: "Did Fred come for him?"

"No. Fred's wife phoned. It sounded like Fred's wife, she's been here once or twice. I gave her Derek's message, but I think it was Fred she was really after. She's like that, keeps tabs on him. You know."

Bassett smiled. "Where Derek was, Fred was sure to be, eh?"

A smile came back. "Not far behind, anyway."

"Have you ever seen Derek wearing a khaki—ex-army—overcoat?"

"A *khaki* overcoat?"

"Mm. For working in. You know." Unconsciously Bassett imitated her.

"Oh! I see." And a headshake. "He wore old jeans and a duffel coat. He kept them at the cottage to change when he got there, saved bringing dust home and messing up his caravan."

"So although he was wearing good clothes when he left here on Friday night, he may have intended working at the cottage. Did he say anything about a job that needed urgent attention?"

"The reverse, actually. He said he could ease off now the original cottage had been made waterproof . . . But why are you asking these questions? If he died of a heart attack . . ."

"Because he may—*may*—have fallen off the scaffolding, banged his head, and suffered delayed concussion," Bassett said. "It happens. Bump on the head. Ignore it. Twenty-four hours later you've got problems. It's a possibility. So you see, even if you had gone looking for him—and found him—he might at that time have been perfectly all right."

"You're very kind," Margaret Gulliver said. "I do feel better for talking to you."

"Good," Bassett said to her lopsided smile.

"And now I've had time to think, no one rang up from Mayberry's yesterday, so Derek must have gone to the shop."

Must he? Bassett asked himself when he was leaving a few minutes later. A new store, new staff, they wouldn't necessarily go chasing up their manager.

He thought of something else, too, and popped back to ask, "Fred. Would that be Fred Ansen?"

He drove to the Hall via the main drive, the route he and everyone else used for the Summer Garden Fête. No band playing now. No bowling for a pig (which nowadays took the form of a bottle of malt or two). No tombola. No laughing children or party frocks. No ice-cream. Or clowns. Or Punch and Judy. Only lawns and autumn leaves and trees; and a house showing signs of neglect. He continued round to the side of the house and under a brick archway into a service yard, pulling up outside the old stables now converted to garages. There was nobody about. He went up the flight of wooden steps which led to the flat above, and tapped on the smart green door. A light tap in case Mrs. Ansen, night worker, was sleeping.

She wasn't. He heard a peevish voice complain, "Oh God, who's that?" followed by Fred's, "Stay there . . . I'll go."

Fred, in shirtsleeves, looked uneasy when he saw Bassett—a typical reaction, Bassett thought, to unwanted Sunday afternoon visitors. "Who is it, Fred?" the peevish voice called.

"It's Mr. Bassett, Glenda!" Fred opened the door wider, a silent invitation to come in.

"Hope you don't mind my calling. I was passing—" Bassett said, stepping into a square carpeted vestibule.

On his left was a coat-rack: a monstrous gap between Fred's outdoor clothes and his wife's. His versus hers? Mucky and clean? And ne'er shall the one dare to contaminate the other? It was blatantly obvious and might have been amusing if it hadn't been somewhat sad. Hers smelt perfumed: colourful townwear, decorative buttons, furry trims . . . An open shopping-bag stood on the floor, incongruous flat ward shoes inside.

"This way." Fred led Bassett into an attractively furnished sitting-room on the right. As Glenda Ansen rose from her chair in front of the television set, Bassett recalled having heard her described as "all paint and powder," and being quoted as saying she "wouldn't be seen dead wearing the clothes women round here wear." And yes, he thought, there was an air of hauteur. A stubborn air. She would continue to teeter on country lanes in crippling high heels, wear fashion boots that leaked rather than wellingtons, suffer the cold sooner than wrap herself in warmers and woolly scarves and thick shapeless weatherproofs. For which, in a way, she was to be admired.

"Mr. Bassett. How nice." But the head tilted on one side and the actressy smile were artificial; and in the eyes he glimpsed hysteria.

"I hope I'm not disturbing you, Mrs. Ansen. I thought Sunday might be the best time to catch Fred. I wanted to ask what the big house did with its waste food, Fred. Wondered if there was any chance of having it for my pigs . . ."

"I'll have a word, by all means," Fred said generously. There wouldn't be a lot though, only Sir Marcus and his housekeeper. Not like in the old days. Seventeen servants they had before the war, as well as outside staff, house always packed with guests . . . His Nibs did do some entertaining, however, and there was the garden waste. "Leave it with me," Fred said.

Bassett thanked them both. "Have you heard about Derek Wilson, by the way?"

"Derek? What's he been up to?" Fred's smile caused him momentarily to look simple.

"Found him dead in the churchyard."

Dead? A fraction of a second's shocked silence, then Fred's chin jerked upwards. "What happened?"

"Heart attack, they think," Bassett said; and Glenda Ansen's teeth came down on her bottom lip as she looked away. Fred nodded absently, some of the colour he'd lost returning: "I told him. Told him not to work every hour God sent, it wasn't worth it, never is in the end. When—?"

"They found him this morning—"

"This morning?" Glenda Ansen seemed to gasp.

"Are you sure it is Derek?" Fred asked.

"The chap from Wyndham Cottage?" Bassett said.

Again Fred nodded. "That's Derek," he said sombrely.

"He was all right, was he, when you saw him Friday?"

"Friday?"

"Friday night."

Fred shook his head. "Not me. I haven't seen Derek all weekend."

"Oh. My mistake. I thought when I was in the Prince William at lunch-time someone mentioned he'd been expecting you."

Fred shrugged a careless shoulder. "I often did have a drink with him on a Friday. But not last Friday."

"You had to get the Rover ready," his wife said. "I was here, remember? It was my night off."

"That's right," Fred agreed; and to Bassett, almost accusingly, "You were there in the Pheasant when his Nibs rang me up."

Bassett let a second pass by, then he stabbed at the space between them with a fist. "Correct. So I was." He smiled and sent a glance to the window. "I'd best be going while there's daylight left. Got to give me pigs and chickens their tea."

"I'll see about pigfood," Fred promised as he showed Bassett out. "Check with the gardeners, too."

"Nice of you, Fred."

The door closed behind him. As he went slowly down the steps Bassett heard Glenda Ansen's sarcastic drawl, "We *have* gone up in the world. Bloody pig scraps now. And why you had to go on about servants, putting yourself on the same level . . . !"

Yet there must be goodness in the woman, Bassett told himself; wasn't her work of a caring nature, looking after the elderly and infirm?

It was on the pretext of cadging pigfood that Bassett went to Mayberry's on Monday morning. He had been thinking over what Margaret Gulliver had said about the store not querying Wilson's absence. If that meant Wilson had been to work on Saturday, he could forget Jessie's little mystery. With Wilson now dead, the truth of what she had seen might never be discovered. If, however, Wilson hadn't been to work . . .

He went in his pig clothes, and in Mary's ageing 2CV to give credence to his request. A sack of stale bread and green leaves wouldn't look as out of place in the "snail" as it would in the back of his classier Citroën. He parked next to the delivery zone and entered the store by means of the loading bay. There, tucked in a corner among towers of Del Monte peaches and Batchelors' processed peas, he came upon a check-out girl hav-

ing a forbidden smoke. "Hello. Could you point me in the direction of the manager's office, please—"

The girl looked at him askance; and burst into tears.

Homeward bound, Bassett pondered on what he had learnt
from the girl, whose name was Susan and who had quickly
recovered her composure under Bassett's gentle handling.

Derek Wilson had lived with his parents and managed a
small Mayberry's shop on his home estate until he moved to
Glevebourne seven weeks ago. For the first two weeks he was
on paid settling-in leave, afterwards he helped organize the
shop, interviewed staff, et cetera. He'd known for six months
previously that the Glevebourne shop would be his; apparently
Mayberry's always promoted their own managers, and brought
in some other existing staff, transfers from smaller shops coun-
trywide. They had done that here. Derek Wilson was from Manchester, the deputy manager was from Nottingham, and the
accounts adviser, Miss Smith, from Sheffield.

The deputy manager was called a floater. He would assist at
Glevebourne until the shop got off the ground, then he was to
farm himself out as required—to cover holidays, sickness, that
kind of thing . . . Some rivalry there—between Wilson and
the deputy manager. Apparently the deputy had applied for the
shop, Wilson got it.

And that was why, the girl said—and here had come the
information Bassett sought—the deputy, the creep, phoned
Head Office when Mr. Wilson failed to arrive on Saturday.

She—all of them!—thought he should have contacted the
Prince William to see if Mr. Wilson was ill; but no, he jumped at
the chance to feather his own nest by laying the poison down
for Derek. She overheard him asking Head Office if there was
any reason why Derek shouldn't be at the shop, and making
snide remarks about him tinkering at his blessed cottage instead
of doing the work he was paid to do . . . And all the while
Derek was ill: and now he was dead.

At home, Bassett changed into his walking tweeds and made
once more for Wyndham Cottage. The key he'd filched from
Wilson's caravan was in his pocket.

He was right: the key did open Wyndham's back door.

He let himself in.

He found no khaki overcoat. No scaffolding ties. No storm lantern or even a container for paraffin. Wilson had used Camping Gaz before his electricity was installed: a Gaz lamp and an opened pack of refills were on the floor in a bedroom.

Which left Wilson's car.

This was discovered in a lay-by serving a popular walkers' path. It was, in police jargon, clean.

But still the car was taken for forensic examination: for by then Derek Wilson's death had become a murder inquiry.

CHAPTER 8

"Murder, Harry. Stab to the heart from behind, with a slender weapon about the thickness of a knitting needle. I'd say a long ice-pick if there'd been such a thing. Death virtually instantaneous. And knowing what and when he ate at the Prince William on Friday I'd say he expired two, not more than three, hours after he'd eaten. Which puts his death at between eleven-thirty and half past midnight the same night, Friday."

Dr. Jim McPherson gave this information to Bassett on the telephone.

"No offence, Jim, but how come he had to be undressed before you found the stab wound?"

"Did you touch him?"

"In the graveyard? No."

"If you had, if you'd looked at his back, you'd have seen what appeared to be a small snag in the cloth of his anorak. You might not have spotted *that* till you brushed off the dust. Very small puncture. Clean through anorak, sweater, T-shirt, and vest. When I talk of a knitting pin I'm talking circumference. Must have been a lot sharper. Went in like the old proverbial hot skewer through butter. But I'll be able to tell you more later on."

Bruising? Had Wilson been manhandled or in a fight? Had he been killed elsewhere, transported, and dumped in the churchyard?

Nothing to indicate either, Doc said. "On the face of it the man was taken unawares, stabbed in the back, caught as he slumped, and lowered on to the gravestone . . . But as I said, I may have additional information after some proper forensics. Anything specific you want me to look for?"

Bassett said no, not at the moment. "But keep in touch, Jim."

"Don't worry. If I get stuck I'll seek your advice."

This reply pleased Bassett although it was said half in jest. He and Jim McPherson had met at Glevebourne police station in the spring, and had liked each other on sight: kindred spirits. Both men revelled in solving problems, Doc being as keen to probe a corpse for answers as Bassett had been to identify his murderers. But where Bassett's official detecting days were over, Doc was still endeavouring to get into Forensics; and many had been the summer evenings spent together, Doc bringing his fun-loving Old English sheepdog for a frolic on the hills as an excuse to drop in for drinks and a chat about crimes solved almost entirely in a laboratory.

Not that this would be one of those cases. A stabbing was a stabbing, in Bassett's opinion. An exact description of the murder weapon might be useful. Other than that . . .

He reflected on the time of Wilson's death. Midnight on Friday, give or take half an hour either side. Jessie saw a something—call it a skeleton—five hours later outside the dead man's cottage. Timewise, therefore, if Wilson himself was not the "skeleton"—and Doc's information cancelled this out—he could nevertheless have put the skeleton there, before midnight. But he could not—repeat, could not—have been responsible for removing same between Jessie's racing home and returning with husband Jan.

"I went to touch him," Jessie had said. *"I would never have done*

that if the thing hadn't looked near enough human." His idea that Jessie had mistaken a coat and a lump of rock for a near-human shape hovered . . . and was rejected. Scrub a trick of the mind, too.

Suppose then what Jessie saw was Derek Wilson's killer. He hears her coming and fakes a horrible sight to despatch her, pronto. Far-fetched? Not necessarily. He hears her approaching . . . feels trapped . . . mind's in a whirl . . . he's already irrational . . . dabs dry cement or plaster on his cheeks, adjusts his face and false teeth to affect a grisly grin . . . plays dead, and lets the lamp and mist do the rest. Feasible? Only just. It would have been far quicker to extinguish the lamp and duck out of sight till Jessie had gone.

Also it posed another question: What would Wilson's killer be doing at the cottage five hours after he had bumped Wilson off? Looking for something?

For *five hours?*

Time of death: roughly midnight on Friday . . . Friday . . . There was something odd about that conversation he'd had with the Ansens, Bassett thought now. True, it was he himself who had highlighted Friday by asking Fred if Wilson had been all right when he saw him. But hadn't the Ansens concentrated a little too much on what Fred had been doing on Friday night?

He telephoned Archie Wood at the Golden Pheasant. "Archie —Friday night, that phone call for Fred Ansen . . ."

The caller had definitely been Sir Marcus; Archie had recognized the voice. Fred had spoken the truth. There Bassett left it while he went about his chores.

Leaving the French windows open in order to be able to hear the telephone, Bassett repaired to the garden and began raking leaves. Time passed and he was at the bottom of the garden, rake idle, studying his hens luxuriating in dust baths, when Helen Geeson trotted down the path towards him. "Stay there!" she called. "I don't want to interrupt your work, I'll come to you."

"A constant source of amusement, my hens," Bassett said,

when she was standing by his side. "They remind me of people."

"And I suppose they all have names." She laughed.

Bassett pointed some out. "The fat ginger one—she's Thelma, after a chubby redhead I sat next to at school. The one with the spindly legs and long neck is Dorothea. The kind little motherly one has to be Jessie—"

"Speaking of whom," Helen said seriously, "I've been hearing about the joke someone played on her. Poor Jessie. A fright like that. It would have been all the same if she'd had a weak heart."

"Jessie tell you about it herself?"

"No, they were talking about it in the shop. And about that poor man Wilson. Is it true Jack Carter found him?"

"Not true," Bassett said. "Jack happened to be in the churchyard when the Barnett children found Wilson."

"Jack! Going to church?" Helen said incredulously; and immediately repented. "Sorry, I shouldn't have said that."

"I'm a bit of a heathen myself," Bassett admitted. "Apparently Jack goes every Sunday to his parents' graves."

"Yes, he'd do that," Helen Geeson said after a short pause. "Someone once told me the graves were tended all the years he was elsewhere. Oakleigh isn't my church, you see; mine's Hollybush . . . People don't change, do they, not deep down. He always did have a big heart. Tough, strong, but sentimental . . ." She smiled.

Later, though it lasted only a second, Bassett was to remember this smile as a brave smile. But at the time the telephone intervened. "There's your phone," Helen said superfluously. She dug into her bag. "I'll leave you to it. I came to give you this." She handed him a Foyle's Handbook on labradors.

It was Bob Greenaway. "Doc's told you we've got ourselves a murder . . ." He spoke falteringly and the last pause was heavy before he continued, "Was it you spotted leaving Mayberry's this morning? Sneaking out the back way?"

"Sneaking out be blowed. Scurrying, tail between me legs! Banished by one Miss Smith! I went to scrounge pigfood."

"Oh." Bassett could hear him perking up. "We'd been asking ourselves how come you were on the prowl before the fact of murder was established."

"I *was* curious," Bassett confessed. "Curious to know if Wilson had gone to the shop on Saturday."

"Well, now you do know. This sheep rustling—I've suggested looking into it, but the guvnor isn't impressed. He's halfway convinced we've got a domestic killing involving Wilson's family. There's a vaguely threatening letter in Wilson's file from a sister-in-law who asked for a loan on the strength of his legacy, and had been refused. Guv likes it. His theory is that the brother was here to apply pressure on Friday night, killed Wilson during an argument, and nipped home to Manchester on the motorway, nobody the wiser. Perfect motive. Perfect opportunity. Our hardest task, he thinks, will be to break the killer's alibi, he's had a whole weekend to arrange a cast-iron one. So . . . I'm off to Manchester. Andy's staying here to handle this end. And I—er—" There Bob Greenaway stuck.

Bassett helped him out. "You wouldn't mind if I gave Andy a hand. Unofficially, of course."

"Not even that. But if you do indulge in a spot of snooping . . . ?"

"I did get one snippet from Mayberry's," Bassett volunteered. "Rivalry between Wilson and his under-manager." He passed on what Susan had told him. "My own view is that if the under-manager had killed Wilson his attitude when he contacted Head Office would have been different. He'd have had nothing to gain by putting the skids under Wilson—Wilson being dead —and so would've been more inclined to do the seemingly decent thing and cover for the chap. But it may be worth checking out, tell Andy."

While Bassett was speaking, the crackle of papers being shuffled had come down the line. "Name's Peter Harvey. Alibi looks unshakable," Greenaway advised. "But I'll pass the info on. And can I tell Andy you'll be keeping your ear to the ground?"

"You can. But give me what you've got, Bob. Bring me up to date so's I know where I'm at."

Bob Greenaway obliged. "The murder weapon hasn't come to

light yet. I've a couple of men still searching the area. All they've come up with so far is a plastic bucket, scrubbing brush, and cloth; probably got left behind after someone cleaned a tombstone, and got blown into the rough . . . Frederick Ansen and David Mellor—know them? They worked part-time for Wilson. Ansen was with his full-time employer, Sir Marcus Clarkson, at the time of Wilson's murder. Clarkson fetched Ansen from the village pub—it says here that you were there when he phoned. Ansen went direct to Clarkson Hall, was with Sir Marcus until after midnight. Fact substantiated by the housekeeper . . . The lad, David Mellor, isn't so lucky. What do you know about him?"

"Not a lot," Bassett said.

"Mm. Mother died when he was six. Father's in a wheelchair, multiple sclerosis. The lad's officially unemployed—he says officially a layabout—because he won't leave the village to find work, refuses to commute any distance. Why? He looks after his dad. Does odd jobs as and when, and is studying at home— correspondence courses. Was with his father all Friday night from five o'clock onwards, but no verification apart from his father's.

"I had to have the lad in this morning for questioning. A Mr. Glass, lives at Cherry Trees next door to Wilson's place, inadvertently let slip that he'd overheard the lad rowing with Wilson last Wednesday, and threatening him in some fashion. The lad explained himself and we've let him go, but if nothing comes of Manchester the gaffer may well favour him as prime suspect—"

"This Mr. Glass—why'd you say 'inadvertently let slip'?" Bassett asked.

"He's a blabbermouth. Pain in the backside, frankly. Fall over himself being helpful, no matter who got fed to the crows in the process. He'd been away all weekend, so didn't know Wilson was dead. Didn't ask why the inquiries, just rabbited on full of his own importance. Dropped the lad in it and was sorry afterwards. Get the picture? . . . Beware telling him any of your private business, for as sure as God made apples, the day would come when he'd get you hanged."

"But not himself."

"Not himself," Greenaway agreed. "He and his wife left on Friday afternoon for a Mini-Break. Got back Sunday. He's in the clear, it checks out. As to Friday and the scene of the crime—no help from the vicarage. The vicar and his housekeeper are both heavy sleepers. The farm that backs on to church grounds—hang on, name's here—"

"Stokes," Bassett prompted.

"Stokes's Farm, yes. They heard nothing, saw nothing, which isn't surprising, there's a fair stretch of meadow and a number of outbuildings between the Stokes's homestead and church boundaries. Again, I thought of your rustling. Could Wilson have got himself tangled with rustlers, and died in the middle of a set-to? But Stokes has cattle close to the farm, his sheep are farther afield on land bordering the hills. Also, there's no evidence to support any sort of fight or confrontation. No roughed-up ground, no heavy-heeled footprints and the like. The killing appears to have resulted from a sly vicious blow . . ." Sounds of pages turning. "And that's about it."

Bassett was on his way out when the telephone rang again. This time it was Jessie. "Oh, Bassett, I've done a dreadful thing! It's Davey. The police had him in—at the police station—all morning, questioning him. Somebody reported overhearing him and Mr. Wilson having words last week, and they think Davey killed him. Thankfully they hadn't enough evidence to arrest him, but he's not to leave the district, he's high on the suspect list."

Having foreknowledge, Bassett was able to say, and make it sound light, "This early on he's probably the only one on the suspect list, Jessie, so stop worrying. Now, what's this dreadful thing you've done?"

"I just didn't stop to think," she said agitatedly. "You were the first person I thought of when I learnt Davey was in trouble. I'm afraid I told him to come and see you, you might help him."

"He's worried?"

"His dad is. Davey being with his dad all Friday night is no alibi. At least . . ." She hesitated.

"At least it's considered dubious."

"That's right. You knowing the ropes, I thought you might explain how the police work, give Davey some kind of reassurance he could pass on to his dad."

"That's no dreadful thing! I'll be pleased to see the lad. Jess?"

"Yes?"

"Could Davey have done it?"

"Never. Never in a month of Sundays!"

"Fair enough. You understand, though, that I can't give reassurance without first asking questions myself?"

"I understand, Bassett. Thank you."

Don't thank me yet, he thought. "Does Davey know about your find?" he asked, although he knew the answer.

"Not the details. Somebody told him I'd found a skeleton, but I passed it off as a joke."

"Did you tell the police about it?"

"No. Should I have done? I did think of it, but I thought they'd think I was a nutcase. Or else trying to divert attention from Davey . . ."

"Jessie—" In spite of Doc saying the man died where he was found, Bassett had to put this to her now: doctors, even good doctors like Jim McPherson, had been known to make errors. "Jessie—has it occurred to you that what you saw may have been Mr. Wilson's body—?"

"As soon as I learnt he was dead," she said forthrightly. "I thought and thought and thought, but I can't alter what I said before. I know what I saw, and it wasn't anybody's *body*. And it wasn't anybody taken ill—"

And then she said, and it seemed as she spoke that the very air around Bassett was motionless, drained of all life-giving qualities, "It was like something out of the grave."

Something out of the grave. The words repeated themselves inside Bassett's head.

Had Jessie been there she would have seen his expression change—the one in the eyes, the one that reveals all. But she wasn't with him to see; she heard only the silence, and as if interpreting this as embarrassment on Bassett's part she gave a nervous laugh, an attempt at levity. "The police will be after me, though, I think. They're bound to get to hear about it. Everybody seems to know about it now . . ."

"Unfortunately, Jessie"—and now Bassett's eyes held a questioning twinkle—"you have only to tell one person a secret for it to be a secret no longer." He left it there, up in the air, and listened for Jessie's response.

"I didn't tell anyone. Not a soul. Except you and Jan. And Jan swears he's kept it to himself."

Bassett said, "So have I."

"Oh, I believe you. It's very odd, isn't it?" Jessie said soberly. "The only other person who could've spread the tale, the only other one who knew anything about it—was the person who put it there."

"Very odd, Jessie. In fact downright intriguing."

CHAPTER 9

Bassett pinned a note to his front door—"Davey: gone to Wyndham Cottage"—before setting off on foot. He had gone no further than a hundred yards when he saw Davey coming towards him. He watched the way the youth walked, straight-backed, no slouching, no scuffing of feet; noted the smart pale trousers and anorak and, as he drew closer, the spotless white at his neck, the polished shoes.

"Mr. Bassett—?"

"Davey Mellor?" He hadn't seen the young man this close before, and he liked what he saw: the no-nonsense, already masculine body, the set of the chin, the groomed hair that was neither sandy nor gold nor mouse, the open friendly face which left him surprised when he failed to find a single freckle. "I'm on my way to Wyndham. Walk with me."

Davey turned, fell in step. "Tell me about this row you had with Derek Wilson."

"It wasn't actually a row," Davey said. "He ticked me off for leaving concrete in the mixer, called me slipshod, and I took exception. I'm not slipshod, I made a genuine mistake. I thought the concrete would peel out when it was dry."

"Like certain plastics and fillers." Bassett nodded. "I know. How much did you leave in?"

"A fair amount, unfortunately."

"Then it's no wonder he ticked you off. He'd have had a hell of a game chipping the stuff out. However, you bristled, lost your temper—"

Davey shook his head. "I didn't lose my temper," he said calmly. "It's not the kind of row they're trying to make out. Derek told me not to bother coming any more, mistakes like that he could do without. I trailed after him up the yard calling, 'Oh, don't say that, Mr. Wilson, sir! Don't give me the push!'— but I was fooling, doing a Uriah Heep, whining and fawning. Any other time he'd have laughed. This time he ignored me, went into the house, and slammed the door. That was when I shouted, 'I'll be back! Don't fret!'—something like that. But I wasn't threatening him, I was laughing."

"Being cheeky, in other words."

"Not really," Davey said deferentially.

"How old are you, Davey?"

"Eighteen."

"What day did you have this disagreement?"

"Wednesday," Davey said. "Wednesday is my dole day. It's also auction day in Glevebourne and I occasionally pop into the auction rooms while I'm there. I often pick up a bargain I can clean up and sell at a small profit. Derek was there that day. He bought some items of furniture and brought them to his cottage in his lunch hour; gave me a lift, and I helped him carry the things in. It was afterwards that he spotted the concrete mixer."

"This was last Wednesday? Therefore when you called 'I'll be back' you were saying you'd be back this last weekend as usual. What do you do, Saturdays and Sundays?"

"I did," Davey corrected, not impolitely.

"So you intended turning up for work last Saturday." A pause. "Did you?"

"No." And a rueful shake of the head. "That was what started me looking bad to the police. I'd said—or meant—I'd be there as usual on Saturday, but I hadn't gone. They wanted me to confess that I'd stayed away for the simple reason that I knew I'd be wasting my time."

"A bright lad would have turned up anyway, to allay suspicion," Bassett observed. And Davey was undoubtedly bright. "Why didn't you go?"

"For one thing, the party."

"The one you were dressed up to go to on Saturday night?"

"An all-night party," Davey said wretchedly. "I'd have had to pack in work at around four o'clock to get Dad comfortable, and have a bath and get ready. I felt guilty as it was for leaving Dad on his own all night, but he insisted I go, I don't get out much. Aunt Jess was going to drop in late-on and again next morning, but I wanted to be sure he had everything to hand before I went off to enjoy myself . . . I didn't want to have to rush, didn't want him thinking he was a nuisance . . ."

"I see." Bassett turned his head to smile, but Davey was seeking neither praise nor sympathy; he was staring straight ahead, and speaking once more.

"Sunday, too. I knew I'd have to rely on someone to bring me home, and an all-night party . . . ? There was no knowing when anyone would be fit to drive. If I appeared on Saturday morning and told Derek I could only give him a limited day and couldn't guarantee Sunday, he might have told me to get lost and mean it, I thought. Whereas if I forgot this weekend and turned up next he might just have relented." A glance was flicked Bassett's way. "Might even have been stuck without me, and I'd be ace again."

"Of course!" Bassett said lightly. "You say you'd have wanted to finish at four on Saturday. Wouldn't that be normal knocking-off time these dark nights?"

"No, we were working indoors."

"Doing what? May I ask?"

"Me? Labouring mostly up to now," Davey said. "But I was

looking forward to painting, I'm not bad with the old paint brush. And Derek was teaching me plastering. We were a smashing team," he said with a burst of enthusiasm. "Fred was a dab hand at carpentry—"

"Fred?" Bassett feigned ignorance.

"Fred Ansen, the chauffeur at the Hall. He did a course in carpentry when he was made redundant but couldn't find a job—"

"Who else works there?" Bassett asked.

"Nobody at the moment," Davey replied.

"He was a grocery manager," Bassett said. "Getting Saturdays off before Mayberry's opened for business would have been relatively easy. Once the shop did open—what were the arrangements?"

"He was going to get in touch with us on Friday nights to give us instructions."

"Get in touch personally? Or by phone?"

"He'd have had to see one of us," Davey said sagely. "Fred or me. To give us the key."

"Did he get in touch with you on Friday?"

"No. That's the other reason—" Davey broke off, looked down at where he was walking.

"Say it," Bassett commanded.

Davey looked up at him. "I was going to say that was another reason why I didn't turn up on Saturday. But it's not true. I'd forgotten all about him getting in touch."

Bassett was thoughtful for a moment, then, "Righto," he said. "Tell me about Friday night. Where were you?"

"At home with my dad."

"Anyone see you? Anyone phone?"

"No. Crazy, isn't it? I can't blame the police for thinking there's something fishy about me . . . On the night of the murder I *conveniently* spend the entire evening playing dominoes with my dad. I give him all my time—till after midnight. I don't go to my own room to study or read because I dislike leaving him alone too long. Yet twenty-four hours later I spend the whole night partying! I didn't engineer anything on Friday. I always stay home with Dad—because it's the only night of the week nobody else visits him. But how do I convince the police?"

There was an edge to Davey's voice which Bassett found disturbing. Eighteen, no job or immediate prospect of one. No mother, and the responsibility of a chronically sick father on his shoulders. A young man going nowhere, worn down by duty, perhaps torn between what *he* wanted to do and staying with a parent dependent upon him—could that be an answer? Frustration? Bitterness he managed to keep under control for most of the time? *Had* he been with Wilson on Friday night, and been told that what was said on Wednesday held, he wasn't wanted, goodbye Davey . . . another rejection?

"David," Bassett said quietly. "People have always experienced hard times. My dad saw two World Wars and a Depression. I've known the tail end of a Depression and one war. Things are improving. What we have at the moment is a recession. People do care, some even understand. Until it costs money. Sympathy is expensive . . . And frustration breeds violence."

Silence; their strides shorter, slower. On their left the fringe of Bluebell Wood, on their right a gold bracken-covered rise and a thousand shades of autumn. A rabbit ran into the lane ahead, stood tall for a look-see, and darted back into a thicket.

"I'm not a violent person, Mr. Bassett. I didn't hit Derek; I didn't kill him. I didn't see him on Friday."

They ceased walking, turned to face one another. "Besides, I daren't get into trouble. I don't even fiddle my dole money, I declare every penny I earn. Well, almost every penny." His candour was refreshing. "I want to join the police force, that's my ambition. I'm keeping fit and studying at home . . . I couldn't tell them that, couldn't risk the mockery . . . I come into some money when I reach twenty-one. No fortune, but I aim to use it to move Dad and me to a town, where he can join a Disabled Club and get a bit more out of life than he's getting now, and I'll be able to do something about my own future. I accept it may never work out as planned," Davey said with a shrug and a half laugh, "but where's the harm in trying?"

Bassett looked at him long and hard. "Eyes, ears, common

sense. Got those?" he said gruffly. "If you have, you'll make it, laddie." It was all he could think of to say.

"What about the famous intuition? Hunches?" Davey quipped.

They both laughed. "Essential," Bassett said. "They'll tell you no, and they'll be right—hunches come from experience. But experience starts the day you start, so—eyes, ears, and common sense. Come on."

The land opened out a little, becoming flat, grassy. The cluster of cottages that included Wilson's came into view, splashes of scarlet and purple in one of the gardens, the vivid orange of late marigolds in another. The scent of wood smoke mingled with the fragrance of burning leaves. High overhead a kestrel wheeled gracefully. Peace. And yet . . . ? Those bright eyes in the sky were the eyes of a killer; whose victims would not see beauty, only terror.

Sand, gravel, and paving stones still blocked access to Wyndham's front door; the scaffolding ties were still missing, the scaffolding loose . . .

"Know anything about that, Davey?" And the ground underneath. "Someone's been digging there."

"Yes . . . it looks like it." Davey frowned. "But you dig trenches on a building site, you don't dig like you dig a garden . . ."

"You didn't see it done?"

"No . . ."

"So you don't know how long the scaffolding has been like that? Isn't it dangerous, left loose?"

"Very." Davey didn't understand it. "Derek was hot on safety. He'd done a safety-at-work course for the shop, and was always lecturing Fred and me. Although Fred said that was because we weren't insured."

Bassett nodded, let it go. "Looks as if the finished article was going to be rather grand. He's excavating into the hillside—"

"That's what I thought at first," Davey said as they strolled towards the bottom of the building site. "All he's doing, though, is tidying it up ready for a supporting wall."

"To prevent earthslip, you mean."

Closer to, Bassett saw that rough steps had been hewn out of the shored-up wall of rock and earth. Steps . . . to where?

To a high meadow . . . woodland . . . a chimney puffing out feathers of smoke. Two figures, a man and a woman, emerged from the near distant edge of the wood, two brown and white Jack Russell terriers jigging in their wake. Bassett watched the couple for a few minutes, placing them as the solitary couple who had been in the Pheasant on Saturday night. Instinct told him they were making for that chimney. He tried to recall the house to memory, for he must have seen it at some time from the road; but to no avail.

He went back down the steps.

He hadn't wandered this far previously, he'd had no wish to tread on pegged ground in case he tripped and messed up Wilson's calculations, but that was before he knew Wilson was dead, therefore unable to complain. Now he trod where curiosity dictated, Davey at his side. They inspected the concrete mixer with its residue of concrete; timber, bricks, tiles, and an ornate fire surround rescued from demolished buildings; a pile of stone similar to that which had been used already; and a heap of shuttering. A few paces farther on two old doors lay on the ground weighted down with strategically positioned bricks.

"There's a well underneath," Davey explained. "We were filling it with rubble." They removed the bricks, lifted one of the doors . . . Rubble, yes. And earthy smells.

Something—or someone—behind them, too; sensed rather than seen. "Don't look now," Bassett said under his breath, "but I think we're under surveillance." Their backs to the watcher, they replaced the makeshift well cover, and as they did so contrived to sneak a peep. "Mr. Glass from next door," Davey groaned softly. "I wouldn't mind betting he's the one who shopped me to the police. I don't particularly want to speak to him."

"Why not? Afraid of him?" Bassett growled. "After me. One, two, three. Ready?" He stood up, turned, feigned faint surprise, raised a hand in a neighbourly wave, and called, "Hello, there!"

"Mr. Bassett, isn't it? Oh! and it's you, Davey—" The man was clearly discomfited, and tried to mask this by being affable. "I didn't recognize you in those clothes!"

Davey looked down at himself. "I can be smart, Mr. Glass. I don't always dress like Wurzel Gummidge."

"About this morning. I'm sorry if I caused you any trouble. I could tell I'd said something I shouldn't by the way the police latched on to it. They'd been asking about who worked here, and I thought they were referring to contractors—"

Davey cut him short. "It's all right, Mr. Glass." He thrust both arms forward, fists touching. "No handcuffs," he said coolly. "Anyway it was Friday, the night of the murder, they were concerned about, not Wednesday. If you'll excuse me, I can see Tod—"

"Yes, well, I couldn't help them there," the man said to a retreating Davey. He turned to Bassett, a face full of frowns: "My wife and I were on holiday all weekend. We'd no idea why the police were asking questions—"

"Many people know you were going to be away?" Bassett inquired.

"Nearly everybody . . ."

Naturally. He'd have told them.

Yet chatterboxes have their uses. "These cottages. Used to belong to the estate, didn't they?" Bassett said conversationally.

"Oh yes. You mean Sir Marcus's—? Yes, his family owned everything in sight once upon a time. The whole village, farms, shops. They've been selling piecemeal since before the war, I believe. Why this one stood empty for so long I wouldn't know. It was an eyesore, quite spoilt the look of the green—"

"So Wilson bought this direct from the estate. Do you know that for a fact?"

"Oh, well . . ." Doubt crept in. "I'm only going on what Derek told me. The agent told him it was an estate worker's cottage till the end of the war, a succession of families had it in the 'fifties, local people mainly, waiting for council housing, plus a family who eventually emigrated. And then it was empty for—ooh! twenty years, save for when a young couple rented it cheaply while they were saving a deposit on a house. We knew them. They moved out a week or so after my wife and I moved in. We're next door—" He cocked a shoulder. "Cherry Trees. Ten years we've been here. Of course we bought privately. Ours hadn't belonged to the estate for donkey's years." Making it sound as though buying privately was somehow more worthy.

He flung an anxious look towards where Tod and Davey were standing talking. "I could do with a quick word with Mr. Arkwright while he's here. He makes Christmas holly wreaths, did you know? I want to order one—"

"Let's go see him, then." Bassett thought, Is the man seeking my permission, for heaven's sake? "You missed the tale of the milk lady's fright then, Mr. Glass? Not being here for the weekend . . ."

"Those bones?" The man's face began to light up: now *there* was something on which to expound. But he checked himself.

"Who told you about them?" Bassett asked quizzically.

"My wife. Oh, you mean who told her. The postman, I think, this morning. A joke, wasn't it? Somebody getting their money's worth out of a Hallowe'en costume . . . Tod! Are you doing holly wreaths this year?"

"Tod." Bassett touched his hat. "See you when you've finished with Mr. Glass?"

Alone with Davey, the other two having moved towards Cherry Trees, Bassett said, "The furniture Derek Wilson bought at auction—what was it?"

"A coffee table, a blanket chest, and a Victorian boudoir chair."

Correct, they were in the cottage. "Valuable?"

"Don't think so."

"Anything inside the blanket chest?"

"Only dust."

"You looked?" Bassett said curiously.

Davey grinned. "Aunt Jess once bought a chest of drawers for a pound and found one drawer was full of embroidered linen."

"Good for her! Wilson had no such luck, though, you say. So no likelihood of him having snapped up an item for a fiver someone else knew to be worth five thousand. He did something, though, Davey. Did, said, saw something that provoked an attack on his person. Any ideas?"

None.

Bassett searched Davey's face. He saw no guile, no cunning; only a tiny shadow of—uncertainty rather than fear. And yes—something of an entreaty.

"Of course, the quickest way to prove your innocence is to find the actual killer," he said. "That would take time and a certain amount of dedication. Unfortunately I keep pigs and chickens, and they are like all creatures including you and me. If they are to thrive and enjoy life, no matter how short, they need love and attention. It's not enough to feed 'em, clean 'em, and lock 'em up safely at night. You've got to talk to them, touch them, show that you care . . ."

His hangdog expression caused Davey to laugh. "You'd like me to look after your livestock."

"Help out, at any rate. Provided your dad can spare you?"

"Tomorrow? No problem."

They made arrangements for next day, Tuesday. Then Davey departed and Bassett strolled on the green waiting for Tod Ark-wright.

CHAPTER 10

He hadn't long to wait. "Davey gone?" Tod asked.

Bassett said yes. "Tod, how ill is his father? Is he incapacitated?"

"If you mean can he get about—answer's no. But he can do some things for hisself, excepting bad days." The old gamekeeper looked perceptively at Bassett. "Davey's not a-using his dad as an excuse, if that's what you're a-thinking. Works hard, the lad does, and keeps a beady on his dad without it sticking out a mile."

"Without his dad realizing he's nursemaiding him, you mean."

"Ar. That all you wanted to ask me?" Tod said with disgust.

"No." Bassett surveyed the elderly cords and hacking jacket, took his eyes back to Tod's face, brown and wrinkled as a walnut. "I've been asking myself what Wilson did or saw that upset someone sufficiently to want to kill him."

"Ar, I've been wondrin' an' all. About Davey. They took him in—"

"Only for questioning."

"But think on. The lad worked for this 'un, Wilson. Sheep-stealing took up again the same weekends they was a-working here. The night the lot of us sat up and they forgot to show theselves, Davey was at an all-night shindig. Think on—" Tod wagged his head long-faced, as he might have wagged a finger. "He couldn't be at a party and out a-rustling, could he? What do you say to that?"

"I thought you liked Davey," Bassett said quietly.

"That's got nowt to do with it. What d'you say to what I just told you?"

"I'd say Fred Ansen also worked weekends for Wilson," Bassett replied slowly. "I'd also remind you why we sat up watching for rustlers on Saturday—because they hadn't struck on Friday. Now, you think on, Tod. Suppose thieves did attempt a steal on Friday—I don't know whose sheep, but suppose Wilson spotted them and was running to the nearest farm—John Stokes's, say, to alert them, and was tackled and killed before he got there. Wouldn't that account for our wasted Saturday and the thief-free Friday? They'd abandon Friday's attempt, they weren't likely to hang around after killing a man. And they'd have to be extremely thick-skinned to return the following night—"

"No need to carry on!" Tod's face cracked into what was for him a broad grin. "I knew I could rely on you, you'm a good'un."

"You old—!" Bassett swore. "Playing devil's advocate."

"Just a-thinking like a few others'd be a-thinking, mebbe. What was that you was saying about Wilson?"

"Rustling aside, what has been done—upset—altered?" Bassett pointed to the stonework. "That stone looks local. Know where he got it from?"

"Smelly's."

"Quarry?"

"Cottage. Derelict. On Top Hill."

"The one you said was haunted?" Bassett said quickly.

"You won't find nobody local going up there anyroad, let alone dismantling it. It's there Wilson's a-fetched this stone from, though. The agent give his consent, seeing as it was doing nothing. I did hear, mind, that Sir Marcus was none too pleased."

"Sir Marcus?"

"Ar. It's on his land."

"Is it now? I thought that was Forestry property."

"Not Top Hill. Belongs to the estate. And mebbe his Nibs is agin interferin' with things best left alone."

"Left alone? Do you mean entirely, or because he planned to sell eventually . . . ? Is he hard up, Tod, for all that he employs a chauffeur? I suppose a chauffeur is a status symbol . . . ?"

Tod chose to reply to the last two questions. "There's hard up and there's hard up," he said lugubriously. "There's thee and me —me, anyroad, has to exist on less than he pays out for heating. Ar. But Fred's no status symbol. His Nibs had no alternative. He lost his licence."

Bassett said nothing.

"There's a goodly number of haunted houses in these parts," Tod went on informatively. "But Top Hill is best known, as you might say, 'cause it's of our time."

"Our time. You mean what happened there happened fairly recently?"

"Recent as far as history goes, not way back like Gurney. Smelly and his young wife lived there. One day Smelly upped and axed her to death, then he disappeared. She's buried in Oakleigh Churchyard. Ar"—he nodded—"same boneyard they found Wilson, only not among the ancients. Where Smelly vanished to nobody knows, but they say he never left the village. There's some as claim his wife's brothers done for him—tore him to pieces and fed him to the pigs, others that he hid in a foxhole and still roams up there after dark. They still yarn about it, ar—and laugh at theselves an' all—but you'll get nobody up there unless they be dragged. He mocked—this'un, Wilson. See where it got him."

Bassett looked pensively at the old gamekeeper for a few moments. Belatedly Tod met his gaze. "How do I get up there?" Bassett said then.

Tod stared. Waste of breath talking to some folk, he seemed to want to say.

"The woodman's track, through the new pines," he said at last. "That's the track Wilson used. I seen his car and trailer up there."

They looked at each other again. "No use my asking you to come with me, Tod?"

"You can *ask* as much as you like . . ."

A mummified body so-called, the demolition of a house with a history of a grisly murder, a dead man sitting on a tombstone.

Bassett mused as he walked down Long Lane towards home. A mummified body. "Like something out of the grave," Jessie had said. *Out of the grave.* According to Tod, the man Smelly killed his wife, disappeared, but never left the village. What if he never left the house? Murdered by his wife's brothers? . . . And suppose Wilson unblocked a recess, a walled-up cupboard, or whatever; uncovered the body; and took it to Wyndham with a trailer-load of stone?

But why shift the body? Why not leave it where it was and notify the police?

He gazed ahead, scanning the scenery; the track up to Top Hill was not yet in sight.

Suppose Wilson had his reasons. Wilson and who else? For there remained the tantalizing question: Who removed the body after Jessie fled on Saturday morning? Not Wilson, Wilson was dead, himself sitting on a tombstone waiting to be found. Who, then? Who first got rid of whatever it was Jessie saw and then started spreading the tale of joke bones?—they had to be one and the same. And where was the body now?

Was there a connection between the mummified body and the tombstone on which Derek Wilson was found? . . . He ought to go and look . . . but he brushed away any sense of urgency, reminding himself of his pigs and hens and where his priorities lay; the afternoon light was fading fast, he had things to do at home, first things first . . . The truth was he'd no desire to roam around a graveyard in dusk or darkness, thank you.

Could the body have been taken back to Top Hill? The track remained hidden but he could see the hill now, the middle slopes, the top was enshrouded by mist; and even as his eyes narrowed in an effort to trace the shape of a tumbledown cottage, the mist visibly descended, in places seeming to rush rather than creep down the hillside, as if anxious to clasp the hill and its secrets in a protective embrace.

He'd leave Top Hill till tomorrow, too.

Later: Who on earth would hang on to a name like Smelly? he asked his pigs.

It was mid-morning the following day before Bassett went to view the haunted cottage on Top Hill. Davey had arrived early. His father was being treated to an outing, courtesy of the Round Table, leaving Davey free to stand in for Bassett all day if necessary. They had worked together steadily for a couple of hours, Bassett with an eye on the mist which stubbornly hugged the hills; they had spent a lazy half-hour with Sally and the coffee-pot, and at last the mist had begun to disperse. Davey trotted off with a sickle and a sack to gather dry bracken for nest-boxes: Bassett wiped the windscreen of the little 2CV.

He drove up the track as far as the entrance to the pine forest, parked between the woodman's Land-Rover and the first "Private Property" notice he had seen in a long time, and followed the woodman's tractor trail up the hill on foot. Old tracks. The ground was hard, only surface damp. Impressions of different tyre tracks appeared here and there. When presently these veered off course, so did Bassett, for these, he guessed, were made by Wilson's vehicle and trailer . . . Soon the pines gave way to deciduous trees. Bassett noted lazily that this arrangement was topsy-turvy—it was usually deciduous trees on the lower slopes, pines above them—but he was disinclined to dwell on the phenomenon; on anything which varied from the normal.

When clumps of nettles became part of the undergrowth, he knew he was nearly there, nettles denoting human habitation past or present. His eyes strained for a glimpse of Smelly's cottage, but it was some minutes before he was able to make out part of a stone wall through the trees. Then—suddenly—the trees opened out and there it was.

He stopped and stared. He had expected a dilapidated, even crumbling building, bits missing, pinched by Wilson—but not this, not a ruin, not something that looked a victim of the Blitz. Two outer walls had all but gone, there was no roof, no windows or doors. Was this it—? Perhaps there was another?

Yet this was where Wilson's tracks led. And yes—Bassett's gaze rested on an obviously recent crop of stone—this was where Wilson was getting his stone from. When Tod said the murder here was "of our time" he had thought Tod meant within the last twenty or thirty years, but this building must have been rotting for at least twice as long. Blame misconceptions of age: Tod was pushing eighty, so the 'twenties would have been of "his time."

He climbed on; reached the top. "Hell of a spot to build a house," he muttered to himself. "Beautiful views. But so alone—" He finished with a snort. He had just remembered the man's name was Smelly.

He was looking now at the ruin. The ground all around was littered with long-ago fallen stone and masonry, remnants of wattle-and-daub and worm-eaten timbers. The floor was a bed of flourishing saplings and weeds. No sign of recent digging.

But there was a deep alcove partially boarded across.

No, not an alcove, a short corridor through to a second room. Which supplied little of interest save for, miraculously, traces of plaster and faded wallpaper on the inner walls. Bassett followed the ruin round. It was bigger than he had supposed, and—"Ah! an outhouse!" Which was not a ruin. Remarkably, the outhouse had a roof. "I begin to see," he muttered again to himself. "Wattle and daub originally, added to maybe more than once, and finally renovated to the then modern standards many moons ago." How many moons? No matter. The building would have had a thatched roof. Once that fell in, it wouldn't have taken long for the rest to disintegrate. But the outhouse was slate-roofed, could last for ever and a day.

Moreover the outhouse had a door: decaying, the bottom nibbled by rodents, but a door nevertheless. Padlocked.

Why padlocked? The lock had a soft iron hasp, which had been forced, so that the padlock if turned sideways would slip through. Bassett had one like it on a shed at home. Five seconds, and he was pushing the door open, wider and wider, letting in the light. A sweet, sickly odour invaded his nostrils. Simultaneously something long, fast, and furry shot across his feet, causing his backside to twitch and sweat to ooze. It was only a grey squirrel. Yet he was loath to move . . . From the security of the threshold he darted glances into the outhouse, focused and looked again: an old-fashioned oil lamp stood on a wooden box in one corner, loose soil was heaped in another; in between— dark brown stains on a once-lime-washed wall. Dark brown stains splashed . . . He looked at the floor: earth . . . a large damp patch in the middle. That loose earth in the corner— thrown up by a burrowing animal? At last he stepped inside, and staying close to the walls he went to look: saw no compensating hole. Stooping down, his back away from the door so as not to block the light, he found traces of human footprints . . . Traces because examination revealed that someone had attempted to obliterate the footprints by scattering soil over them. They had almost succeeded.

Bassett's interest increased. He worked his way to the opposite corner, pausing to look at the stains on the walls and twice bending to pick up small items of debris. Arrived at the crate, he lifted the oil lamp and shook it, inspected two spent matches. Slowly he returned to the doorway, from where he ran his eyes over the ground, the ceiling, walls . . . He recollected the conversation he'd had with Jack Carter and John Stokes about sheep rustling, and a new awareness came to him.

Forget mummified bodies and old murders here. True, the outhouse may have been the site of the Smelly murder, the padlock fitted originally to prohibit morbid sightseers—but those stains on the walls were brown, therefore relatively recent, bloodstains. Old stains would be black. There was oil in the paraffin lamp. The spent matches were fairly fresh. The debris was in fact sheep's wool. The damp earth in the middle of the floor? He hazarded a guess that the damp was caused by blood and other animal fluids, that underneath the damp surface a hole had been dug which now contained sheepskins and innards. He wasn't game at this stage to find out.

He began pulling the door shut, to lock in what he had found, when it occurred to him: How many skins? Too many sheep had been stolen for this to be the burial place of all the skins and leavings, the hole would have needed to be a whopper. By the same token the thieves would have been taking risks if they buried sheep remains outside, where wildlife might unearth them and scatter fragmentary evidence. Where else would they dispose of waste? he asked himself as he finally shut the outhouse door and refitted the padlock.

He sought a well but would have been surprised to find one: Smelly and those who lived here before him were more likely to have tapped a stream for water. Anyhow, discovering what the thieves had done with waste was not a priority: what concerned Bassett more just now was *who*.

He strolled in a circle round the top of the hill, halting every now and then to gaze down upon the countryside lying peacefully below. There, the church. There, the big house, Clarkson Hall. There, there, there—sheep. Grazing sheep in every direction. How easy would it be to draw sheep up here? Very easy. Rope one, lead it, others would follow, 'twas the nature of the beast . . . So. Walk the sheep up here on their own four legs— into the outhouse—the slaughtershed. How to get them down again? Carcases were weighty. Carcases *plus* waste . . . Bassett edged closer to the ruined cottage, reducing the circle, and began inspecting the ground. In two places he found what he was seeking: impressions criss-crossing Wilson's vehicle and trailer tracks. The first, a few yards from the outhouse, he had spotted earlier; the second set, running on to grass and petering away, nevertheless provided a clue. He thought he knew now what had made them: cart wheels. Out-of-date wooden wheels with iron tyres.

Gurney's cart. But no ghostly thing.

The angle of impressions running on to grass indicated that the cart had journeyed in a different direction from Wilson's trailer . . . But Bassett's attempt at following, trying to pick up the trail farther on, had to be abandoned; it was too spongy underfoot. You could really only chase tracks made in mud.

He strolled a while longer, his gaze travelling the line of the woods described by Tod. His own and many of the other cottages were hidden from view . . .

Suddenly he realized the outhouse was directly behind him. He had just been inside, knew it contained nothing that could possibly harm him, yet still he gave it a swift backward glance and moved to where his back was less vulnerable . . . Who would come here at dead of night, for heaven's sake? Who would come to this dark, eerie place lit only by moon and stars? Not outsiders, surely. Not townies coming off the motorway for a quick kill and back with their spoils to the city. Wouldn't townspeople bred on neon and noise and the security of buildings and pavements be more disorientated, more nervous, than even superstitious country folk? He thought of Tod's tale, of others possibly hearing and doing nothing . . . Dead of night, everywhere black, sounds of wheels floating on the air . . .

Enough to give anybody the screamers!

He returned to the simple query: Who? Not outsiders. Three or four beasts at a time wouldn't be worth a gang's while, not with the risks involved. Surely not locals: the villagers here were too honest to steal from each other. Which left—inevitably—locals who had once been town-dwellers; and who mocked at superstition. Like Wilson.

He began the descent to his car. Wilson must've seen inside the outhouse, he reasoned; he defied anybody to go weekend after weekend to the ruin and remain incurious about that padlocked door. It might have been Wilson who forced the lock. Why hadn't he reported what he found? He pictured Wilson opening the door—maybe hoping to see old furniture, antiques, something he wanted anyhow—seeing bloodstains, smelling

smells, turning pale—Oh my God! the scene of the axe murder!
—and shutting the door again post-haste . . .

Balderdash! The man would have had to have been a complete innocent, and utterly without the nerve to mess with a
haunted cottage in the first place, for that to be his reaction.

Suppose then, for the sake of argument, Wilson didn't see the
outhouse; say he was *vaguely* superstitious, or simply in a hurry
to meet his restoration deadline. Anyhow he went to Top Hill
for stone and stone only, didn't bother to look any further—
until the one occasion when he did go walkabout, found the
outhouse, forced the padlock . . .

Could that be why he had to die? Because he did tell someone? The wrong someone? And that someone killed him.

Or did he identify the cart tracks, remember where he'd seen
a cart to fit . . . ?

Or . . . ?

Bassett grunted. That brother of his . . .

He reached the 2CV, stood for a moment looking back up the
hill, got into his car, and drove home.

Five minutes later he was heading for the sounds of sawing
coming from the direction of his woodshed.

CHAPTER 11

"I've timed it right, I see!" Bassett looked from the newly
stacked logs to Jack the Poacher's sweaty face and beard to Davey, axe in hand, a split section of tree-trunk at his feet. Grins
were exchanged all round. "That tree branch we carried off the
hill," Jack said. "I've sawn them, Davey's chopped them."

Bassett pushed his hat to the back of his head. "All that from
one branch?"

Davey laughed. "You had a delivery of logs. We've split and stacked them, too."

Bassett grinned, pleased. "Very grateful, both." He rubbed his nose with a knuckle, betraying how pleased he was, brought one eyelid down in a kind of wink, and trying not to feel awkward, said, "Methinks I'll only be a nuisance if I hang around here. So how about if I go and organize a pot of tea. Eat cake, Jack?"

"Just the ticket!" More grins, and Bassett's initial embarrassment evaporating. "We've nearly finished. Sally's gone shopping, by the way."

Which meant that Bassett had to make the tea himself. He did so with expertise and, while the tea brewed, spread a cloth on the kitchen table, brought out the cake, plates, and knives.

Davey was first in, hot from his exertions, clearly happy with the results. Bassett kept the mood light when, while Davey was having a wash, he told him he'd been up Top Hill. "Wanted to see where Derek Wilson was getting his stone from."

"Smelly's."

"Mm. How on earth did he know it was there? It's completely hidden till you get right up to it, and it's off the walkers' routes, not a place you'd find by accident." He gave Davey a clean towel out of a drawer. "I've been here two years and only learnt of its existence the other day, he was here a few weeks and seems to have known of it almost straight away."

Davey shook his head, foxed. "Unless he asked. Or knew about it before he came."

Bassett picked that up. "From his brother? He's a brother in Gloucester or Hereford, I believe . . . ?" Popping a question mark on the end: to no avail. Davey knew nothing about a brother, nothing at all about Wilson's family apart from what Derek had told him concerning connections with the building trade. As far as he was aware, these relatives all lived in and around Manchester.

"Did you ever help him fetch the stone?"

"Not me," Davey replied with a cross between a shudder and a shrug.

"Did he ask?"

Davey's nod was an amused one. "I told him it was haunted."
Bassett smiled quizzically. "What did he say?"
"What you'd expect. Load of rubbish."

Bassett watched him rinse out the bowl, wipe the sink, put the towel to dry. Work denims today, and a shirt and sweater that might have been his second-best they were so smart. In deference to him? "Have you never been up to the ruin, Davey? When I was a lad the very mention of a haunted house would have been a spur. Ah!" Seeing the youth's expression. "Out of bounds, eh?"

No, habit, Davey said. Nobody went up Top Hill, there was nothing to go for, really. No restrictions were placed on villagers, Sir Marcus allowed everyone access to estate land provided no damage was done; but Top Hill? Nobody bothered with it, it was just one of those things. "I dare say the legend has *something* to do with it," he confessed. "That and serpents . . . Adders," he explained with a grin.

Then, seriously, "I did used to go exploring on Top Hill when I was little, of course I did. But it was crawling with adders. A friend of mine was bitten. And his dog. We gave it a wide berth after that. There were so many other places to play it wasn't worth the trouble."

"Did the dog recover?" Bassett genuinely wanted to know.

"Oh yes. He was sick for a fortnight but he got over it, he was a little toughie. Never went sniffing adders out again, though."

Presumably the friend recovered also. They talked dogs for a time, Bassett telling Davey about the pup he would be having soon, Davey reminiscing about the dogs in his life.

It was Davey himself who brought Bassett back on course. "Derek did have permission to take that stone," he said loyally. "And I would have gone with him if he had asked me again."

"Who did go with him?"

But Davey's attention was drawn to the sound of a sharp rap on wood. "Here he is!" he exclaimed as the door opened.

"Help yourself to a wash, Jack," Bassett said welcomingly.

"Done. Used the tap outside." Jack slung his jacket over the back of a vacant chair and thrust out his hands like a small boy for inspection. "Brushed the sawdust off me boots too—" Presenting one, to Davey's amusement. He drank thirstily from the mug of tea Bassett gave him, and winked his approval. Then, sitting down next to Davey: "You behaving yourself?"

Davey laughed: "Don't I always?"

"We were talking about the stone Derek Wilson was using," Bassett said, cutting man-size wedges of cake.

"Oh yes!" Davey's head shot up from watching the knife. "Fred Ansen helped him fetch it."

"Smelly's cottage?" Jack said a moment or so later.

"Yes. Tod says the owner killed his wife with an axe, then disappeared; might have been lynched by her brothers."

Jack nodded. "The lynching could be true. But Smelly wasn't the owner. I heard the story when I was a kid, from what you might call the wise old man of the village. According to him— he could spin a good tale, mind!—Jack Smelly was an educated man, a poet and traveller, handsome as a dog fox, wonderful raconteur when you could catch him standing still, but as nutty as a fruitcake." He rolled his eyes, making it plain that the choice of words and flamboyance were the old storyteller's, not his. "The old master of the manor found him in Italy, where he'd been ill for some time, took pity on him, and brought him home; gave him Top Hill Cottage to live in while he wrote his poetry . . . He married a local girl, a doctor's daughter named Louise. Eighteen months later he killed her with an axe. He was seen chasing her with it. Her body was found. He never was."

Davey was agog. "I never knew all that. Was he really a poet?"

"So it's told. Poets tend to favour solitude, and he definitely got it on Top Hill. I think it was a woodman's cottage previously. Or a charcoal-burner's. Before the pines were planted. When the hill was covered with proper woodland."

Bassett said, "You heard the story when you were a kid, Jack. So when did it happen? Pre-war?"

"And the rest. Pre the First World War."

"So the old master wasn't Sir Marcus. His father?"

"Grandfather."

"A seventy- or eighty-year-old crime," Bassett murmured.

"You're looking for a connection between Derek Wilson's death and Top Hill?" Jack asked shrewdly.

"I was. Until you just told me how long ago . . . I had a theory that Wilson uncovered Smelly's remains. And whoever killed Smelly silenced Wilson. But all those involved will be dead now, surely. Or too old to care."

"What about relations?" Davey ventured.

"Descendants who care enough to kill?" Bassett said. "How would long-lost relatives—I take it they are long-lost, murder usually results in relatives scattering far and wide—know if Wilson had found a skeleton?"

Davey suddenly shot bolt upright. "I've just come in! You think—? The one Aunt Jess—?"

"It was a thought," Bassett admitted.

Jack echoed his own argument earlier. "Why would he shift the thing?"

"Exactly," Bassett said. He waited for further comment. None came. "I understand Sir Marcus wasn't too chuffed about Wilson having the stone. Why his displeasure, any ideas? Could he have been told a different version of the tale, Jack? That Grandpapa bumped Smelly off, for instance? How would that go down? Family pride? Sensitivity to Grandpapa's dirty deeds receiving a public airing? Far-fetched, would you think?"

"Not if it were true that the old master had been up to no good. But who could possibly prove that now? Or want to?"

Good point, Bassett acknowledged. "Smelly's wife is buried in Oakleigh Churchyard—" He pulled a face. "Was that his real name, for God's sake?"

"Never heard him called anything else," Jack said. "As for his wife—'Louise, beloved daughter of Thomas and Jane Whitehead' is all you'll find on her tombstone." He anticipated Bassett: "It's nowhere near where Wilson was found."

"So much for that," Bassett grunted.

For no particular reason, it was merely somewhere to look while he marshalled his thoughts, he stared at Jack. It wasn't until Jack half-turned in his seat and thumped Davey playfully on the shoulder saying, "Haven't you work to do?" that it registered: those twinkling far-seeing eyes of the Poacher's had lost some of their shine.

"Why'd you get rid of him?" he asked Jack when Davey had departed, to "dig a few rows."

"Because you were about to move on—to Wilson's cottage and its history."

"A history which includes you?" Bassett said equably.

"Up to a point, yes."

"You're not obliged to tell me anything—" Bassett began.

Jack shook his head. "I sent Davey away because I'm not a bloke to speak his business in public. If you've questions to ask, ask them. What do you want to know?"

"All right. Would you know why Wyndham stood empty for so long after the others on the green had been sold?"

Jack's smile was low on humour. "If it hadn't been Wyndham it would have been one of the others. Rumour has it that Sir Marcus's empty properties are hidden assets to be put on the market as and when. He never advertises, probably has his agent circulate details to interested parties. You don't need me to tell you about waiting lists for cottages."

"It was an estate cottage until the war?"

"And during. People named Bentley. Their son Tom and I were pals. We even tried to join up together when war broke out."

"Tried?"

A lopsided grin from Jack. "We were too young. It was early in 1943 before we finally made it into uniform . . . Tom's parents still had Wyndham up to then, but Tom married before he went away, his parents moved out, and Tom and his wife took over the tenancy of Wyndham."

"And after the war?"

"Tom didn't make it. When I got back in '46 I learnt that Tom had been posted missing, presumed killed. Molly had held on to Wyndham but she wasn't living in it. She had moved in with her mother—"

Molly? Bassett had heard the name spoken recently. He remembered where.

"—And there she stayed, she and the new husband she married in 1947. Her mother was ill, died in 1949."

Jack paused, began again on a sigh. "I wasn't here but I was told it was 1950–51 before the furniture was removed from Wyndham. Both cottages—Wyndham and Molly's mother's—had been offered to them for sale; they chose her mother's eventually . . . From then until the 'sixties the cottage was let to anyone who wanted it. Stopgap tenancies by people prepared to put up with no amenities. Young couples, evacuees who fell in love with this part of the world and came to stay, POWs. Short let, low rent till they found something better. Then one year it fell empty and stayed empty. Regulations apparently. It was no longer fit for human habitation, the Hall couldn't meet the cost of renovations . . . A couple of teenagers camped out there a few years ago, otherwise that's it. I never heard of any scandal touching any of them."

Scandal? Bassett regarded his friend thoughtfully, the feeling growing that Jack had somehow managed to manipulate the conversation; had volunteered information . . . answered some of those questions that had never been asked. Information about his pal Tom's war service, for example. And Tom's marriage to Molly.

"Tom's wife . . . ?" Bassett said slowly.

"She's the woman I spoke to in the Pheasant the other night."

"I see," Bassett said.

He did see. At least he was beginning to.

"I must be going." Noiselessly, almost gracefully, Jack rose from the table, retrieved his jacket, and thanking Bassett for the tea and cake, moved towards the door.

"Jack—?" Bassett said; and when the other turned, "What service were you and Tom in?"

"The army," came the dispassionate reply.

"Together?"

"We saw each other only once after joining up."

"Tom was killed in action, you said."

Jack turned back to the door, sent the reply over a shoulder. "Missing, presumed killed, Bassett."

Outside, Jack straightened his shoulders, filled his lungs with fresh air. Only then did he pull on his jacket. Only then did he intimate things untold.

"Go and see Winnie Allsop at Home Farm, Bassett. She was a friend of the Bentleys." Their eyes locked briefly. "If there's anything to know, Winnie knows it."

Bassett drove to Home Farm, lying halfway between Oakleigh and Glevebourne, by the scenic secondary-lanes route, a route so devoid of buildings and people Mary had once joked, "Passport ready! Foreign border coming up!"

Nor did Home Farm intrude. The house itself was a crooked old building, but charming: all brown, with black beams and picture-book windows; ancient when the oaks all around were acorns, as quaint as the visions it conjured up of mediaeval England. A neat drive was flanked by dark green, glossy rhododendrons. In spring the ground around them would be awash with daffodils and narcissi. Bassett followed the signs—FREE-RANGE EGGS FOR SALE—round to a small walled garden and a side door. In summer this would be ajar boasting a triangle of polished red quarry tiles; hollyhocks would be in flower, and sweet peas, and sweet williams, Canterbury bells, scabious; and roses at every movement of the eye. There were still a few roses to be seen . . . The door, in November, was shut. Bassett knocked and went in.

In summer, blind Winnie would be sitting in this room in her rocking-chair knitting blanket squares for Oxfam. "Through there, me dear," she would say to passing trade, directing customers into the packing room next door. "Help yourself and put the money in the jug." Seldom was she cheated . . . Bassett glanced appreciatively at the glass-fronted cabinet and its rows of leather-bound business ledgers, cherished tomes from a bygone age: at the solid roll-top desk he coveted, and the leather-backed chairs that went with it. An office once upon a time, and spotless, the faint pleasant smell of carbolic not there to mask grime, for although Winnie was blind she was a real stickler for hygiene, more so than Sally. In the place where her rocker stood in summer there was now a table, with a centrepiece of rosehips and autumn leaves on lace.

"Anybody home?" Bassett called.

"In here!"

The sitting-room on the other side of beads and a door marked PRIVATE. A lovely room with heavy gold curtains, bronze chrysanthemums in a copper bowl, a huge coal fire blazing merrily; and Winnie in her rocking-chair surrounded by knitting wools the colours of a rainbow. Before she went blind, Winnie loved colour. Charlie said she did still; she could *feel* the colours of things around her for all that she could no longer see them.

When her nose twitched as if she was accustomed to identify people by smell, Bassett recalled that the first time he came here the old lady had sniffed and announced, "You keep pigs!" He nearly laughed today when she said, " 'Tis you, Harry Bassett!" —until he remembered he had called out. There was nothing wrong with her hearing.

" 'Tis I! But what's all this! Making a fuss of yourself, aren't you? Fire up the chimney, fur boots, shawl. And winter's miles off. You're getting soft, Win!"

Bassett, like most people, adjusted his manner to suit his company. With Winnie, a down-to-earth sometimes coarse country 'ooman, he could be plain-speaking, occasionally rude; same as she. "I thank my lucky stars I've got the wherewithal!" she retorted as he plonked a kiss on her fire-toasted cheek. "Winter'll not take me. Oh! that nose of yours is cold." She tucked in her chin and shivered.

Bassett massaged the offending lump of soft putty in the middle of his face. "It's mild out . . ."

"Well, come and sit yourself down. Put a lump more coal on if it needs it."

It didn't. "You're looking very glamorous, Winnie." Bassett shaped himself into the armchair opposite and took off his hat. "Had your hair done . . ." Beautiful white hair piled on top of her head.

"Cold to the neck," the old lady grumbled. "And you haven't come here to dole out compliments! . . . Nice of you to say so, all the same," she added, lowering one eyelid over a sightless eye to give Bassett what he knew was designed to be a saucy wink.

Then her voice changed again. "You want something. To do with that murder. Charlie's told me about it. Lot of queer things going on, more than meets the eye by the sound of it."

"You're very astute, Winnie."

"Don't know what that word means. All I know is it stands to reason—a foreigner moves in [she meant stranger] and starts knocking places about left undisturbed for half a body's lifetime, somebody else resurrects Gurney, in a manner of speaking, a new murder on top . . . Can't all be coincidence, can it?"

"You've a nice turn of phrase yourself, Win." And for astute read: Wise old bird.

"I've been talking to Jack—"

"Jack Carter? Poacher Jack?" Winnie stiffened slightly.

"Yes. He gave me a brief rundown on past tenants of Wyndham Cottage. I've a feeling he'd have liked to tell me more . . . He sent me to you instead. He said you were friends with the Bentleys."

"The Bentleys, ar." The old lady sucked her lips, rocked herself for a moment, then, "Did Jack tell you about Tom?"

"He said he and Tom were pals, that Tom married a girl called Molly before they went off to war, and that Tom never returned, killed in action."

"*Believed* killed in action. That's what *they* said, the girl and her mother." A scrawny finger waggled towards knitting wool down by her feet. "There's some burnt orange there needs winding."

Bassett looked, saw a bundle that was neither orange nor brown, bent forward, and picked it up. "This? I thought they'd done away with hanks." The old lady ran both hands over the wool, felt for a strand, rubbed it between thumb and finger, and nodded. "This is it. 'Tis cheap, that's why it's in hanks. Ideal for what I want, though." From a pinafore pocket she produced a pair of blunt-nosed scissors, felt for the string holding the hanks together, and snipped. "You hold it, I'll wind while we're talking."

The two of them sitting by the fire, knitting wool between

them, reminded Bassett of wet afternoons when he was a boy, and his own mother . . . And Mary.

Only the conversation was very different.

CHAPTER 12

"The Bentleys came from up north looking for work during the Great Depression," Winnie said. "Mr. Bentley got fixed up as under-gardener on the estate—loads of staff they had in them days—Mrs. B. helped in the house. They weren't country folk but they settled in as if born to it. Tom was their only child. They wanted the best for him, better than they'd ended up with, so when little Molly moved to the village and the two children took a liking to one another, they couldn't have been more delighted. Molly—her folks were schoolteachers, all set to send Molly to university. The Bentleys thought Tom'd be encouraged by the friendship to do well at his own schooling and spend less time stargazing." She paused, moistening her lips with the tip of her tongue. "By stargazing they meant spend less time with Jack Carter.

"Ar—they was young 'uns together," she said, nodding. "A threesome that lasted for years despite Jack's upbringing. I won't say breeding because breeding he's got; but he was a ragamuffin, poorer than the rest of the village poor, and that's saying something: in those days half the farm labourers' offspring were arse-out-of-pants, poor little beggars. Jack was even worse off—he was one of them kids respectable folk tell their children to keep clear of. And in that light all the other folk was respectable."

Jack's father, said Winnie, was a Bad Lot in capitals by the time the Bentleys and Molly's folks entered the scene—a drinker and not above thieving, a foul mouth on him, and lazy. He hadn't always been like it, and when he was on the wagon and you saw him sober, you'd see the man he used to be. He came from good stock, was smart with his learning, inventive by all accounts, and in his young days wasn't short of cash. What ruined him no one ever knew. An invention, some said; he was robbed of it. 'Twas probably the truth: one day he left the village, eyes ablaze with unspoken dreams, six months later he returned, in the old lady's words: done for.

"Whatever it was destroyed him, Bassett, his dear little wife stood by him, she loved the man. It broke her heart watching him sink deeper and deeper, and 'twas for her he tried to reform, credit where due. But 'tweren't no good. He'd disappear for months, turn up again sober, with money in his pockets, and she'd take him in and love him. Oh yes!" Winnie's voice rose and fell and the wool was wound fast or slow in tune with her emotions. "You'd hear them singing and laughing for days on end, little Jack an' all!—then one day it'd be quiet and you'd know he'd hit the drink again. There was more bad times than good in the finish, and the bad times got longer.

"Jack saved them from starving. That's where he got his name from—the Poacher. Poached everything. Wood when there was none to be got from common land. Rabbits, wood pigeons, pheasants . . . He had to. And when he had spare he'd sell them to buy his mother something fancy like a tablet of scented soap. He worked too, make no mistake. One or two would give the lad jobs; he'd work himself to a standstill for a handful of coppers. Got canny though, learnt to stick up for himself. Learnt the hard road but by the time he was twelve he knew his worth, never let anybody put on him after that. A man afore he was fifteen. There's some as said he should have gone then—left home. 'Twas weakness, they said, him sticking to his mother. 'Tweren't weakness, it were strength.

"But let's get back to him and Molly. 'Tis them, the three on 'em together, Jack was on about when he told you to come to me. Tom and Molly took a liking to one another, as I said. They both took a shine to Jack. They'd meet secretly and Jack would take them exploring. There weren't an inch of hills and woods for miles around they didn't end up a-knowing. In them days children could be gone for hours and nobody need worry, not like today, but Joan—Tom's mother—did worry, she told me. Then she found out Tom and Molly went with Jack and that settled her mind. She knew if they did meet harm—sprained an ankle, fell out of a tree, got bitten—they couldn't have been with anyone more capable . . . You hear what I'm saying? Ragamuffin or not, Joan Bentley thought Jack was to be trusted. And rightly so."

Winnie suddenly leant forward and fixed Bassett with her sightless eyes. "Now you be thinking what's all this to do with recent goings-on? I'll tell you—"

One hank wound, another was started.

"Molly. Molly O'Neal. Poor Molly. Life seldom measures up to our expectations—Jack's father said that to me once. Molly's father died when she was fourteen. Her mother carried on teaching at the village school, but from then on was ailing. Couldn't stand the 'ooman myself, she carried on as if she was the only person ever to lose a loved one. Took to her bed in the finish. Putting paid to Molly's hopes of university; she left school and taught herself cookery. Tom never did come up to scratch, he got an office job in Glevebourne. Jack, the brightest and ablest of the lot, got himself fixed up with horse-breeders name of Knight. Gone long since, the Knights.

"When war broke out, Tom and Jack was that restless! Thought it'd all be over afore they had a chance to show their mettle. But their time came, as soon as they was of an age they joined up, matter o' weeks 'tween them. And Tom married Molly. Lovely wedding it was, you'd never have known it was wartime. Tom went to win the war, Molly went to work at the big house, they'd taken in evacuees. The Bentleys—Tom's folks —moved into a farm house, and Molly took on Wyndham Cottage to make a home for Tom to come back to . . . Nobody was exactly staggered when Tom and Molly wed, but for my money Jack was always the better man . . . Now—" A gentle tug on the wool. "Ask me the first thing that enters your head, Harry Bassett."

"Was there ever anything between Molly and Jack?"

Winnie pounced. "That's the one! We're treading the same furrow. I'll say this much, and I'm not mischief-making, what I'm saying is all part, parcel, and baggage—the girl wanted Jack but hadn't the guts to fight for him. 'Twas the mother wanted a ring on Molly's finger, and Tom was her choice—the mother's. Stupid 'ooman. 'I'll die happy now my Molly's got her man,' " Winnie mimicked spitefully. "Bah! Tom? Jack could've eaten him for breakfast. And 'twere years afore the silly'un did die. I swear she only went then to spite them as'd said there was nothing wrong with her . . . Still, the deed was done, Tom and Molly got wed, and Jack danced at their wedding.

"I didn't see Jack again till after the war. He came to see me. Cut up about Tom, he was, but more than that he was uncommon hurt about Molly. He'd gone to offer condolences and also . . . let's be honest . . . to let her know he was there, available. He always was a shy man, and I believed him—still do— when he said he didn't push it. Folk were a-picking up the pieces everywhere, all Jack had wanted to know was—was there any hope for him; if so he'd wait till she was ready."

The rocker jerked violently, then stopped. "Him! Him! Molly said. She could never marry *him!* Wiped the floor with him, she did. Poor Jack couldn't understand it."

The rocker started slowly. "Couldn't understand it," Winnie repeated softly. "And that's putting it mildly. A man like Jack— you'd have expected him to pack his bags there and then and go off to make his fortune. He'd no family to worry about. Mother and father both gone. But he stayed for nearly a year. My fault. 'Twas my fault. I kept him here. I felt so heartily sorry for him I said something I shouldn't've.

" 'Tis not what it seems, Jack, lad, I said. Don't ask me to explain, I said, just believe me. Molly probably *can't* take up with you, Jack, lad. Then I told him that I thought—but couldn't prove any more than he'd be able to—that Tom was still alive—a deserter."

Winnie stuck out her chin. "I don't hear any surprise, Harry Bassett."

Bassett shook his head, forgetting the old lady was unable to see him. "Mind telling me why you think Tom Bentley was a deserter?"

"For one thing there was never a telegram from the War Office. I had that on good authority." She passed the second ball of wool to Bassett, picked up another hank. "None of this need go further, need it? The authorities aren't going to worry about what Tom did forty years ago, but I'd as soon not stir anything for him."

"I'll only use it as a last resort, Win."

"Good enough." They began the next hank. "For one thing—no telegram. For another—I was at Tom's mother's when Red Hatters turned up: looking for him or I'll eat my own hat. We're a contented bunch round here—or bone idle, unadventurous, call it what you like, not much else to do but mind one another's business. 'Twere worse them days. Everybody waited to be told what it was all about, the Bentleys having fit in so well and being as chatty as the rest—but never a word."

"They didn't confide in you?"

"No. That's what decided it for me, us being such good friends. All Joan ever said on the subject was, 'Don't ask me, Win. Don't so much as whisper Tom's name in front of his father.' "

"Suppose Tom did desert, Winnie—"

"His father would have killed him. No! I don't mean that, I mean he'd never have condoned it. Him, fathering a cowardly son!"

"He'd have turned Tom in?"

"He'd have sent him back to give himself up!"

"When exactly was this?" Bassett asked.

The old lady sucked her lips before answering. "I've been trying to remember. Ever since Charlie started telling me things. The best I can do is summer 1944."

"Was Jack home on leave around the same time?"

Winnie snapped, "No, he was not."

Bassett watched until the flying wool calmed down, then: "Where are Tom Bentley's parents now?"

"Went back up north the minute war ended. Joan and I writ

for a year or two, then Tom's father died and Joan married again. We lost touch, can't remember her last address."

"You remember the town, though. Was it Manchester?"

"Durham," said Winnie. "Is it Manchester where he comes from—the murdered man?"

"Derek Wilson, yes."

"A city. You can lose yourself in a city. Know what I'm saying? I've had my thoughts." The head of white hair bobbed up and down. "Tom Bentley, deserter, changed his name. Or stole a dead mate's name. Thought of it first I did when that MP was in the news, the one as faked suicide and used dead men's names to get a passport. Never forgot Tom, I haven't. What if Tom's new name is Wilson, and the Wilson who bought the cottage was his son? And the son found a photograph or papers that'd slipped under a floorboard or something . . ." She tugged on the wool. "Well?"

"It's a possibility, Winnie. This is the last hank, by the way . . ."

"Meaning you don't think much on it."

"I didn't say that," Bassett chided. "Matter of fact, I was thinking about Tom's wife. She remarried too—"

"Ar, she did. Turned Jack down flat, wed somebody else in 1947. I thought about that a lot an' all. Had to, didn't I, considering what I'd told Jack. If anyone in the village had any doubts about Tom being killed in action—her marrying again put a stop to the tittle-tattle. You following me?"

"I follow, Winnie. If Tom was alive—a deserter—Molly wouldn't have been free to remarry."

"Not unless she divorced him. And in them days she'd have had to wait. Seven years, weren't it, for desertion or assumption of death? I don't think she did wed that new man of hers in 1947. She might be married to him now but I think in 1947 they was just living together. None of us got invited to the wedding. They went away and came back man and wife. They'd only met six months afore. He'd knocked on her mother's door asking for directions. On a walking holiday, he said, bed and breakfasting. They took him in, he stayed a fortnight, and next thing—he'd got a job in Tewkesbury and a few months after that Molly was wearing a new wedding ring."

The beautiful white hair seemed suddenly to droop and the old lady's face seemed to age all at once, startlingly. "Oh, Bassett . . ." she moaned. Dropping one end of the wool he was holding, he leant over and touched her hand. She clutched at his fingers, held them tight. "I do a lot of thinking sitting in this chair. A lot of thinking . . . Ar, and remembering . . . I haven't always been blind. I've seen things, heard things . . . Ar. And one of the lessons I learnt on my father's knee was: Be sure your sins will find you out."

What was she trying to say?

Into Bassett's head flashed a picture of Molly and her husband in the Pheasant, obviously uncomfortable . . . watchful . . . mouthing words spoken by Davey and his pals . . .

"What are you trying to say, Winnie?"

"I'm just a-telling you my thoughts." She released his fingers, fumbled for the half-wound ball of wool in her lap. "He got himself work in Tewkesbury, she got herself a new wedding ring, and from that day to this they've lived their lonely little lives tucked up in a cottage that was her mother's. Altered it into something worth a bob or two, I know, but why stay there? I've often asked myself that an' all, seeing as they cut themselves off like a pair of hermits. Why didn't they move to Tewkesbury where his job was? Why not move altogether if they wanted to be *that* separate from the rest of us?" She shook her head, controlled a low sigh. "Oh, I don't know . . . I'm tired of thinking."

The last of the wool trickled through Bassett's fingers. "That's the last of the burnt orange done, Winnie. I'll put some more coal on the fire." He banked up the fire, replaced the guard. "Nice bit of coal you've got here."

She was rocking gently, her hands at rest in her lap. Whistler's Mother. And when next she spoke, her tone had changed again, become decisive. Sad too; but decisive. "Charlie told me about Jessie Podwojski's fright the other morning. Didn't you think it worth a-mentioning?"

"Never occurred to me, Winnie—"

" 'Allowe'en joke somebody played on her, Charlie said. That right?"

"Ar. Something like that." Bassett injected a smile into his voice although he knew she was testing him.

"Luminous paint, Charlie said, according to her at the shop. Paint on a coat to make it look like old Gurney—his skeleton. Charlie took it all in, but you know my Charlie. Was it a joke?"

"Seems to have been."

"Don't flim-flam! What kind of coat was it?"

"An army overcoat, Winnie."

The rocking-chair halted abruptly. The old lady closed her eyes. Bassett thought he saw a tear . . .

"Go and see Artie Anderson, Bassett. You'll find his address in the telephone pad. Tell him I sent you. Artie used to be Oakleigh's village constable."

Bassett nodded to himself: he'd have thought of it himself eventually. If Tom Bentley had deserted, the local constabulary would have been informed.

"Well, go on, you great clod! Pass us them knitting pins and get going . . . And Bassett—? Get there afore t'others get on the trail. Things get twisted and lies get told. Look after Jack Carter. He's a good man, is Jack."

The rocking-chair was set in motion. A low quavering sound came from the old lips: Winnie was humming a tune.

CHAPTER 13

Artie Anderson lived in Glevebourne, at an address not far from the offices of the *Glevebourne Gazette;* which suited Bassett very well, since he could cover two errands at once. But he parked as usual in the police station car park: no charge, no hassle for space in town, and anyhow he wanted to see Sergeant Andy Miller, the third item on his list.

Andy wasn't in. Bassett left a note for him at the desk. It read:

Please get everything you can on Wilson's parents, especially his father. Am particularly keen to know if any connection with people named Bentley.

St. Katherine's Court was at the other end of the short high street, a collection of black-and-white buildings comprising the Ancient High House, now part museum, part art gallery, a row of almshouses converted to craft shops, and a tiny appendage which housed the newspaper offices.

The offices were closed. A telephone number was provided for emergencies. Bassett made a note of this and carried on across the cobbled square fronting the ancient buildings, down narrow Church Lane, and up to the double row of modern old people's bungalows built behind the old almshouses.

They were neat little bungalows, compact, no doubt designed for convenience. Fluffy white curtains at many of the windows; polished wood, not painted front doors. An elderly bloodhound was draped over a doorstep, head on paw. A tabby cat teased him from the windowsill above, insolently safe in the knowledge that its fat pampered little body was out of reach. In appreciation of Bassett's "Hello, old lad," the dog's tail gave two hopeful thumps and then relaxed, only doleful eyes moving to follow Bassett as he ambled past. The whole was somehow sleepy, restful, yet not without fun. No. 6 was the bungalow he wanted. This one, with lively potted scarlet geraniums along the windowsill.

The door opened slowly in response to Bassett's thumb on the bellpush. A disembodied head peered timidly from the gap: pale-complexioned, with silky silver hair cut pudding-basin fashion, and rheumy eyes behind steel-rimmed spectacles.

"Mr. Anderson?" Hat in hand.

"Yes . . ." And thin, tall, wearing a collarless shirt buttoned at the neck and many layers of woolly jumpers under a badly fitting cardigan: this Bassett observed as the door opened a further foot.

"Mrs. Allsop directed me to you. Winnie Allsop. I'm interested in people name of Bentley who lived in Oakleigh during the war. Winnie said you might be able to help . . . Village constable, weren't you?" Bassett smiled.

But the other was shaking his head pleasantly. "It's my dad you want."

This feeble old man's *dad?* Good grief! How old was his dad, for heaven's sake!

"Who is it, Arthur?" And now there were two of them; two silver-topped, blue-eyed, wizened bespectacled faces at the door. They might have been twins. "Someone to see you, Dad." Bassett made a mental note that Anderson senior was the one with a stick. "Sorry to bother you. Name's Bassett. I'm a retired bobby like yourself—"

Magic words! "Come in! Come in! Put the kettle on, Arthur! Or would you fancy a drop of rum?"—whispered conspiratorially. And, "Come to the fire! Take your coat off or you won't feel the benefit . . ." And more, overwhelming Bassett with hospitality. The excitement invigorated them, gave them permanent smiles and red mounds of pleasure high on their cheekbones, so that now Bassett recognized them—they were garden gnomes come indoors for the winter.

"The Bentleys, did you say? Yes, I remember them. Arthur! This is private. Go and make that tea!" And a shake of the stick.

"Winnie's right," old Artie said, when they finally got down to it. "It happened so long ago it can't do any harm to talk about it now. It never was openly talked about, though I think some of them guessed. The odd hint was dropped but I never bit, used to quote propaganda sheets, soon nipped mischief in the bud. What was that one about loose talk? 'Ssh!—a fifth columnist may be listening.' You'll know the one I mean."

"*You* knew Tom Bentley was a deserter, though . . ."

"Part of my job to know," Artie said, puffing out his chest a little. "I had to see his folks and young wife, keep my eyes peeled. The trouble was the authorities would inform you when a serviceman broke loose, but they never followed up with the outcome. He could have been caught or have given himself up, served his ninety days and *then* got killed in action for all I know. Somehow I never did think so."

"Why?" Bassett asked.

"Hard to say," the old man replied reflectively. "Let me put it this way—after the war men came home who'd been prisoners-of-war, in Jap hands, some of them. They never discussed their experiences. They might now but they didn't then, they knew most folk would accuse them of exaggerating. Men who had been through hells like Arnhem—they never said much. What they all did talk about were their pals who *didn't* come back. Hardly a mention though about Tom Bentley. It was as if the word had spread that Tom Bentley was taboo."

"Winnie suggested that Tom's father would have refused to harbour a deserter."

"Stan Bentley was proud of his soldier son, yes. On the other hand—" Artie lifted frail shoulders, tapped with remarkably straight fingers on the arm of his chair. "Many a village lass was threatened with the workhouse and, after they went, the street, if she got herself in the family way, but when it came to the crunch . . ."

Bassett nodded agreement. "Can you recall the circumstances?"

"Embarkation leave. He was supposed to be coming to young Molly. He never arrived . . . Excuse me. Where's that boy?"

Boy? Bassett stared in silent amazement as old Artie shuffled to the door, called belligerently, "Arthur! Where's this young man's tea?" and disappeared. He stifled a grin, shut his ears to muted sounds of bickering, and thought of soldier Tom heading for home on embarkation leave—and never arriving . . . Who said? His wife? Parents? . . . Which home would he have aimed for first? A youngster—a kid, they'd call him today, but then he was a man; and married. He'd go to his own home surely, to the waiting arms of his bride . . . He never arrived. Implication: *nobody* saw him; none of the villagers.

Old Artie returned, chuntering. "Young whelp. Half asleep, that's his trouble . . ." And Bassett had difficulty keeping his face straight: he'd known women who bickered like this, never elderly father and son. "Where was I?" Artie said. "Oh yes. Tom's leave—"

"Were they expecting him?" Bassett said.

"No. No, they weren't. He hadn't told them he was coming."

"Presumably his travel warrant was taken up . . . Must have been, yes, they'd have checked."

"Knew he'd set out for home," Artie said.

"How would he have travelled in those days? Train to Hereford? Malvern? Or were there village stations pre-Beeching?"

"He'd have come by train to Malvern, bus from there. Loads of buses—"

"Not late at night, though?"

"That's true," Artie said, nodding.

"Remember how unreliable trains were?" Bassett said, thankful for the opportunity to release that held-in grin. "The hours they stood outside main-line stations during airraids? Suppose Tom's train arrived after the last bus to Glevebourne had gone, what would he do, hitchhike? Or walk the eight miles of hills he knew so well? . . . If I had been Tom, I'd have walked the hills. Agreed?"

"Walked the hills, yes. He'd have been home before dawn."

"If I had it in mind to *disappear,*" Bassett continued, "I would definitely choose the hills. That ruined house on Top Hill—abandoned many years ago, I understand—?"

Old Artie beamed a row of false teeth. "Jack the Ripper's—"

Gave Bassett a start. "Eh?"

Artie said, not without glee, "Jack the Ripper was what they called a man named Somelli when he killed his wife with an axe—"

He was interrupted by "Boy" Arthur bringing in a tray of tea and three tots of rum. While teas and rums were being handed round, Bassett asked, "How do you spell that?"

The old man grinned. "You've heard him called Jack Smelly. It's Somelli. Giacomo." He spelt it out. "He was Italian. Turn of the century, twenty years after the Whitechapel murders, but the Ripper was still in people's heads, and when Somelli killed his wife, well, you might guess. Folk were very suspicious of foreigners in those days. The master had brought him from Italy, he was a gent like the Ripper . . . People clung to that and him being 'different,' meaning he kept himself to himself, as proof positive. Accused the master behind his back of bringing the Ripper home from exile. Who's to know they weren't right? I don't know the full ins and outs, though, it's my dad you'd have had to see. Happened in his time."

Artie's last words coincided with a look towards the door in response to a small noise on the other side. Bassett glanced sharply in the same direction, and such was his mood in the company of the Andersons he said irreverently, unable to help himself, "He's not with us, is he?"

"Hope not," Boy Arthur mumbled joyfully. "He's been dead thirty years." Next second he was dancing a practised fandango, legs skilfully avoiding his father's attempts to fetch him one with his stick; and Bassett was having trouble with his face again. But tea and rum tasted, and praises sung, Boy Arthur went to collect the newspaper from the front mat, and Bassett brought the conversation back to its former footing.

"Top Hill Cottage . . . You must have known it when it was reasonably habitable. What condition was it in during the war?"

The old village constable was quick. "Tom Bentley didn't hide out up there. I checked regularly."

"Haunted," Bassett said mildly.

"You'll always get some daft noodle keeping a spook tale alive."

"But why that one?" Bassett said. "I can understand original fears and people keeping their distance—Somelli had vanished, meaning they didn't know where he was—meaning he could jump on them from behind a tree. But those fears would have died with the passing of time. What kept the Somelli legend alive?"

"Or revived it? And when? And could the ghost, say towards the end of the war, have been the real live Tom Bentley?"

Bassett looked at old Artie with silent admiration. "Suppose Molly harboured her deserter husband, mightn't he have hidden on Top Hill until Molly considered it safe, and then moved in with her and stayed out of sight?"

"Wouldn't have been easy." Boy Arthur put in his two penny-worth. "She had followers."

"Followers?"

"Anything in trousers," denounced Arthur. He sipped tea and stared into space, a knowing smile dimpling the corners of his mouth.

"Bucked her ideas up after—" Artie glared at his son.

"Yeah. Butter wouldn't melt," Arthur muttered. "Got herself a new husband and started acting lady-of-the-manor, too good for those she'd grown up with. Toffee-nosed—"

"She did give that impression," old Artie admitted. "Even gave Jack Carter the cold shoulder, yet the three of them—Molly, Tom, Jack—had been inseparable. Do you know Jack? He came to see us the other week, brought the rum, matter of fact . . . Fond of Jack, Molly was. They both were—Molly and Tom. Knew him, you see; knew the real Jack. So did I. Many's the blind eye I turned on his bulging bag of rabbits and black-berries—yes, gather blackberries from a gentry's hedge, he'd like as not have you for it. Although it was for his mother mainly I played dumb. Lovely woman. And Jack was a good son, he'd have done Molly proud. But there you are, she didn't want him. So—"

"Could have been the other way round," Arthur put in. "Could have been Jack who turned *her* down after he learnt a thing or two—"

Artie senior glared again. "Where'd you get that crackpot no-tion? If you'd seen Jack—! I've never seen a man so cut up! He looked pole-axed." The last word was almost inaudible. "All these years," he said, staring beyond Arthur. "All these years and I've only this second thought of it. The one place I only ever checked the once was Jack's old house. Too far from Molly's, you see, she'd be bound to have been seen taking him food, too chancy, I thought. But he could have holed up there . . ."

And if Tom could get home unseen, Jack surely could, Bassett thought. And there were more reasons than one for a man to look pole-axed.

"Molly still there?" Artie inquired. "Never thought she'd stay, you know, she had nothing to stay for after her mother died.

Except maybe the beauty of the place . . . Yes, yes. Could have been that that held her. And getting her mother's house at sitting tenant price," he added sagely.

The conversation drifted on to the subject of community policing, past and present, which was what Artie had wanted to talk about all along. Out of courtesy and some deference, Bassett stayed longer than he intended, the anecdotes flowing freely, Bassett's admittedly relating more to his grandfather's experiences as a village policeman in Hampshire than to his own; but at last it was time to go.

Both Andersons accompanied Bassett to the front door, where old Artie said, "You didn't tell me your interest in the Bentleys, and I won't ask. But about Tom holing up in Jack's old place—forget it. You lose track, but when I think back forty years I can remember I went all over. If Tom had been anywhere for any length of time, I'd have picked up the scent. As for Molly, she was only a lass," he said indulgently. "My wife explained it to me: a young girl, had little enjoyment out of life after her father died and her mother declared herself an invalid, discovered she liked being loved—you know what I mean—and couldn't get enough of it. She'd probably never have gone off the rails if Tom had been there. He wasn't. Other men were—"

Nicely expressed, thought Bassett.

"—And I think she suffered for it. It could have been for Tom that she stuck it out, originally, a kind of atonement; and in case he came back."

"Huh. Didn't stop her getting married again, did it?" Arthur muttered darkly. "Got wed again in 1947."

Bassett retraced his steps to the *Gazette* offices deep in thought. He had a sneaking suspicion that towards the end of his visit at least one of the Andersons had caught on.

The newspaper offices remained closed. Returning to the police station, Bassett added to his note to Sergeant Miller:

Andy—when you've time will you dig into *Gazette* archives for anything appertaining to Bentley, resident Oakleigh. Critical dates: 1943 to 1947. Wedding '43 or '44: photo-

graphs would be useful. Senior Bentleys left Oakleigh '45 or
'46. Query: any farewell messages? Will phone you tomorrow.

Afterwards he sat in his car, frankly at a loss to know where
to go next. His mind was in a state of mild confusion . . . He
began to sort himself out. He'd started the day with Top Hill and
sheep rustling. Jack and Molly and Tom Bentley had intervened; and Winnie and the Bentley family; the Andersons and
Tom and Molly Bentley . . . It was obviously Molly he should
go to see next.

But Derek Wilson—who was he?

He decided to take advantage of Davey's baby-sitting his pigs
and chickens, and pursue Derek Wilson's possible connection
with Top Hill.

He headed for Mayberry's.

CHAPTER 14

He couldn't see his little checkout girl so he went to the wine
and tobacco kiosk and purchased two bottles of whisky, one for
himself and one for Davey to take to his dad. Mr. Mellor's visitors would drink it if he himself wasn't allowed to. "I wanted a
word with Susan," he said to the young fellow who served him.
"Is she here today?"

It turned out that the girl Bassett had found tearful in the
loading bay the previous morning wasn't a checkout girl, as he
had surmised, she was a trainee accounts clerk. "I'm in the
office," she told him when in due course she arrived at where
he was waiting in a quiet corner of the store. "Thank you, Deb-
bie—" to the shelf-filler who had fetched her. Then back to

Bassett, and a small gasp of surprise, "Oh! Are you the gentleman—?"

On whose shoulder she had wept yesterday, yes. Bassett smiled. "I came to see how you were feeling. You were so obviously fond of Mr. Wilson."

The girl shrugged shyly. "I'm afraid I made a fool of myself. But when you leave college wondering will I, won't I get a job, will I or won't I be forced to travel, which I don't want to have to do for the moment, and someone gives you a chance on your own doorstep, it's natural to feel fond of that person. I'm ashamed to say I was also thinking selfishly. Derek liked me but the deputy manager doesn't—or didn't, he's changed his tune a little since. I needn't have worried, silly me; Miss Smith assures me my job is safe."

"The redoubtable Miss Smith."

"You've met?" the girl said, wide-eyed.

"Briefly." He raised an eyebrow: Remember?

"Yesterday," the girl said brightly. She paused, said soberly, "This is very nice of you," and gave him a most bewitching smile, which quite bowled him over—although he was well aware that her happiness was due to her "safe" job. "I'm sorry I haven't been able to do anything about pigfood yet, Mr.—er—"

"Bassett," he prompted. "And you are Susan, whose friends call her Sue. Susan—or may I call you Sue?—is there anywhere we could talk in private?"

"In private?" She was suddenly looking at him wisely. She was a pretty little thing, neat and business-like, older than the sixteen he had imagined yesterday; nearer eighteen or nineteen, he guessed now, and probably clever. "I thought you were a pig-keeper." She inclined her head. "You're not, are you? Are you a policeman?"

Bassett made comical eyes at her. "Yesterday you met a policeman pretending to be a pig-keeper. No, not pretending—I do keep pigs. However . . . Today you see that pig-keeper acting the part of a policeman."

Susan laughed. "You've lost me. But if you *are* a policeman—"

"I'm not," Bassett confessed. "I'm a retired detective with a private interest in the case."

"All the same . . ." Bright eyes told of private debate going on in her mind. The debate came down in Bassett's favour. "What about the loading bay again? I'll be able to hear the phone from there. We are all at sixes and sevens and I haven't had a lunch-break yet, so I'll take a short one now. Go the back way, I'll meet you there."

"Miss Smith's gone to the bank," Susan said when they were together once more, "or I'd have begged a proper break and suggested we have a cup of tea somewhere."

"You work with Miss Smith?"

A nod. "She's teaching me my job. I'll take over the paper-work when she returns to Head Office. She's very strict but I get on well with her. That's why I'm glad of this opportunity to talk to you. You see, I have some information which may be evidence. But this is my first job, and I intend to work for advancement. If I go to the police—officially—it could get back, and they might not like it—"

"You mean Mayberry's may take a dim view of your going over their heads?"

"Yes."

"Haven't the police questioned you?"

"Well, no. Not really."

"If what you have is evidence—"

"I'm not sure it is. It *might* be. Derek had a funny phone call . . ." There Susan faltered, as if in doubt about how to proceed.

Bassett gave her an indirect nudge. "Did you share an office with Derek Wilson?"

"Yes, I did. With Miss Smith as well, but she isn't in the office all the time, she flits around other shops."

"It was you then who answered this particular call," Bassett said kindly. "Tell me about it."

"It was last Monday or Tuesday—I'm not sure which. Derek wasn't in the office, I had to go and find him. He was in the shop, perfectly fine till he picked up the receiver. He listened, went vivid red and swore. 'I'll do him!' he said. I didn't hear anything else because the deputy manager came in, wanting my help with an invoice. But after he'd gone I saw Derek sitting —well, stunned. I asked if he'd received bad news. He said it was a deal that had gone wrong. Then he picked up the phone, dialled, tried several times, and got no reply. He'd cooled down by then so I offered to keep trying for him. But he said it was all right, he'd try again later. Whether he did or not I wouldn't know, but . . . It might be important, mightn't it?"

"Indeed it might, Sue. Have you any idea what kind of deal?"

"Sorry, no."

"Did the caller supply a name?"

"Paul."

"Paul who? Relative? Friend? Brother?"

"Sorry again. Don't know."

"When you answered the phone the man on the other end said what? 'May I speak to Derek?' Or did he say Mr. Wilson?"

"He said, 'Get me Derek, will you, love.' I said, 'Who shall I say is calling?' and he said, 'Tell him it's Paul.' "

"You found Mr. Wilson, told him. What was his reaction?"

"He was pleased. I said, 'You're wanted on the phone, somebody named Paul,' and Derek said, 'Oh, good.' "

"And when later he said 'I'll do him,' he was saying this *to* Paul, about someone else?" Susan said yes. "Did it sound like a genuine threat?" Bassett asked.

"I didn't think so, not really. He was cross, but not that cross."

"I see." Bassett spent a moment or so digesting this, then, "In a nutshell—Mr. Wilson was expecting good news, received bad, and someone else, a third party, appeared to be responsible. Sound reasonable?"

"Yes, it does."

"And you're sure Mr. Wilson didn't say something like, 'Oh good, the man from Bird's Eye?' In other words the deal, as far as you know, had nothing to do with a discounted consignment of, say, frozen peas he was let down on?"

"I doubt if it was anything to do with the shop," Susan said.

"Head Office deal with bulk buying, discount contracts, and so on. If it had concerned the shop I think he would have told me, had a good old moan."

"Right-o!" Bassett said matter-of-factly. "My advice is to tell the police if they approach you again. Choose your moment, use tact . . ."

"You think so? All right. I'll do that. I'd hate to jeopardize my position here, but if I do it right, as you say . . ." She bounced a perkier look at Bassett: "Yes. I can do it. Thank you. I've rather monopolized the conversation, haven't I? *You* wanted a private word with me."

"Mm." Bassett nodded and smiled. "Bit of quid pro quo now. Tell me: did the police take anything away with them?"

"Only Derek's things out of his locker."

"What about his desk? Notebooks, jotters—" Susan began a slow headshake. "Did he not have a pad to jot down notes to himself? Reminders? Names, telephone numbers—"

"Like his desk diary? They didn't take that. It was on my desk. It's there now."

"I wouldn't mind having a look at it," Bassett said. "On the off-chance of finding something," he explained. "Desk diaries invariably end up as scribbling pads—phone in one hand, scribble away with the other. We all do it. I could write my wife's biography from a collection of our telephone pads. The number —or numbers—Mr. Wilson tried to get through to after Paul's call. They may be in there. He may have had to look them up sometime."

"And written them down. I get you." Yet Susan hesitated.

"If the diary's absence from your desk is queried, you can safely say the police collected it," Bassett began; but Susan waved that away. "It's not that. Derek doodled, the diary's a mess. What I mean is, you'll need me to do some deciphering, and I really can't stay now. I could take it home with me to-night," she said helpfully. "You don't live in Glevebourne, do you? No, you can't do, not if you keep pigs. Could you come back in the morning, early?"

"How early?"

"Eight o'clock? That will give us twenty minutes before I have to start work."

"I'll be here."

And with that Bassett had to be content.

As Doc McPherson's surgery was in Glevebourne, it crossed Bassett's mind to call in on him also, but it was already mid-afternoon, he was chasing daylight, and he was anxious to locate Molly. That is, he wanted to pinpoint her home from the road now, while certain ideas were in his mind. Molly had priority.

There were many houses in and around Oakleigh which meant little to Bassett. He met people out, knew them to speak to, some he and Mary would have claimed to know well; but often they had no idea who lived where, which house belonged to whom. Jack, for example: Bassett was in total ignorance of where Jack lived. Molly . . . ? Following a spot of reasoning, which included those chimneys seen from High Meadow, he headed for Oakleigh Village main road and carried on towards Pepper's Farm, looking out for a sign he had seen frequently: ACCESS TO THE OAKS ONLY. The journey wasn't without a moan or two, muttered under his breath, "A good copper should know where everybody lives in his manor," countered by a reply that could have come from Mary, "But you're retired (dear), remember?"

He reached the sign. Was this it? If so, no wonder he hadn't been able to recall the house to memory: it was completely concealed from the road . . . And who could blame anyone for not wanting to leave, he thought, as he drove slowly along the access lane: the house was a beauty, a totally rebuilt thatch cottage with gardens so expertly landscaped they might have been fashioned by Nature herself to complement neighbouring hills and woodland. He parked on the turning area at the bottom of a long winding path to The Oaks' sculptured front door, and continued on foot. Flowering roses and primulas marked his way. Roses everywhere; past their best, but must be gorgeous in the summer . . .

Grass on his right now: sweeping lawn . . . and a newly

planted curving border bed of shrubs or bushes . . . Roses again, he saw as he drew nearer; what else? He stopped to read some of the labels. "Blessings: coral pink, fragrant." "Bettina: orange, fragrant." "Bonsoir: peach pink and fragrant." And one called "Peace . . ." He stood for a few moments surveying the soil; then he continued up the path.

She must have seen his approach for the door opened as he reached it, but if she had witnessed his looking at the rose labels she gave no indication. "Name's Bassett," he said, smiling and raising his hat. "We are neighbours." He motioned in roughly the direction of his own home. "Disgraceful state of affairs! I don't know your name, yet I ought to . . ."

"Willoughby. I'm Molly Willoughby." She spoke softly, with a trace of apprehension; she recognized him, he could tell.

"Ah, then you are Julian's wife—"

"My husband's name is Graham." She showed neither pleasure nor displeasure, merely a kind of wariness. Take away that wariness and you might have a zombie. Yet this state must have been temporary, her skin was too good, her grey hair too healthy, and she did possess laughter lines. "I have seen you about," she said; and as this seemed to establish bona fides, "You'd better come in."

But only just in. He wiped his feet on the mat, her glance and small hand movement suggesting this was expected of him. They stood in a square entrance hall about the size of his parlour. Heat belted out from the walls. A swift look at the balustraded stairs and into a room whose door was ajar revealing a predominance of velvets and polished woods told him that this was one of those houses where you would be shy of rumpling a cushion. And where were the Jack Russells?

"Graham isn't home yet."

Bassett smiled. "It's really you I came to see. I wondered how well you knew Derek Wilson, the new owner of Wyndham Cottage."

"Knew him? Not at all."

"Oh." Bassett affected some surprise. "I don't know where I got it from, but I felt sure you sold him the cottage."

"No."

"Oh." And now he portrayed disappointment. "I understood Wyndham used to be yours. I hoped you might have had an affection for the old place, and been interested in the alterations Derek was making." He gave her one of his best smiles. "You did used to live there once?" But he made it sound casual.

"When I was married to my first husband. He died in the war."

"I'm sorry—" Bassett began humbly. Molly Willoughby cut him short. "No need to be. It was a long time ago."

"Yes. Yes, of course. You've heard Wilson's been killed?" This time Bassett spoke with a hush in his tone, and sidelong, like someone dying for the other to say no so that he could have the doubtful satisfaction of supplying the gory details. Molly Willoughby, of course, replied yes, she had heard; as he'd known she would. "I wonder," he said, then, "if Wilson had found something, something left behind, lost, buried even by a previous occupant—might he have come to inquire of you?"

"Why should he?" she said after a fractional pause. "Dozens of tenants have passed through Wyndham. Why come to me?"

Her attention wavered, drawn by faint sounds of a car outside. "That will be Graham. I usually open the garage—" A foot was poised ready for flight.

Bassett intercepted the glance she threw towards a door on her left. "Mrs. Willoughby," he said sheepishly, "I've been out all afternoon. May I use your bathroom?"

For a second he thought she was going to refuse, but really, who could? She watched him slip out of his shoes, said impatiently, "Well, if you must; upstairs, second on the left," then she herself made a controlled dash.

Upstairs, Bassett found the bathroom, opened the door on luxury and perfume, then continued to the landing window and looked out.

From here, this height, he could see into Wyndham's backyard. Not distinctly, but with the aid of binoculars—and full light . . .

More car noise. The car going into the garage, he guessed. Ah. The Jack Russells were barking; happy barks; someone was getting a right royal welcome . . . He peeked into bedrooms, a

linen room, and a sewing-room, flushed the toilet in the bathroom, rinsed his hands . . .

Downstairs he opened two doors and looked inside: luxury
throughout, and he was right first time, not so much as a pin
out of place. A lovely home but not for him. He liked rooms that
looked lived in . . . Muffled voices . . . He dived for the centre of the hall and his shoes.

They came in walking huddled together, from their attitudes
looking for all the world as if Molly had described him as a
molester or worse. "Here he is, Graham." He imagined the ac-
cusing finger: "This is him."

Yet seconds later he was obliged to revise his opinion. Graham Willoughby's arm round Molly's waist had to be there out
of affection, and the flush in her cheeks was surely because
Graham was safely with her, her man, her protector and pro-
vider. There was no animosity in either pair of eyes now when
they looked at Bassett. Wariness was there, yes, and perhaps
anxiety, but so overworked and diluted as to be scarcely detect-
able. "Hello!" Graham Willoughby said, thrusting out a hand to
shake Bassett's firmly without letting go of Molly.

"Hello!" It suddenly came to Bassett with something of a
shock that the Willoughbys weren't middle-aged, they were old.
As he was old. Pensioners now, or very nearly. And lovebirds
still. Why not? For God's sake, why not? Two unto themselves;
they had no need of others . . . He felt a catch in his throat.
Not for the Willoughbys, however, this momentary emotion.
For himself and Mary.

". . . Regret we can't help about Mr. Wilson," Graham Willoughby was saying. "We only spoke to the man a couple of
times."

Bassett nodded, clearing his throat. "So your wife explained."

"We were sorry to hear of his death."

Oddly enough Bassett believed him.

Molly Willoughby murmured something about the oven, and
left the two men talking about the current spell of glorious November weather, and forecasting what to expect from the on-
coming winter. That was all they talked about. Nothing further

was broached on the subject of Wyndham Cottage or Derek Wilson.

Some purpose had been served, however. When Bassett left The Oaks, Graham Willoughby's face was imprinted firmly on his mind.

It was almost dark now. Bassett thought longingly of his fireside and his supper.

CHAPTER 15

Bassett was putting lamb chops under the grill when the telephone rang. It was Doc McPherson.

"Harry—did you come to see me today?"

"I was going to but I ran out of time."

"That explains it. I thought I spotted you in town, thought I'd somehow missed you."

"Got something for me?"

"I gave you time of death—"

"Uh-huh. Around midnight on Friday. The murder weapon you likened to a knitting needle."

"Correct. We now know it had a chisel end, so we say a long narrow screwdriver. Upward thrust. Had the weapon been blunter or bigger I would be saying look for someone who knew where to make the insertion—clean between the ribs, soft tissue all the way. Understand? But—long, narrow, sharp—it could have been done by virtually anybody. A lucky blow. Unlucky for Wilson, of course . . . Nothing else at the moment except traces of sheep's blood on the dead man's clothing."

"Which clothes precisely?" Bassett inquired. "Underclothes?"

"No. Jacket and trousers. Why underclothes?"

"Trying out an idea, Jim, that's all."

"He could have brushed against a bloodstained object. Brushed lightly but traces are there. Blood. Fat."

"That's put me off me tea! I'm already off pork and chicken. But thanks, Jim. Keep in touch."

He had finished his meal and was enjoying a quiet pipe with coffee and a glass of whisky when Andy Miller came on the telephone.

"Andy. How're things? How are they doing up in Manchester?"

"Not very well . . . These notes you left at the desk. Want some answers? Haven't done anything about the archives, I've organized that with the *Gazette* for tomorrow, but Wilson's background—what exactly do you want?"

"More than I wrote in the note," Bassett said. "I've worn me thinking cap since then. Tell me: did Wilson buy that cottage or did he inherit it? Also, was he by any chance granny-reared—?"

"How did you guess—that he was granny-reared?"

"He has two brothers and a sister, if my memory serves me right," Bassett said. "Yet Gran leaves him the bulk of her money. Why? He's Gran's favourite. Why? When Mum can't cope it's often the case that one of the children goes to live with Gran. Sometimes the youngest, sometimes the oldest. Which was he?"

"The oldest. Brought up by Gran for the oldest reason in the world—his mother was unmarried when she had him."

"Wilson is only a half-brother, then?"

"No. His mother married his father when his divorce came through."

Bassett reflected on this for a second, then, "Have you checked his father's past? I'm after a change of name, something faintly shady in his background."

"Don't think you'll find anything," Sergeant Miller advised. "He works for the Home Office, not much escapes their vetting. I did do some checking on your behalf—no Bentley anywhere."

So exit Wilson Senior as Tom Bentley in disguise, so to speak, and therefore also Derek Wilson as son of a deserter.

"As to Wyndham Cottage," Andy Miller went on, "Wilson did purchase. Cash. The deeds et cetera were in the file from his caravan. Gran's money just about covered it."

And so exit Gran being Mrs. Joan Bentley, Tom's mother, and Derek having inherited Wyndham, fibbing about it to Mr. Glass. Joan Bentley buying the property *in absentia* when it was up for sale in the 'fifties had been one of his many theories.

"Any help to you?"

"Disposes of several possibilities," Bassett said. "Thanks, Andy." Without thinking, he put the receiver on to its rest.

In fact, Andy's information disposed of the best of Bassett's theories. Having regard to what he had learnt from Winnie Allsop and the Andersons, he had pictured Tom Bentley arriving unannounced on leave in the middle of the night and catching Molly in bed with another man. They fight. The other man is killed. Tom, cognizant of the Somelli superstition that stopped people from venturing too close to Top Hill, buries the body there, and takes off. In due course he changes his name to Wilson and starts a new life. Derek Wilson is his son . . . When it is known that Derek's job is bringing him to this area, Dad tells Derek his guilty secret, and Derek acquires Wyndham: either by approaching the estate and making an offer—the cottage isn't on the market but a visit to Oakleigh shows it to be vacant and semiderelict—or by inheriting from his grandmother, Joan Bentley . . . It is through his father that Derek learns of the existence of Top Hill Cottage: collecting stone for re-use provides a perfect excuse for going to Top Hill—but his real motive is to exhume the body and hide it for good, under the foundations of his extension. Learning that Mr. and Mrs. Glass are going away last weekend, he elects to do his grisly work then, when there is no risk of Mr. Glass sticking his nose through a hedge . . .

He had liked it as a theory, as far as it went. Now he had to scrap it. Granted, there had been holes in his follow-up speculations: he had toyed with the idea of the Willoughbys having seen Wilson with the body, for instance; but he knew now they could not have seen from The Oaks what Wilson was doing at night, the view from their landing window would only be clear in broad daylight. He'd toyed with the Willoughbys being responsible for removing the body, that is Jessie's skeleton, after Jessie hared off . . .

But why go over that now? He would have worked to fill in

those holes if Derek Wilson had been a Bentley. He was not. So think again, Bassett old lad, he instructed himself.

The telephone rang. It was Andy again: "Is there a conspiracy going on in your village?" The sergeant was naturally a trifle hesitant in view of Bassett's former rank.

"Conspiracy?"

"We've been getting whispers about ghosts, skeletons, and some carriage or other charging round the countryside at night, but that's all we can get, whispers. And then in the middle of a conversation you put the phone down on me."

"Did I?" Bassett apologized. "Not intentional, Andy. Sorry. You were saying? Oh yes. Ghosts and skeletons. That started with Gurney—"

"Gurney? No one of that name on my list . . ."

"Got himself knifed—"

"When was this?" Andy said almost frantically.

Bassett grinned into the mouthpiece. "Calm down and I'll tell you. Listen carefully . . ." He began telling Andy the legend of Gurney, Tod Arkwright fashion. Halfway through, the Sergeant guffawed. "Nuff said. I fell for that, didn't I? Village superstition—"

"Hard to separate superstition from fact sometimes, Andy. Stick to facts is my advice." *And leave skeletons to him.*

They both laughed, Andy saying, "I thought you were holding out on me!" and Bassett answering, tongue in cheek, "Would I do that!" Then it was back to business.

"Seriously, I may have something for you," Bassett said. "Derek Wilson's brothers. What line of business are they in? Is one a butcher, by any chance?"

"How did you know? One's a teacher, lives in Chester. But the other's not twenty miles away. *He's* a butcher."

"He's not in the book," Bassett said. He had checked after leaving Susan: no Wilson in the trade directories under farmer or butcher.

He wouldn't be, Andy explained. He was a butchery manager. Managed a B. D. Jones branch of butchers.

His Christian name? It was Paul.

"Then I do have something," Bassett said. He recounted the

gist of his conversation with Susan, and, "I think Derek and brother Paul were involved with sheep-stealing. I think the deal that went wrong related to dud sheep . . . Three of the last four stolen were ewes in lamb. To a butcher—mutton; small returns for the thieves, and an end to their activities if they had any sense. They'd know the farmers would be on full alert from then on—"

"In the event a costly mistake all round." Andy was all for pulling Paul Wilson in for questioning. Paul was alibied for Derek's murder, but they could probably get him for this.

"Don't," Bassett said. "Where's your evidence?"

"Those traces on Derek Wilson's clothes—"

"Could be attributed to his visiting his brother's shop."

"An excess of meat in stock. Something. Books that don't balance?"

"A non-starter, Andy. He'll have outlets on the QT. Hotels, restaurants . . ."

"What do you suggest, then? He could be a lead."

"What we want, Andy, is that third person, the one who slipped up on the choice of sheep stolen . . ."

"You sound as if you know who he is."

"I've some ideas. But nothing concrete," Bassett said. "So play ball with an old codger, will you? Leave it for twenty-four hours. In the meantime, if you want to get Wilson's troublesome phone call on record, go to Mayberry's and ask for Susan. But not before nine o'clock tomorrow morning. Be diplomatic. Protect Sue's job, in other words. Will do?"

"Will do. Do you still want the *Gazette* info on the Bentleys, whoever they are? Where do they fit into all this?"

"I don't believe they do." Bassett silently cursed himself for delaying his reply half a second too long. He added quickly, "My interest in them is purely private." Which actually was no lie.

Then he adroitly switched subjects once more. "Paul Wilson's alibi, Andy . . ."

Apparently Paul Wilson had admitted to seeing brother Derek on the night of the murder: the two had met outside the Prince William when Derek arrived there after work. Paul had given

Derek money, presumably the roll of notes the barlady, Margaret Gulliver, saw in Derek's possession later. Paul claimed this
was repayment of a loan. Derek had then gone into the Prince
William, Paul had driven on to Newent, sixteen miles on,
where he was in the constant company of twenty or so Rugby
supporters attending a charity function which lasted until well
after midnight. This had been checked out.

"Speak the truth for most of the time, a lie when told will
invariably be believed," Bassett observed. "The money could
have been the pay-out for the previous weekend's load of meat.
However . . ."

Afterwards, while reheating his coffee—he couldn't drink it
cold—Bassett reflected on that third man, the one whose neck
Derek had been threatening when he said, "I'll do him." There
was only one person it could be. He gave a name to the man
. . . then perversely told himself he could be wrong. He could
also be wrong about Jessie's skeleton. Wrong on which count?
He had told Andy the Bentleys had nothing to do with Wilson's
death, had told himself there remained a faint possibility that
they had. Which was it to be? Which was he going to plump
for? All right, so Andy's information seemed to rule out any
family link between Derek Wilson and the Bentleys . . . yet
there was *something* . . .

He took his coffee and a newly lit pipe out on to the porch
and stood looking at the stars. Soft grunts, thuds, could be heard
coming from the pigsty. He smiled, visualizing a friendly argument over who had prime place in the warm straw bed; or
perhaps an adventurous mouse had moved too close to a snor-
ing snout. No sound at all from the henhouse: all asleep on their
perches, bottoms facing the window he had constructed all
along one side.

Something . . . he mused. Wilson started it all. There was no
trouble here, it was quiet, peaceful, everybody minding his and
her own business—within village standards, of course—then
Wilson moved in. Something Wilson did, said, saw, acted as a
trigger.

A chill crept into Bassett's bones. He returned to his fireside,
to the shabby, luxuriously comfortable armchair he'd been

breaking in for twenty years, now beautifully moulded to his shape. He sank into it, waggled his toes inside his slippers, old but also blissfully comfortable; and thought of the Willoughbys. It occurred to him that their house almost exactly fitted the description of the house Wilson's fiancée wanted . . . A passing thought: replaced by one of Mary laughingly calling his armchair and slippers his security blanket. Not true, he chuckled. It was Mary who had been his security . . . but he couldn't stay with Mary too long, it hurt too much.

Back to Wilson and the something he had done; and to sheep rustling—and what the thieves had done with their waste.

The well in Wilson's backyard . . . a moment of rising excitement; which subsided as fast as it came. Worth checking: but would you? he asked himself. Would you hide the evidence of your crime in your own backyard? An ongoing crime? Fine if you could camouflage or concrete over the site immediately, or be there to keep an eye on it, but Wilson wasn't . . .

He went suddenly stock-still, staring into the fire. *"Hide the evidence of your crime in your own backyard,"* he murmured softly. *"In your own backyard . . ."* His head slowly filled with pictures painted by Winnie: of three happy children—two boys and a girl and permanent summer. A girl growing up, with a boy on each arm: two playmates turned handsome suitors; who both went away to be soldiers.

What really happened to the missing soldier?

What was he like?

Bassett had asked Andy to look for a wedding photograph in the *Gazette* archives. He needed a photograph in order to be able to "see" Tom Bentley, for a name without a face was like solving a murder without a body. All he could "see" at the moment was a child. And a shape without substance, wearing army uniform . . .

And a bundle of bones.

An army greatcoat—and a bundle of bones . . . screaming for attention . . .

He sat deep in thought. The fire died down and was banked up again. It was about then—when the fire blazed anew—that Bassett realized there were too many pieces in the puzzle. It was like when you were little and couldn't for the life of you get the jigsaw right. What was a piece of fire-engine doing in a cowboy picture? Eh? Until it hit you that your pal Jimmy Brown had mixed them up, put two jigsaws in the same box; he'd sold you a pup when he'd swapped his jigsaw for your Dinky toys.

The pieces of sky were hard to separate so you began in the middle with the colours . . . Ergo, take away Smelly's crime, that happened too long ago. Take away Gurney and his ghostly chariot—No, put that on one side . . . with Dickie Debbs's Wood.

His task might have been simpler if he had known the victim. Learning all he could, getting to understand what made a victim tick, had always been an essential part of his investigations. *But which victim?* He continued to find Jessie's skeleton of far greater interest than the dead Derek Wilson. Naturally he would never have confessed to this if he had been an active member of the force. Perhaps it was to his advantage—he wasn't official, therefore his mind was free to take him where it would.

It took him in two directions. After a long time spent thinking, he knew he was looking at two crimes: sheep rustling and a falling out among thieves on the one hand, and a wartime forty-odd-year-old mystery, possibly murder, on the other. And that the two crimes *were not connected* except by a place—Wyndham Cottage.

He woke up stiff with cold; he'd fallen asleep in his armchair. He had no idea how long he had slept, he only knew he was too weary for the cold to force him up to bed; too numb even to shuffle to the fireplace and poke at dying embers. He closed his eyes: two minutes, then he would make the effort. The cold intensified, he began to shiver. What time was it? My God! Four-thirty in the morning. He'd done a Jessie! Too late now to go to bed, he'd oversleep, and he mustn't do that, he had an appointment with young Sue. He propped his eyes open, pulled on his jacket, flung a scarf round his shoulders, filled the kettle and plugged it in. While the water came to the boil for tea, he stirred what was left of the fire, added twigs, used bellows to help them catch, and fed the flames with logs.

After two mugs of reviving tea he lit the fire under his pigfood boiler and prepared the hen's mash. By six forty-five the pigsty had been roughly cleaned by lamplight, the pigs fed—he never ceased to marvel at their readiness to tuck in whatever the hour—the hens were enjoying their hot mash, and he had scooped the thin lens of ice from the water dish on the bird table; chopped suet and mixed in seed for the tits, finches, and Henry his tame garden robin; and served it, calling, "Breakfast!"

By seven o'clock he had run his bath, had slid a thick slice of bread and butter out to the first of the day's panhandlers: a grey squirrel who tapped on his window every morning begging for his share; and had made himself a teabag mug of tea, which he took with him to the bathroom.

By seven-thirty he was beginning to feel human.

He got in his Citroën, pointed it towards Glevebourne and Mayberry's.

CHAPTER 16

Derek Wilson's desk diary, as Sue had implied, was a mess. Wilson had used it to note down all sorts of memory-joggers: scraps of telephone conversations, phone numbers, invoice numbers, representatives' references, et cetera. And he was a compulsive doodler. Fortunately, however, the diary had been in use for only seven weeks, and the early entries concerned mainly shop-fitters and the like. Sue made short shrift of the remainder. She was able to isolate and identify all but two numbers: 692 and 705. Both had been jotted down several times throughout: once, an early entry, with a doodled *O*, once with a

stylized doodled *Fred*. *O* for Oakleigh, Bassett reasoned. *Fred*—
for Fred Ansen?

Today, Wednesday, was Davey's dole day. Bassett had offered
him a lift into Glevebourne but Davey's signing-on time was
eleven-fifteen, and when they said eleven-fifteen they meant
eleven-fifteen, not five to eleven or five past and certainly not
eight o'clock. Bassett was mulling over that little bit of bureau-
cracy among other things when he arrived home. No special
reason, he was simply tired, fuzzy-headed, and finding it diffi-
cult to concentrate on one thing at a time. True, he had separated the crimes, had separated fact from fiction—you see? he
couldn't even get that right, there was no fiction as such—but
Wilson and the skeleton, sheep-stealing and deserter Tom Bentley remained intertwined in his mind.

Unless he pulled himself together, this was going to be what
Mary used to call a "bitty day."

The real truth was he continued to be more fascinated by
Jessie's skeleton than by Wilson's murder, and he didn't know
what to do about it. Guilt was his companion for a while.

Normally when Bassett heard Jessie's Land-Rover and he was
unoccupied, he would go to the door or at least call out. Today
he was slow to react and so was silent . . . Jessie was so quiet
herself, however, two days running now, it came to him that
she might be avoiding him. No cheerful cry: "Morning!" but
swiftly up the path, an almost furtive placing of bottles in the
porch . . . Scarcely a sound.

He wondered. Was her behaviour due to shyness after making
a fool of herself, she might think, the other morning? Or had
she, once the shock of finding a mummified body wore off,
recollected long-ago murmurings about a missing soldier? She
would have been a teenager at the time. When he was a teenager he had ears like radar, and inquisitive was his middle
name. He could still remember things overheard when he was a
child, he'd acquired a knowledge that would have horrified his
elders. Was that it? Was Jessie afraid he might start probing?
And that she might inadvertently re-open wounds?

On impulse he trotted to the gate in the hope of catching her.

But he was too late, the tail of her Land-Rover was vanishing round a bend.

The post van drew up in Jessie's wake. "Not much for you today, Mr. B.!" Bassett received the *Reader's Digest* envelope: six more lucky numbers. Postman Sam's cheerfulness was contagious, the tonic Bassett needed. The two chinwagged, about Christmas a-coming, carol services, the weather, all wondrous events if Sam's enthusiasm was any measure.

"Hear about the milk lady's bones?" Bassett asked when other topics were exhausted.

"I did, yes." Chin on chest. "Sorry I cracked so many jokes about it after I heard about old Wilson. No connection, I suppose?" A rhetorical question.

"Where did you hear about it?"

"Ooh . . . Could have been anywhere."

"The Hall, I'll bet," Bassett said amiably. "I hear they're a gossipy lot." He'd heard no such thing.

Sam nodded happily. "I do have elevenses there." Ruminating. "Not on a Saturday though, or the collection boxes are emptied too late." Rural postmen being responsible for both collections and deliveries. "If I'm not back in town by half past eleven on a Saturday, the mail misses the train. But hang on—" His contemplations paid off. "It was Mrs. Willoughby. I remember now. She was in the garden with the dogs. 'Heard any more about the missing skeleton?' she said. 'What skeleton?' said I. She laughed and told me somebody had been playing jokes on Jessie."

"Saturday morning, did you say?" Bassett's manner cast doubt on the day.

"Had to be Saturday," Sam said inoffensively. "Any other day of the week I'm only too ready to chat like we are doing now. Saturdays it's deliver the post and run. Any hold-ups and the old stomach starts churning."

"I know the feeling," Bassett commiserated. "Nothing worse when you're running late."

"Oh, it wasn't that. Usual time for The Oaks—nine to a quarter past. But I have to stick to time, that's the problem. Because of the train. Yes, it had to be a Saturday, I remember now, because I only listened to the bare—oh!—bones I was going to say. I ended up late in the finish. Usually do," Sam said merrily. "And having said that—" He reached for the van door handle.

Between nine and a quarter past, Bassett mused, as he waved cheerio. The puzzle pieces were beginning to fit snugly into place.

And he was back on form.

Shortly afterwards Bassett exchanged town clothes for old trousers and tweed jacket, a tasteful old trilby, sturdy boots, and scarf. He slid a small but powerful torch into a pocket, and as an afterthought grabbed a walking stick.

First stop—after pinning a note to his door for Andy Miller, and a short chat to Miss Piggy and Barrington-Smythe—Wilson's cottage.

He went straight to the disused well, removed the makeshift covers, and shone the torch down. The well had been filled to a dozen or so feet from the top. He had hoped to push some of the surface rubble aside to get an inkling of what was underneath, but it was no good, too far down . . . Jessie had said she stumbled over rubble first time round; on her return visit the rubble had vanished. Tossed down the well? He played the torch into every crevice, every hollow. Or scattered? Scattered, he decided. Hadn't they found the plank she mentioned, moved to a different position?

He replaced the well covers, dusted off his hands, strolled round the site. He was about six feet away from the steps Wilson had carved in the bank rising from the bottom of his garden when he spotted the button lodged between stones on the ground. He stooped and picked it up. A brown button, with a brass ring on the back. He stared at the tiny object thoughtfully, scanned the site, brought his gaze back to the ground where the button had lain; and presently climbed the earth steps to High Meadow, and stood for a few minutes just looking. Then he strode out across the grass towards the edge of the woods and The Oaks' chimneys.

Had Molly Willoughby perhaps seen him? Had she by chance

looked out of her landing window? He thought he saw her in the distance, and quickened his pace. Would she see him now, note the direction from which he was walking?

She saw him. She was out with the dogs: wellingtons, head-square, colourful rubber ball moving to meet him . . . Would she stay on course . . . stop . . . answer that one question he needed to ask her . . . tell him what he wanted to know?

"We meet again," she said as they drew level. Her voice was controlled, her eyes betrayed faint alarm and for the fraction of a second they met his seemed to search, probe his mind. But even as he halted and wished her a polite good morning she sped on, calling shrill instructions to the Jack Russells.

Bassett sighed and watched her go.

He had progressed half a mile along the main road to the village when an old Morris Minor pipped its horn and pulled up alongside. Reverend William Brewerton stuck his head out of the window. "He moves in mysterious ways His errands to expedite. I've been hoping for a word with you. Have you time? I could give you a lift . . ."

"Where are you headed?" Bassett asked, sliding into the passenger seat.

"Would you believe the church?"

Bassett grinned. "Drive slowly then and drop me off near the post office if you will. My destination is the Hall."

"This dreadful business," Willy said as they drove on. "I've been sick-visiting for two days. It wasn't until last evening that I learnt that poor man Wilson had been murdered. Is it true? Was he murdered?"

"He was, yes."

"And have sheep been stolen? I ask because people can and do frequently get hold of the wrong end of a tale."

"There has been some rustling," Bassett said. "Yes."

"Then the rest of what I've been told must also be true, I fear. Those weird noises in the middle of the night—" The curate flicked Bassett a glance. "Made by thieves carting off their spoils?"

"Who told you that?" Bassett voiced the first of two names which jumped immediately to mind: "Tod?"

Willy moved one sports-jacketed shoulder and his lips, a reluctant gesture of affirmation. "Last Friday in the Pheasant," he said slowly. "Tod's yarning . . . Fred seemed nervous of a ghost. Is that how you saw it?" He sounded vaguely worried, vaguely sad; and went on without waiting for a reply, "It is unfortunate that Mrs. Ansen is so bitter, so unready to adapt to their new situation."

Bassett said nothing.

"She is quite unapproachable . . . Yet I understand they think highly of her at Rosemead. That is the nursing home where she works."

"Yes," Bassett said.

"I called on them when they first moved into the Hall flat," Willy said. "Fred was very pleasant. He has since confided that privately he rather enjoys his new mode of life. No rush, no push and shove. No great responsibilities. No longer any guilt feelings about the struggle to keep up with his contemporaries, latterly his inability to do so." His tone went up a notch. "He'd done it, you see. He had succeeded once. He had worked his way up from nothing to management level. He and Glenda had once been buying their own house, new car; they had experienced the thrill of money to spend, holidays, a good wardrobe and table—all the things their parents never had."

Again Willy flicked a glance at Bassett. "Fred's father worked the whole of his life far harder than people nowadays know how, and died little better off than when he was born. Whereas Fred had tasted a decent standard of living." A finger lifted off the steering-wheel. "He, personally, had succeeded. It was not his fault he was made redundant. Given the chance he would succeed again. He knows he may never get that chance, but he's in a way content. Because of that knowledge of himself. *He* knows he is not a failure. The knowledge is his salvation."

"Wise man," Bassett said inadequately.

The curate nodded, moved a shoulder and his mouth as before. "Mrs. Ansen is, I think, still suffering from an element of shock and stress." He spoke with slight emphasis, seemingly choosing his words carefully. "She remembers best what they have lost. Not only their home and former standard of living, but also prestige. She is, no doubt rightly, resentful of the fact that their reward for half a lifetime's hard work and responsible citizenship was unemployment followed by a return to poverty conditions. The future they had planned, she and Fred, no longer exists."

The curate fell silent as they drew up outside the post office. Bassett unclipped his safety-belt but made no move to get out of the car. He felt intuitively that Willy had more to say when he could find the right words.

He found them. Turning his eyes steadily to Bassett, he said, slowly, deliberately, "It is a great pity that Glenda Ansen has become unhealthily money-conscious."

Once more a silence.

"And Fred," Bassett said at last, "would do his utmost to please her."

Reverend William Brewerton looked out of the windscreen, saying nothing further.

After a minute or so Bassett touched his arm. "Thank you for the lift, Willy." He got out of the car.

There were four lanes, drives to the Hall, but Bassett again chose to arrive by the main drive: he wouldn't have minded bumping into Sir Marcus. He saw no one.

He found Fred in one of the garages leathering Sir Marcus's Rover. "Nice day for it, Fred."

"White takes some looking after, though," Fred said wearily. "If it's about the pigfood—"

"It isn't," Bassett said. "I was wondering what you could tell me about Wilson's cottage."

"How do you mean?"

"For instance, whose will it be now?"

Fred shook his head. "His girl's, perhaps. He was engaged." He rinsed the chamois in a bucket of water and wrung it out. "Done. Half an hour to dry and then I'll give it a wax." He wiped his hands on a rag, took out his cigarettes. "He could have had an agreement with his girl. Dunno. It's not the kind of thing you discuss. Smoke?" He proffered the packet.

"Pipe," Bassett said. "I like a pipe in the evenings." He smiled. "Any of his family live round here?"

"Don't know much about him at all," Fred said, lighting up. "We didn't have that much to say to one another."

"You did work for him at weekends—?"

"As long as it didn't interfere with my duties here."

"Sir Marcus raised no objection?"

"Why should he? I use my own time."

"You worked with Davey Mellor," Bassett said shortly.

"Yes."

"Did you know they had Davey in for questioning?"

"They questioned me too," Fred said through a cloud of smoke.

"But you are in the clear," Bassett said when the cloud dispersed. "You were here with Sir Marcus at the time of the murder. The housekeeper and your wife were also here. Davey is not so fortunate. He has only his father to vouch for him."

Fred stared for a moment, then lowered his gaze.

"About Friday," Bassett said. "Davey claims that he—Wilson —arranged to get in touch with you both, to give you instructions for Saturday. What time did he get in touch with you?"

"Get in touch?"

"Mayberry's had opened. Wilson's Saturdays were no longer free. He had to let you know what work he wanted doing—"

"Yes. That's right."

Had he forgotten? Patiently Bassett repeated the question. "What time did he get in touch with you?"

"He didn't. Didn't come nigh." Was it a polite dismissal Fred had in mind when he picked up the bucket of dirty water and took it to the drain across the yard? A thick-skinned Bassett stayed put and edged idly along the workbench, not looking for anything specific, not touching anything, and transferring his attention to Fred when the chauffeur returned.

"You already knew where to find the key then, Fred?"

"Key?" Fred tore his eyes away from the workbench.

"The key to Wilson's cottage."

"Look, what is this?" Fred turned mildly nasty. "Saw me leaving on Saturday morning, is that it? After I had said I had to take his Nibs to Cheltenham. OK, if you're that keen I'll tell you—" He deposited the bucket noisily under the bench. "I did take his Nibs to Cheltenham, as I said. He was going to be there all day, might even stay overnight, so I came back here, no sense hanging around Cheltenham. I went straight to the cottage, as I was, in best clothes, to see if Derek had left a message. If he had, if there was work for me, I'd come and change. If not, I'd stay as I was, watch the match on TV, and wait for the boss's phone call. OK? I wasn't surprised when the arrangements about the key went haywire. As you said, Mayberry's had opened, Derek had a lot on his plate. I took it for granted he was giving the cottage a miss for one weekend. OK?" he demanded.

Bassett raised both hands in mock submission. "OK," he said mildly. He moved towards the exit, turned, said as if he'd that second thought of it, "Did you hear about the joke somebody played on Jessie?"

Fred's slow smile appeared to be genuine, for all that there were shadows at the back of his eyes. "She's tough. Would have scared the daylights out of me. Find out who did it?"

Bassett grinned non-committally, turned once more to go. "Bassett—" Fred forestalled him. "Sorry I was a bit short-tempered."

Bassett gestured: Think nothing of it!

He looked back one more time, just after he hit the open air, to see Fred idling sideways along the workbench in much the same fashion as he himself had done earlier. He walked home thinking of Derek Wilson's desk diary.

Davey was there before him. He left off hanging over the pigsty wall and came to meet Bassett smiling broadly. "They're great!" —jerking a thumb. "Almost human! And don't they love to play!"

"Knocking chunks off you in the process! Dad all right?"

"Fine. He sends his thanks for the whisky. You've had two lady friends looking for you. A nice one called Helen came to ask if you could use some greens. For them." Meaning the pigs.

"I think it was you she really came to see, though." The smile took on a wink, causing Bassett to grunt, "You said two lady friends. You are of course merely using a figure of speech—"

"The other was that Mrs. Willoughby. Funny woman. First time she's ever spoken to me. She said she'd catch you some time, it wasn't important. Although I've probably answered her query for you." Davey wrinkled his nose. "I think she's only just found out about Derek, or at any rate when he was killed. A bit upset, I think. 'On *Friday* night?' she said. 'And *when* was he found? On *Sunday* morning? It took them long enough to find him, didn't it? Poor man.' "

Davey wondered why Bassett stared at him oddly. He was not to know that his last words had stirred a hazy memory deep in the recesses of his mind . . . Stirred, struck a spark . . .

"How about a bite to eat, Davey! I brought some hot crusty bread from Home-Bake this morning. Tasty Cheddar. Pickles compliments of Sally. And a drop of red wine. How's it grab you?"

"Can't be bad!"

Bassett had decided to give Davey what the lad might call "a piece of the action." He talked while they ate.

"You want to be a policeman, Davey."

"Yes."

"Couple of pointers for you. First—professional ethics. Need I spell that out?"

"No. I know how to keep my mouth shut."

Bassett nodded his approval. "In a nutshell. Second—objectivity. If you are, say, confronted by a friend or relation wearing handcuffs, remember you're a policeman first, a mate et cetera second. With certain reservations which need not concern us for the moment. Need I go on?"

"No."

"Right. Listen carefully." Bassett explained about the desk diary, and, "I was most concerned about telephone numbers or numbers which may be telephone numbers. There are two. One linked with an O—for Oakleigh, I think. One with a *Fred.* I'd like you to help me find Fred."

"Fred Ansen?"

"I think so." Bassett nodded, cut himself another slice of Cheddar. "But I may be wrong."

Davey chewed, swallowed, wiped a crusty flake from a corner of his mouth. "Why don't we dial the numbers, see what we get?"

"We'd get the Hall. I looked them up. They have four: one to Sir Marcus's private quarters and three more. What's the staff situation there, any idea?"

"Housekeeper. Fred Ansen. Two gardeners. And Polly who cleans, mornings."

Bassett twitched an eyebrow. "That all, a place that size?"

"That's all. I know because I tried there for a job. They had seventeen indoor servants before the war, and as many gardeners, Aunt Jess says. Their walled garden was fantastic—like that Victorian one on television. But two gardeners—only a corner gets cultivated now."

The gardeners were named Cyril and Danny. They had estate houses and private telephones. Polly's husband's name was Frank: they lived in a gate lodge and weren't on the telephone.

"Right," Bassett said. "Four numbers to the Hall. One to private quarters. Say one to the Ansens' flat, one for the housekeeper. The fourth, say, for guests. Among whom there may on occasion have been a Frederick . . . The housekeeper may have a gentleman friend named Fred . . . What I'd like you to do, later on"—Bassett was thinking of night-worker Mrs. Ansen sleeping—"is to try them, deviously . . ."

They had finished eating, and had just switched on the one o'clock news when the doorbell rang.

Reverend William Brewerton said, "Would you care to come with me, Bassett? I think we've turned up Gurney's cart."

CHAPTER 17

For the second time that day Bassett clipped on the safety-belt in
Reverend Willy's car. Both men were pre-occupied for the short
journey, each with his own thoughts. Presently they entered the
approach lane to the church, a loud toot on the horn bringing
Jack the Poacher out of the vicarage. They drew to a halt near
the church gates, Jack catching up with them as they got out of
the car.

"Along here." Willy motioned ahead. "There's a separate entrance on the other side of the church, we don't have to go via
the churchyard." And when they reached the entrance, "This is
seldom used nowadays. It dates back to when the church was
surrounded by fields and worshippers travelled from every direction on foot and in wagons."

Bassett saw dark walls, cold shadows, grey grass, and crumbling drunken headstones of indeterminate age . . . Then they
came to a hedged pathway, wide and again grassy. Ancient,
large and impressive tombstones could be glimpsed through
gaps in the hedge on their left; on their right John Stokes's farm,
its outbuildings and large amounts of corrugated iron unseen
from the road, hidden by this, the cold, dull, north-facing aspect
of the church. At the end of the path—a weather-bleached hut.

"Scouts' hut," Jack informed Bassett.

The lock had been forced, like the lock on Top Hill. Inside the
hut, which was remarkably free of damp, was a treasure trove
of scouting equipment: bundled bell tents, ropes, spades, flags
complete with sectional flagpoles, steel dixies big enough to take
a bath in; all manner of camping gear of the old-fashioned,
heavy-duty, pre-war variety, not an inch of nylon or aluminium

to be seen. Plus boxes of miscellanea which at another time would have had Bassett, for one, in rooting mood . . . Also in the hut were half a dozen trestle-tables, two dozen or more stacked wooden folding chairs, and under a sheet of tarpaulin, the thing Bassett had been brought to see—a monstrous contraption with four-foot-high wheels.

"Bring back memories?"

Memories of this and others like it being manhandled round an unsuspecting countryside by Attila the Hun and his horde of Bombay-bloomered, grubby-kneed, big-hatted fiends, yes. "Led by a bugler! Don't forget the bugler!" "Remember raw chips and burnt sausages?" "Black handkerchiefs and socks pulled under to hide the holes!" No wash. No checking for dirt behind the ears. And the cocoa! Always the cocoa.

The contraption was, of course, a Scout cart.

"Tod's ghostly wheels," Jack said, holding one end of the tarpaulin clear.

"It certainly fits Tod's description."

"Iron tyres, you mean?" Willy's query. "But to what purpose exactly?"

"Transport of meat, Willy. I think the rustlers used it. Killed the sheep in Top Hill Cottage, brought the meat and waste down the hill in this." The cart was empty and virtually clean save for a small smudged bloodstain here and there. "Packed in plastic . . . That bucket and scrubbing brush the police found, Willy— has anyone claimed them?"

"No, they are in the porch."

Bassett tapped the side of the cart. "Someone was going to give this a scrub. Was. He didn't make it. Not that it would have mattered, Forensic would still have lifted traces. They'd have done better to burn the thing. How many people know about this hut?"

Nearly everybody, it seemed. But it was opened only once, maybe twice, a year. The last time was in July for the church fête.

"Surely that was held in the grounds of Clarkson Hall?" Bassett said.

It was, but the weather was unpromising, so Sir Marcus

erected a marquee. He sent to the vicarage for some extra chairs and tables.

"Do you remember who fetched them, Willy?"

"The outside staff . . . Fred brought them in the van," he added with some reluctance.

"Don't let anyone touch this," Bassett requested as he and Jack replaced the tarpaulin.

"How can I prevent it? If they come again—"

"They won't," Bassett said kindly.

"No. No, I suppose not," the curate said unhappily.

As they left the hut, he offered to run Bassett home. Bassett accepted until they reached the car, when he changed his mind. "I think I'll walk after all, William. I've only been to the Hall via the main drive. What are the other drives like?" He was looking at Jack when he finished speaking; Jack therefore replied.

"You've probably walked on them without realizing, Harry. Two of them run through the woods."

"There is a short cut." Reverend Willy looked at Jack. "The one I take when I collect my eggs and milk."

"I'll show you," Jack told Bassett.

"What did William mean about eggs and milk?" Bassett inquired as he and Jack set off together.

"Goats' milk and bantam eggs," was the reply. "He collects a supply twice a week from the Hall."

"Ah." Grazing Herefords lifted their heads, lower jaws chomping steadily, side to side, and watched the two stride past. "I'm curious, Jack. How come Willy has the living at Oakleigh? I was under the impression that country parsons had to look after two or three parishes these days, and stagger services."

Jack's bearded chin moved slowly up and down. "It came to that here, services down to one a month. Then Sir Marcus's old mother stepped in—bought her passport to heaven, some said." The badger beard spread itself round a smile. "Engaged her very own vicar, our William, by arrangement with the Bishop; paid his salary and expenses; and left money in trust for the arrangement to continue after her death. He's not the incumbent."

"Which is why he's called a curate. Thank you, Jack."

"I won't insult your intelligence by asking if you thought Willy—"

"And I won't insult yours by answering."

They grinned at each other; came to the end of the approach lane. "This short cut—"

"Servants' Walk," Jack said, leading left into the village main road. "I went up Top Hill this morning."

"Yes—?"

"I found what you found, and agree with you about the cart. No problem getting sheep up there—walk them up. But getting dead weight down, dodgy. They wouldn't dare drive a vehicle up the foresters' track for fear of someone seeing the lights or hearing the engine . . ."

"Also mud," Bassett said. "A bogged-in handcart could be dragged out, a van would require a tractor or tow-truck."

"Were the sheep killed to feed hungry bellies?" A characteristic question from Jack.

Bassett shook his head. "I think not."

"Then we can forget the unemployed in the area."

"Who thought of the cart first?" Bassett said shortly. "You or Tod?"

"Who's to say? I thought of it on Top Hill, got to William and found Tod had already planted the seed. I had followed the tracks . . ."

"Good at tracking, eh?" Bassett threw a grin.

"Plenty of experience." Jack grinned modestly back. "Also, once I *had* thought of it, I *wanted* the signs to show up within sight of the hut. Did Wilson catch them at it?"

"What do you think?"

"I think he was mixed up in it."

They strode together, in step. Jack's beard gave a twitch. "Makes sense, doesn't it?"

"Makes sense," Bassett said. "I'm wondering where they dumped the waste. Find that, we may find our murderer. You know this area well. Have a think for me."

"I will." They veered into a private lane. "This is it. Servants' Walk coming up."

"Part of the old North Drive," Jack said. "Tradesmen's entrance in the old days. Whole thing's half a mile long. Over there—the woods that run into your Bluebell Wood. Over there"—turning an arc—"Top Hill. But we go this way." He directed Bassett to a gate-wide gap in a tall hedge. Metal gateposts remained, thick rope slung between them to denote a barrier. Jack unhooked one end of the rope to allow them passage. "The path runs right round to the Hall's service yard."

Bassett had never met a Servants' Walk before. It was what its name implied, Jack told him; and a short cut by accident. In the good old days servants were never to be seen coming or going, preferably never seen at all. Food had to be cooked, beds made, rooms cleaned—but never within sight of master, mistress, or guests; it was considered "not nice." Hence the Walk. Even the tradesmen's drive had been off-limits.

Thick growth, untrimmed ivy, and other creepers either side of the Walk produced a tunnel effect, causing Bassett to think: Pity the poor little skivvy on a dark winter's night hurrying home after her monthly afternoon off: an owl hoots, a rat dashes across her path—and wasn't this once part of Dickie Debbs's Wood? Not a route for the timid.

They had gone a distance, single file, when Jack called a halt. "Something odd," he observed. "I haven't once had to push a bramble or creeper out of the way." He studied the path, the undergrowth. "Willy Brewerton is the only one who comes here. Or so I thought. But look—broken twigs, damaged greenery on both sides . . . Don't you think it's looking *used?*"

Bassett felt unqualified to pass comment, never having seen the Servants' Walk before. Maybe Willy wielded a machete . . . As for footprints, the path was too thickly carpeted with leaves for him to pick any out.

Jack, however, began delicately brushing away surface leaves and twigs. He looked up. "You go on, I'll catch up with you. Follow the path, you'll come to a mound. Go round it, you'll see the back of the stables, Fred's flat above. Keep on, you'll come to steps down to the service yard."

Bassett followed instructions. He did have to avoid an occasional clinging weed, but it was near the mound that greenery became a real nuisance. Twice he had to stop to extricate himself. Both times he sensed someone watching him, and he cursed himself for wanting to shudder . . . He looked back but couldn't see Jack; looked up at the Ansen windows, thought he saw a movement, but when no shape materialized, decided it was a trick of the light. Eyes were upon him, though. As he rounded the mound he saw Fred standing watching him from the top of the yard steps.

"Thought it was you," the chauffeur said when Bassett reached him. "What on earth did you come that way for?"

"It is a bit like a jungle," Bassett agreed amiably, displaying a sleeve covered with burrs. He jerked his head towards the mound. "What is that? An old midden? Household refuse heap," he explained when Fred looked blank. "Before the days of dustbins."

Fred opened his mouth to speak, closed it, and looked overtly at his watch. No one could have failed to notice the suit, the polished cheeks, the oversplash of aftershave; the discomfiture. "Won't detain you, Fred. Just wanted to ask who helped you fetch the furniture from the Scout hut—?"

"Scout hut?"

Why does he always repeat what I say? Bassett thought wearily. "Where you got the chairs and tables from for the July fête," he said. "You did take someone with you, in the van? The gardeners, perhaps?"

"Yes. Danny and Cyril," Fred replied distantly. His head went up. "Was that a Scout hut? I didn't know." He cocked an ear to sounds—voices—in the yard. "Look, I've got to go—"

"Fred?"

"Yes—?"

Was it fear or regret that flitted back and forth across the chauffeur's face? He looked thinner, looked as if he'd shed pounds since this morning. "Want to talk, get it off your chest?" Bassett wanted to say. "Just you and me, figure something out?" If he had been investigating in an official capacity he would be saying it. Or something like it. What held him back now was a nagging doubt.

He shrugged, motioned. "It'll keep. You'd better go."

He retraced his steps along the Servants' Walk. Of Jack "the Poacher" Carter there was no sign. He remembered he had no car. The walk home was going to be a long one.

Davey was on the telephone. He put his hand over the mouthpiece, mouthed as Bassett came in, "Parcel for you. On the kitchen table." Bassett gestured thank-you and left the lad to his privacy. It didn't occur to him to query what Davey was doing.

The parcel was a large bulky brown envelope on which had been written, "Are these what you want? Will see you or phone at eight."

Inside the envelope was a collection of black and white, eight by ten photographs: a wedding photograph of Molly O'Neal and Thomas Bentley, and several taken on VE Day—village Victory celebrations captured on film.

Bassett glimpsed Molly on two of them; but it was the wedding photograph that captivated. At last he was seeing the real Tom Bentley . . . Good-looking young man. And Molly was so pretty! . . . Was there a young Jack Carter here? Would he recognize him without a beard? . . . If only he could see all three of them together as young adults. It was their love—their crime?—that . . .

He stiffened. He was holding a photograph in each hand, another lay in front of him on the table. He stayed like that, staring at each in turn for a few moments; then thoughtfully he put them all back in the envelope.

Davey joined him a few minutes later. "I tried those numbers—"

"You did?" Too early, Bassett was thinking: Fred out, Mrs. Ansen sleeping. But the lad clearly had something he couldn't wait to tell him.

He had dialled 692, he said, and got Sir Marcus Clarkson's residence, housekeeper speaking. He asked for Fred. Sorry, Fred had that second left, he'd be out till about five o'clock. "There is only one Fred, is there? I'm calling from Mayberry's, you see, compiling a list of telephone numbers for Mr. Wilson's successor, and require a full name to go with this number." "Fred

Ansen," the housekeeper said helpfully. He was the only Fred she knew of.

"That's what I was just doing," Davey said. "I was going to try the other number next."

"Just—?" Bassett glanced at the kitchen clock. It read twelve minutes to three.

"Something wrong?"

"No. Only that Fred was on the point of leaving when I was at the Hall, somewhere around two o'clock. But—time flies, the housekeeper probably lost track."

"Shall I try the other number now?" Davey asked keenly. "If it is Mrs. Ansen—"

"If it is Mrs. Ansen who answers," Bassett cut in, "she'll love you. For disturbing her beauty sleep."

"I think she'll be up. Fred told us she goes to bed as soon as she gets in so that she can get up in the afternoon and enjoy a spot of sunshine. Otherwise in winter she'd hardly ever see daylight—"

Bassett looked at him quizzically. "Eyes, ears, and common sense," Davey quipped. "I've used my ears." Bassett grunted; and went with him to the telephone. "Let's hear you use your common sense . . ."

Davey dialled 705. He had barely done dialling before a female voice was snapping, "Seven-oh-five." Affecting the Scottish accent he was good at, he asked politely to speak to John, please. "No John here." Phone slammed down.

He dialled again. "I'm sorry, but this is the number John gave me. John Cox—" "Well, it's wrong!" Again the call was cut off.

He tried a third time. Obsequiously. "Dearie me. I'm terribly sorry about this, but John wrote the number down himself. If you're not Mrs. Cox—may I ask you who you are?" She threatened to sick the police on to him.

A fourth and final attempt. All he wanted was her name uttered: "I'm Mrs. Ansen." Or Smith. Or Brown. Or Dogsbody. It sounded like Mrs. Ansen, but he couldn't be certain. For the sake of peace she just might tell him this time.

She did not. She didn't answer.

Davey pulled a face. "Phone the housekeeper again," Bassett

suggested. "Tell her you need to speak to Fred but won't be able to ring up until after six, would she be so kind as to give you Fred's home number."

Davey did this, and got the number: 705.

"Simple when you know," Bassett said. But Davey wasn't so pleased with himself now. "What does it prove?" he asked uncomfortably.

Bassett shook his head. "It proves nothing, Davey." Not even that Wilson and Fred Ansen were partners in crime. "Fred could argue that Derek had to contact him now and then in respect of the weekend work."

Davey stared into space . . . brought his gaze back to Bassett. "I wouldn't like it to be Fred," he said.

"Mm. I know," Bassett murmured.

Six o'clock. Davey had been run home. Helen Geeson had visited and gone. Pigs and hens had been cared for. Now Bassett was alone and recapitulating as he took a cottage pie out of the freezer and popped it in the oven. He set the timer to forty-five minutes. Forty-five minutes to sit and smoke a thinking pipe.

He had to find the skins . . . He had asked Helen for ideas, referring to sheep thefts in previous years. "Disregarding derelict buildings, can you suggest any place in the immediate area where waste could be safely dumped a little at a time? A cave? An underground passage? Big enough to take a quantity, and capable of being sealed after each drop; ratproof . . ." Helen's best suggestion had been a compost heap.

He toyed with—and discarded—the notion of butcher Paul taking complete animals and disposing of the waste himself. Paul wouldn't dare have dead animals as distinct from meat on his premises. Health regulations. By the same token he'd be an irresponsible fool if he carried meat and waste in a van together, no matter how well wrapped. What did happen, then? . . . The sheep are slaughtered, skins and carcases are packed separately in plastic and carted down the hill. The carcases go into Paul's vehicle, the other two—the thieves—are left with sacks of waste.

Where are they when Paul drives off leaving them with a cartload of waste?

Bassett's thoughts picked up Tod; who had hinted, pointed an invisible finger, guided him directly or indirectly much of the way . . . Gurney's cartwheels. The woods, particularly Top Hill Wood and Dickie Debbs's . . . *Why Dickie Debbs's Wood?*

Puzzle pieces: Dickie Debbs's Wood . . . Servants' Walk . . . Jack . . . Clarkson Hall.

The Hall. He had assumed Tod dropped hints because he suspected someone he knew of sheep-stealing and, an old trusted employee of the estate, couldn't, wouldn't, say so openly. What if it wasn't someone: what if it was a *place?*

Suddenly it was there—the answer. The television series: "Victorian Kitchen Garden," the second or third programme. Mary had been fascinated . . . The Hall was nowhere near as big as the stately home depicted on film, but it did boast an extensive walled garden which at one time had provided year-round produce. Ergo, might it not also possess a . . . ?

When Sergeant Miller rang up at eight o'clock, Bassett was quietly confident. "Andy! Can I recap on alibis? Fred Ansen's and Paul Wilson's? Paul's first. At the time of the murder he was at Newent, sixteen miles away, I think you said. At a rugby do. Sixteen miles isn't far at night on empty roads, motoring fast. He could have left the shindig, killed Derek, gone back and not been missed—"

"He could have, but he didn't," Andy said. "We did think of that trick. No go."

"Right. Fred Ansen. Alibied by Sir Marcus Clarkson and his housekeeper."

"Correct. Sir Marcus, Ansen, and the housekeeper were together at the Hall from about nine-forty until well after midnight, when Ansen went to his flat across the yard."

"In other words they alibi each other. What about Mrs. Ansen?"

"She confirmed Ansen's whereabouts."

"I meant where was she?"

"At home, in their flat."

"Mmm." Bassett paused; then, "Someone is lying . . . How soon can you get here, Andy? I want you to help me to look for something." And when the Sergeant hummed and hawed: "Be a feather in your cap if I hand you a murderer!"

There was time for another pipe before Andy arrived. For a second look at the photographs too . . . A far-away gleam entered Bassett's eyes.

He had finished the pipe, was abstractedly cleaning out the bowl when the telephone rang. A few minutes afterwards he was donning warm outdoor clothes. He put the button he had found on Derek Wilson's land into the same envelope as the photographs, tucked the envelope into the front of his coat. Then he gathered up his pipe, tobacco, and torch.

He was at the gate when Andy drew up.

"Slight change of plan, Andy. Follow me to the vicarage. Our Reverend Brewerton's gone missing."

CHAPTER 18

"How kind of you to come! I didn't like fetching you out at this time of night—but the Poacher insisted that you wouldn't mind."

"Quite right, we don't," Bassett assured the curate's housekeeper, Mrs. Blundell. A pale, thin, rather severe-looking woman, many people fought shy of her until they got to know her, and discovered that not only was she kindness itself but also that she possessed a wicked sense of humour. Neither severity nor humour showed now, she was instead a worried lady.

"Something must have happened to him," she said, her dark

eyes full of silent appeal. "This is so unlike him. He would never let his dinner go to waste, out of courtesy to me if nothing else."

"Smells good," Bassett said, tactlessly sniffing the breeze. He took her gently by the elbow and steered her into the living-room. "We can talk better sitting down."

"His favourite, steak and kidney pie," Mrs. Blundell said mechanically. She gestured towards slippers warming in the grate. Bassett recognized the warning signs: any second now she would be fighting back tears. "This is Sergeant Andy Miller," he said, as she lowered herself on to the edge of the settee.

Andy gave her a friendly smile.

"Do sit down, both of you. I'm probably being very foolish about this—"

"You are familiar with William's habits," Bassett said considerately. "So no more talk of being foolish. How long has he been missing?"

"Since this afternoon. I don't know exactly when. He was here when I went out a little before two o'clock—he hadn't long left you and the Poacher, I believe. I got back around four. He wasn't here and he must have been gone some time because the fire had burnt down. I felt sure he had gone to the Hall, his egg basket and milk jug were missing, too. He has two identical jugs, like that one on the table. I got that out to show the Poacher." A blue enamel jug with a lid. "He goes to the Hall for goat's milk—" A hand fluttered. "But you know that already—"

"His car?" Bassett inquired.

"In the garage."

"So he went on foot as usual. You've been in touch with the Hall, of course."

"He hasn't been there. When I rang up at half past five the housekeeper was about to ring me to ask if she should put the milk and eggs in the fridge till tomorrow."

"Have you spoken to Sir Marcus himself?"

"Oh yes. He organized a search party to scour the grounds. He was on the phone shortly before the Poacher advised me to contact you. They hadn't any news up to then."

"Is anybody ill? Might William have called to see a sick parishioner and stayed on?" Bassett retracted even as he spoke. "You will have phoned around, naturally."

"*Every*body . . ."

"Someone who isn't on the phone?" said Andy.

"He would have got a message to me somehow. Most houses have a neighbour with a telephone, and in an emergency everybody rallies, word would have been got to me, I'm sure."

True. Yet Bassett took up Andy's suggestion. "There could have been a chain reaction, a combination of circumstances where everything went wrong. How long has he been missing —six, seven hours?"

"Yes, it's no time, is it?" Mrs. Blundell said apologetically. "Six hours in daytime wouldn't worry me in the slightest. It's simply that it's dark and he didn't get to his destination."

"You've checked the church? Churchyard?" Bassett said. "The hut?"

"Searched thoroughly by the Poacher," was the reply.

The telephone rang. Mrs. Blundell rushed to answer it; returned saying, "Sir Marcus is on his way—"

"They've found William!" Bassett exclaimed.

"No, no, they haven't. But naturally Sir Marcus feels responsible for him—" Perhaps fearful of divulging her employer's private business, Mrs. Blundell stopped and began again, revealing a little of somebody else's. "His chauffeur has to take his wife to work, she's a nurse on night duty. He's going to drop Sir Marcus off here."

A slammed car door shortly announced Sir Marcus's arrival. Mrs. Blundell went to let him in, while the other two rose to their feet. "Any news?" they heard him say. "Saw the cars outside—" Then, "Blast!"—when something fell with a clatter, followed by "I beg your pardon, Mrs. B. These coats aren't meant to be worn indoors, every breath I take I dislodge something."

"Never mind, nothing broken. We've Mr. Bassett here. He's a retired policeman. And a sergeant . . ."

He was bulky even without the sheepskin coat, had a shock of red hair which his Russian hat seemed unable to keep tamed, a drinker's nose, and a deep booming voice: "Hallo there!" and a practised "Nice to meet you!"—to Andy Miller; "You're the expert! Don't believe we've met!"—to Bassett. "Got you the right way round, I hope." His handshake was powerful, his slightly protuberant grey eyes sincere. An unworldly, not terribly bright man by all accounts, but one you couldn't help liking on sight. "Anything I can do, please say!" Clutching his stiff coat around him, he perched on a hardback chair: safer.

"Your grounds have been searched, I understand, Sir Marcus. Does that include the no man's land by the old Servants' Walk?"

"Sorry—?"

"Reverend Brewerton usually travelled along the Walk and past the midden—"

Midden? Midden? Sir Marcus racked his brains. "Oh! You mean the ice-house mound!"

Bassett allowed himself a tiny inward sigh of satisfaction. Yes, he meant the ice-house.

"I never knew such an invention existed," Bassett said evenly. "Never entered my head, to be honest, till I saw the 'Victorian Kitchen Garden' series on TV. Theirs had a tunnelled entrance to a massive domed underground cave. Yours similar?"

"No tunnel, old man. One opening only."

Drawn, Sir Marcus described the Hall's ice-house as simply a huge egg-shaped chamber, big end below ground, little end above. Hadn't been used though for—oh! nearly a century. He himself had been the last to open it, when he was a boy. He and a couple of cousins. He'd won himself a good old rousting when Cousin James fell in. The ladder down into it disintegrated when James was half way down. They'd had to haul him out by improvised rope-ladder. Smooth-sided, you see, like the inside of an egg, absolutely no possibility of anyone climbing out . . . Used to wind stuff down on a platform, but the ratchet and pinion had long since rusted into disuse . . .

"Funny you should have thought it a midden," Sir Marcus boomed finally. "My chauffeur retained a similar impression. He volunteered to remove the lump—shovel it away and level the ground." He was about to smile, albeit weakly, at the memory, but Bassett's rather sharp "When was this?" swiftly changed his mood.

"When? Not long after he began working for me—"

"And you explained what it actually was?"

"Certainly. I say—!"

But Bassett interrupted. "Excuse me, Sir Marcus." While they had been talking, Jack had appeared in the background, having presumably let himself in via the kitchen. Bassett now took himself and Andy to where Jack was hovering in the space between kitchen and sitting-room. Behind him he heard Sir Marcus say, "Couldn't possibly have fallen in, Mrs. B., cover's on tight as a drum."

A few minutes later Jack and Andy had departed, and Bassett was asking Sir Marcus, "Would you mind telling me what your arrangements were with your chauffeur last weekend?"

Sir Marcus seemed bewildered. "Sorry, old man, we appear to have our wires crossed. I thought you were here because of Will Brewerton—?"

"There just might be a connection with the murder—" Bassett began, almost apologetically.

"Good lord!" A second to sink in, then Sir Marcus's chair creaked a protest as he sat back heavily and slung one corduroy-trousered leg over the other. "Damn it, yes! The man Wilson was in the old graveyard!" His expression became vaguely that of a wounded innocent. "Afraid I don't follow, though. Wait. You want to know what I was doing on Friday; that it?" He remained puzzled but genial.

"You misunderstand," Bassett said. "My fault for not making myself clear. It's Saturday and Sunday I'm curious about, specifically your arrangements with your chauffeur. He drove you to Cheltenham—"

"On Saturday morning, yes. I had a weekend engagement, a reunion of sorts." Sir Marcus paused, took Bassett's silence to mean he expected to hear more, and so supplied it. "I knew Fred was doing a spot of work for Wilson so I suggested we leave early, crack of dawn, to enable him to get back and put in a full day. He was to collect me on Sunday afternoon."

Bassett's eyes narrowed fractionally. "Are you saying the weekend was *pre*-arranged?"

"More or less. A fortnight ago."

"Mind if I ask you what the set-up is?" Bassett said forthrightly. There was no time now for playing games, Fred was due back soon. "Between you and your chauffeur, I mean." He smiled. "You seem to be extraordinarily accommodating. No offence intended."

"None taken." But a frown; which lessened as Mrs. Blundell discreetly withdrew. "Point is, old man"—the booming voice was reduced to a resonant whisper—"I can't really afford a chauffeur, have to make sacrifices elsewhere to pay for him. Damn it, I'd drive meself—but I lost my licence. Mother always said the demon drink'd be the death of me! I told Fred—can't pay fancy wages, that nonsense, but the flat's yours for as long as you want it, and if part-time work comes your way, I'll try and fit my needs in with yours; least I could do. When the Wilson thing came up I told him go ahead, build up a list of contacts, get his work known, he could have a thriving little business by the time I got my licence back. It was working well."

"And you gave Fred prior notice of when you might need him outside of normal working hours."

"Whenever possible, yes."

"Now I am going to have to ask you about Friday night, Sir Marcus. Mind telling me all of it, starting with *why* you phoned Fred at the Pheasant . . ."

Bassett could have driven directly to the Hall by the main drive, but he preferred to avoid any stragglers from the search-party. He therefore parked off-road in North Drive, as he had advised Jack and Andy to do. The Servants' Walk seemed shorter second time round. Soon he saw lights ahead and figures moving about near the top of the mound; Jack's beard made him distinctive. Drawing nearer, he saw Jack lie face down—to talk to someone in the bowels of the earth. Closer still and he extinguished his own flashlight and went in by the light of the rescuers'.

"He's alive," Andy said. Jack looked up and grinned; then called down hoarsely, "Reinforcements, Willy! Soon have you out! Give us a hymn while you're waiting!" Incredibly, a giggle came up from below.

"He can't climb a rope," Jack said seriously. "We wanted him to tie the rope round his waist so's we could haul him up, but that's no go either." Down the hole he called, "I'm telling Bassett it's no wonder the scout movement round here collapsed, Willy! You can't tie a blasted knot! Keep singing!" To Bassett: "Poor devil's too stiff with cold to help himself. No feeling in his fingers. One of us will have to go down for him, unless Sir Marcus has any better ideas—"

"We'll manage without him," Bassett said. "I've left him at the vicarage, asked him to stall Fred. I said I'd give him a tinkle when it was clear for him to leave. I'd as soon leave it like that."

They volunteered an obliging Andy for the job. Twenty minutes later the curate was being restored to the land of the living by Sir Marcus's motherly housekeeper, Jack and Andy were putting the mound back to how they found it, and Bassett was on the telephone.

"Bassett here, Sir Marcus. Not a word! I'm a well-wisher inquiring after the Reverend . . . It's all clear for you to return, William is here, safe. But say nothing to Fred or Mrs. Blundell. I'll give you five minutes, then I'll phone the good lady myself. Oh, and Sir Marcus—please on no account invite Fred in for a nightcap."

Three minutes ticked away. Jack and Andy came in, and wrapped their hands gratefully round the mugs of steaming liquid thrust upon them. They were all in the hot and homely kitchen: "The warmest room in the house!" the jolly housekeeper told them. William was there too, thawing out under blankets on a recliner chair pushed up to the Aga.

Five minutes. "I'll phone Mrs. Blundell now. Will it be in order for me to say William is spending the night here—?"

"I shall be cross if you don't," the housekeeper said goodnaturedly, "I've a bed prepared." The look she gave Willy made it plain, gently, that she would brook no argument.

"Is anyone still out looking for William, by the way?"

She replied no. "I told the last resolute handful we thought Reverend Brewerton had been located but no details were available."

"My advice," Jack enlarged. "I guessed you mightn't want the rescue broadcast."

"You guessed right." Bassett picked up the telephone; dialled. "Mrs. Blundell? Has Sir Marcus left? . . . Good. And good news for you—we've found William. Safe and well . . . Yes, all in one piece. But he's very tired, he'll be staying at the big house tonight. He'll explain everything to you tomorrow . . . Yes. Oh yes. Now, I doubt if concerned parishioners will phone you at this late hour but if the phone does ring will you ignore it? I don't want anyone actually to be *told* the Reverend is safe . . . Yes, it *is* mysterious, isn't it? Please trust me . . . Good night, dear lady . . ."

"*She* was mystified," Andy complained.

"Failsafe," Bassett said. "If you had sent William to a slow death and knew a search-party was out looking for him, wouldn't you be anxious to keep track of progress? If asked, a member of the search-party will say that Willy has been located, no details available. No relief to the attacker there. *Located:* but dead or alive? If, on the other hand, it's the vicarage the would-be killer contacts—imagine the havoc wreaked on the imagination by a phone that refuses to answer . . . We shall see how our guilty one looks in the morning."

He was really speaking to everyone present, but he had not forgotten that Andy Miller was perhaps less informed even than Jack. He must soon get some time alone with the Sergeant; who in the meantime played the part of patient observer.

And continued to do so when Sir Marcus bowled in.

"Thought I'd find you all in here! . . . William!" He swept across and gripped the curate's shoulders warmly. "Good to see you safe and sound!" The voice was hushed and full of unspoken questions. William mumbled something about a day trip to Hell, only thankfully the fires had gone out. They laughed but the scene was quite emotional. "Tell me about it tomorrow, William!" Sir Marcus turned to his housekeeper, nodding amiably to the rest of them in passing. "You've organized a bed—?" And to the others, "You have met my favourite lady? Is the brandy out, Dimple?"

"For medicinal purposes, yes!"

Sir Marcus screwed up his face in mock dismay. "Used to be my nanny and continues to rule me with an iron rod!" He glanced around. "Shouldn't we be somewhere more hospitable, Dimple?" he asked her when she handed him a goblet.

But what could be more hospitable than a homely mansion-size kitchen smelling of fruit, spices, coffee, and home baking? The opinion was voiced and applauded, and a further note of levity was struck when Bassett addressed the housekeeper as Miss Dimple. "My name is Dalrymple, actually," she confided in his ear, simultaneously tinkling a little laugh at Jack Carter's unstoppable grin. "But it was always Dimple even after Master Marc learnt to pronounce my name. He was a very lazy little boy."

"You see how little respect I command!" Sir Marcus remonstrated, though not without pleasure. "Now, what's the gen—er —Bassett?"

"It's a longish story, Sir Marcus. If William feels up to it perhaps we could hear what happened to him first. William . . . ?"

William had set out at around half past two for his slow stroll to the Hall, by way of the Servants' Walk as customary. As the mound came into view he saw Fred Ansen. "Fred appeared to be spreading brambles about near the top of the mound. Spreading, not cutting back . . . I suppose it was because of recent events that I paid somewhat more attention than I would have normally . . . He didn't appear to notice me. I think I stood still . . . Before I had a chance to proclaim myself, there was a shout from the yard, and he shot off. I heard a vehicle drive away—"

"Master Marc going to town," informed the housekeeper.

"I'll come back to that," Bassett said. "Carry on, William."

"When I reached the mound I felt compelled to see what Fred had been up to. I poked about, found shall we say a manhole cover, and decided after some thought that Fred may have been applying camouflage . . . I began shifting the camouflage and found a lifting handle . . . The cover was far too heavy for me to lift, but I managed to wriggle it off eventually; enough for me to have a look in. Which is what I was doing when someone pushed me good and hard from behind . . . A terrifying experience. Fortunately what felt like lumpy cushions softened my fall."

"Did you see any part of the person who pushed you? Foot? Leg?"

"No, it happened so quickly. The lid was back on by the time I landed. Although two or three minutes later I thought rescue was at hand: the cover was being jiggled about. But I saw nothing of my attacker, no. Slits of sunlight. Shadows from moving feet. That's all."

"How many feet?"

"I think only two."

"As you were pushed, did you get a whiff of a smell, a scent—?"

"No . . ."

Bassett then went to where Jack and Andy had put the ropes and other rescue equipment outside the kitchen door; returned carrying a crowbar. "This yours, Jack?"

Andy Miller said, "I fetched that from the garage here."

"Did you use it?"

"Didn't need to," Jack said.

"Yet there is damp soil and leaf mould on the end. Show me where you got it from."

Drops of soil and leaf mould on the garage floor.

"You didn't use it—" To Andy and Jack. "William didn't use it. But someone did."

"Crucial question, Willy," Bassett said when they were back in the house. "What time are we talking about?"

"When I was pushed in? Three o'clock, as near as I can say. I left the vicarage at two-thirty—"

"That's what I thought you said."

"—And the steady walk—I do dawdle—usually takes roughly half an hour."

"It was shortly before three then when you heard a car drive off? I was here half an hour or so earlier and almost exactly the same thing happened—a call from the yard, Fred rushing off. I thought he was going out then—?" Bassett looked at the housekeeper.

"Oh, the master seldom gets off promptly!" she exclaimed.

"Head like a sieve. He's worse than a woman for popping back for this and that. They had a number of false starts."

"True, matter of fact," Sir Marcus said candidly.

"Then I needn't ask you, Willy, if there could be any mistake about who you saw."

"It was definitely Fred. But if he—?" He stopped and sank into a puzzled silence.

Bassett turned to Jack. "You never did catch up with me."

"No." Jack told how while he was searching for tracks after Bassett had left him in the Servants' Walk, he recalled Tod's tale about Gurney, and Fred's discomfort; began putting two and two together, and widened his search with the missing skins in mind. The ice-house? He was unaware of its existence. Bassett asked a further question or two, received answers, then turned once more to Sir Marcus and his housekeeper.

"What time does Mrs. Ansen come off duty in the morning?"

"Six o'clock."

"Does Fred fetch her?"

"Oh yes."

"Thank you. I'm ready now to put you more properly in the picture, Sir Marcus. But I would like a private chat with Sergeant Miller first, if I may presume . . . Will you stay, Jack? I shall probably be asking you all to help in the morning . . ."

Reverend Brewerton stayed too; that is, he was in no hurry to go to bed. Twenty minutes with Andy, followed by a private conversation with Jack, then Bassett joined everyone round the kingsize kitchen table, and over soup and sandwiches, deliciously flavoured, the company was apprised of the sheep-stealing story.

"And the skins are in the ice-house, you say? In plastic sacks? Well I'm damned! Don't understand, though, old man. Why do you require our help?"

"Knowing is one thing, proving another altogether, Sir Marcus," Bassett said slowly. "All we have is circumstantial evidence. What we need is proof. Or a confession. Sometimes the guilty cannot wait to confess, and it is a tremendous relief to them when they do. Sometimes the wrong person confesses. Sometimes . . ." But here Bassett halted and began again. "I'm hoping—we are hoping"—he included Andy—"that our suspect will respond to an audience. It may be quicker and kinder all round in the long run.

"So . . . we have to set the stage, if we could do that now? Then all I shall ask of you tomorrow, Jack, William, Sir Marcus, Miss Dalrymple, is to ignore any lie Andy and I may speak and yourselves—simply tell the truth."

CHAPTER 19

During Bassett's time on the force he was known to colleagues and criminals alike as a decent bloke. An apt description, for Bassett seemed to have been born with an understanding of human frailties many men and women take a lifetime to acquire, some never acquire at all. It was in his nature to feel pity for many of those he helped to bring to justice. This was not to say he was against punishment: you take a life, commit a foul crime, you pay the penalty. But vengeance, vindictiveness, even ridicule, were not, never had been, part of his makeup. Thus when Sir Marcus advised, "We've guest rooms," and Dimple smiled, "You are more than welcome," Bassett nevertheless declined. He had to stay awake. The stage had been set but he himself was far from word-perfect; and he must be if he were to get tomorrow's business over as quickly and painlessly as possible.

Andy Miller elected to go home and return in the morning.

"Is this the best room to be in, Dimple, to hear if Fred gets the car out?" The kitchen was next to the service yard and garage, so to speak.

"Or in here—" Dimple opened a door. What had once been a butler's pantry was now her private daytime parlour. "The big window looks out on the top of the drive. I can switch on an electric fire, but there are only two armchairs."

Two would do nicely. And it was here that Bassett and Jack were to spend most of what remained of the night, while the others went to bed. The two men talked in low tones for a time, then all went quiet. Jack slept. Bassett struck a match. The scent of fruity tobacco drifted out towards the kitchen. A thinking pipe, Mary would have called it, indicative of mental struggle.

Time passed. Jack stirred. Bassett said, "Willy's jug and basket —were they down the hole with him?"

"Dunno. Don't think we looked. Will didn't say they'd been chucked down after him."

"Mm. May be up top, then. Nowhere near the mound or we'd have spotted them. Fancy a breath of freshers?"

A movement of air as they crept into the kitchen. Not a sound as the outer door opened and closed. But puffed-out lips and exaggerated shivers as they were hit by cold crispy night air . . . They had looked at the clock on the way out. Ten minutes to four. Ungodly hour to go a-tramping, as Tod would have put it.

Yet worthwhile: they found the jug and basket in one of the Hall's half-dozen dustbins, buried under a stack of magazines and a parcel, which Bassett opened . . . There was no light on in the Ansen flat, but from the foot of the steps they heard muted radio music. Bassett contemplated tackling Fred now, while the chauffeur was on his own . . .

It was not until five o'clock and Dimple, in dove grey with lace and a china brooch at her neck, was brewing the first of the day's pots of tea that he reached a decision. Rightly or wrongly he must see the Ansens together, reactions might be all-important.

Someone thought to ask: What if they've already planned to make a run for it? Bassett considered this unlikely; but as a precaution Sir Marcus, a naturally early riser, would contrive to be in the vicinity when Fred emerged from the flat: if any luggage was in evidence Fred would be stopped.

Shortly afterwards Sir Marcus left the house. Jack followed, keeping out of sight. Jack returned with newly arrived Andy Miller to announce the Rover was on the move.

"That's it," Bassett said. "Go and get William."

Six-twenty. "Jack Carter you've met. And—er—Mr. Bassett. This is Sergeant Miller—" Sir Marcus boomed conversationally as he ushered Glenda and Fred Ansen into the kitchen.

Bassett wondered again: Should he have seen Fred alone first?

But he need not have worried: Fred dashed off a few anxious glances, then settled into what was clearly a state of resignation.

Not so Glenda, whose puffy eyes and smudged mascara could have been due to the strain of night duty. She hunched her shoulders, drew the collar of her simulated fur coat up around her neck, and said irritably, "Well, I'm sorry—but if you think I'm going to join a search-party for the vicar after I've been working all night, you've got another think coming!"

Granted, cups and saucers littered the draining-board. Granted, the kitchen did resemble a mini distress centre. More than one face *looked* distressed. Yet Fred knew better. "Sit down, Glenda," he said quietly. Sergeant Miller held a chair for her. Throwing a daggers look at her husband, she sat, sideways on to the table, legs crossed inelegantly at the knee, an inch of pink petticoat showing. Sir Marcus leant over to speak to her, then began pouring two cups of tea, oblivious apparently of the tart, "I just hope this isn't going to take all day, that's all!"

"Fred?" Bassett indicated a chair on the opposite side of the table. Fred too sat, said a polite if unsteady thank-you for the tea, then, "This isn't about Reverend Brewerton, is it?" He put the onus on Bassett to reply.

Bassett gave it to him straight. "No, Fred, it isn't."

"It's about sheep-stealing, Mr. Ansen," Andy Miller said. No preamble. "Whose idea was it to use the ruin on Top Hill as a slaughterhouse?"

Glenda Ansen rounded on him. "That's your game, is it! Look —go and persecute someone else. Fred's got enough to contend with without this! As for you"—Bassett—"what's it to do with you? You're retired. Why don't you mind your own business?"

"They know, Glen."

"What?" Glenda glowered at her husband.

"They know."

"They know *nothing.* "

"I'm afraid we do," Bassett said. "We know about the killing shed, the Scout cart, about Derek Wilson's butcher brother—" He broke off on that high note.

"What started it off?" Andy asked Fred. "A wandering sheep knocked down, killed when a wall fell in? You opted to dump the animal by the roadside, victim of a hit-and-run, Derek had a better idea, take it to his butcher brother? And cheers! You're not only helped out of a sticky situation, you also get paid for the meat? Any more where that came from, wink, wink—"

"It wasn't like that—"

"You see?" Glenda demanded. "They're bluffing!"

"What was it like, Fred?" Bassett said. "Tell us."

"They know, Glen." Fred wasn't seeking her support, he was stating a fact. He looked at Bassett. "Does Glenda have to stay?"

" 'Fraid so."

Fred nodded, gripped his teacup with both hands, and sipped slowly without raising his eyes. "I'd never been up there, to the ruin, Smelly's I think it's called," he said at last, pausing momentarily and blinking when Glenda hissed, "You bloody fool!" "Knew nothing about it till I heard Derek talking to the woodman, asking if he knew where to get cheap stone. The woodman said there was a stone cottage falling down on Top Hill, ask the agent if he could demolish it.

"We'd fetched two or three trailer-loads—Derek had already collected some himself—when he said, 'Come and have a dekko at this.' He took me to the outhouse and showed me a pair of dried-up sheepskins and skull bones. 'I've heard sheep go missing off the common now and then,' Derek said, I thought he meant we were going to report the find, but no; those remains must have been there months, maybe years, he said, and they must've stunk at one time—yet obviously nobody had done anything about it, thereby proving something else he'd heard—that nobody came nigh . . . We were both short of spare cash, so why not have a go ourselves. He had an outlet if I could line up the sheep."

Fred went on to tell why they shied away from using conventional transport, how they hit upon the Scout cart he had seen in the summer as an ideal alternative. "Push it cross-country with little or no light . . ." And how the success of their first steal set a pattern. The cart was awkward to handle, but it made far less noise than a motor vehicle, what noise there was only happened when they met rock or stony patches . . . It occurred to Bassett that this was an oblique reference to Tod—that Fred was puzzled by Tod's hearing the cart. But Tod had, which was what counted.

"We started with commonland sheep, they were easy to bag. But one Friday night there were men with shotguns and dogs hanging about, so we turned to farms. We reckoned it could be weeks before the sheep were seriously missed, we'd make a bob or two for Christmas, then lay off for a spell." He stopped and looked at his wife: she stared through him.

"You slipped up with the last four." Andy Miller consulted the notes made with Bassett. "They included three pregnant ewes. The end of your enterprise."

Fred said nothing.

"You knew the farmers wouldn't be slow to miss *them*. Derek Wilson was hopping mad, wasn't he?"

"He wasn't exactly pleased," Fred said. "It meant the finish, as you say. We couldn't risk another steal, that was for sure, the farmers would be on full alert, he said; likely lynch us if they caught us."

Bassett said, "When did Derek tell you the bad news?"

"Monday. Monday night. He phoned me—"

His wife fed him a look, was about to say something, something cutting, but changed her mind.

"Wilson phoned you on Monday night," Andy said, "told you the news, arranged for you to meet on Friday as usual, same rendezvous—by the Scout hut. Not to fetch the cart, to scrub it clean, get rid of telltale stains and dirt. Right?"

"That was the general idea—"

"Friday was also payout night for the previous week's haul. When you discovered your cut was a fraction of the amount you were expecting, you picked a quarrel. Wilson said take it or leave it and walked away. You ran after him. Stabbed him in the back."

"I didn't see him on Friday," Fred protested. "I've said it over and over again. I didn't see him. I admit I was going to, I should have gone on to the Prince William, or phoned him there to sort out a time for meeting, neither of us wanted to hang about. But I never got that far. Bassett knows. He was there when Sir Marcus rang me at the Pheasant. Sir Marcus will tell you I came back here—"

"All the same—" Andy began.

"All the same nothing. I admit to the sheep thefts. No point in trying to deny that. But you're not going to pin Derek's murder on me. No way. I had nothing to do with that."

Bassett had been ambling round the room. He paused at Fred's side. "The skins Derek found. Must have stunk at one time, you said. Not necessarily. If the skins were deposited in the outhouse in cold weather, perishable parts eaten by scavengers before they had time to decompose . . . Nevertheless, two skins. You and Wilson handled ten times that number, planned to handle more. Where did you put your waste, Fred? Where—?"

"They buried it, of course!"

"Ah." Bassett looked at Glenda. "Mrs. Ansen. So you do know about it. Where are the skins buried?" Her mouth tightened stubbornly. She began to shake. Bassett turned. "Fred?"

Glenda Ansen's voice was louder. "Don't, Fred! Fred, don't!" What had at first sounded like a command changed to what seemed like a plea. "Don't, Fred. This is bluff. They can't prove a thing . . . Fred . . ."

And when a wife pleads with her husband . . .

Fred had opened his mouth; closed it again. Now he alternately shook his head, flicked glances at his wife, looked down at his empty cup.

"You didn't actually bury them, did you, Fred. You didn't take a spade and dig a hole. A hole was already dug for you. I refer to the ice-house, a ready-made near-perfect hiding-place. You packed them in plastic sacks and dropped them in there. Yesterday I showed interest in the mound you once thought was a build-up of soil and wanted to level. My interest was casual and innocent, yet it worried you. Worried you sufficiently for you to guess why you were brought in here today. Yesterday you couldn't rest until you had made sure there were no telltale signs, nothing to indicate that the cover was regularly interfered with . . . Reverend Brewerton witnessed your actions. He was curious, discovered the opening, wrestled with the cover, and when it was half off leant over to look in the hole—"

Fred's head came up sharply. He stared. Bassett watched the man's jaw clench, watched him swallow, hard; saw the slow understanding dawning, the horror as he began to realize what was coming next.

"—And you crept up behind him and pushed."

No! Fred's mouth shaped the denial, but no sound came out. He was still staring fixedly at Bassett when Glenda said, with some concern in her voice, "You've found the vicar then? In there? In the ice-house?"

"We've found him," Andy Miller said. Simultaneously Sir Marcus and Bassett exchanged silent signals, Sir Marcus tapped on Dimple's door, and Bassett slid into a position from which he could see both Fred and Glenda Ansen in the same second—all it would require would be a flick of an eye. And it was all done so swiftly neither Fred nor his wife could have been aware of what was going on until the door opened and Dimple stepped into the kitchen accompanied by William.

Bassett wasn't watching them, he was looking at the Ansens. He saw Fred's face begin to light up, Glenda's jaw sag, then freeze.

Her recovery was rapid. "You're all right then, Vicar." She even managed a half-smile. But Bassett knew where he was going now. With a tiny sigh, and avoiding all other eyes, he took out his pipe and waited for Dimple and Willy to be seated.

"Fred could not have pushed Reverend Brewerton into the ice-house," Bassett said, tapping his pipe out into a metal ashtray on the table. "He was out with Sir Marcus at the critical time. True, Fred. When William was sent headlong you weren't within a mile of the estate. But you were—" He swivelled, pointed the stem of his pipe at Jack the Poacher. "Yes, you Jack. You were with me for a short distance along the Servants' Walk. Then you sent me on ahead—"

"I told you the reason. I was looking for tracks."

Bassett nodded. "Find any?"

"None of real significance."

"Didn't think you would. Your aim was to *conceal,* not uncover. The Servants' Walk is the route the cart took with its cargo of skins. Alongside North Drive. You went to pains to point that out. 'This is North Drive,' you said—to mark it as different from the route Tod Arkwright claimed the wheels travelled; which was East Drive and Dickie Debbs's Wood. But from where Tod lives the sounds would seem to be coming from East Drive. Why not? Dickie Debbs's, what's left of it, lies between the two . . . You would never have introduced me to the Servants' Walk, but when William suggested it, you had no option but to show me the way. It was you who saw William being too inquisitive after I had gone. You, Jack, pushed him—"

"And a few hours later helped rescue him?" Jack sneered.

"Again, you'd no option after you overheard Sir Marcus and me talking about the ice-house. But the rescue was accidental. What you'd really planned to do was finish Willy off. Dead or alive hadn't mattered when you pushed him in, he'd be dead of cold by morning anyway—"

"And the rope?" Jack taunted.

"Wasn't to bring William up, it was to get you down inside. The crowbar, which you've since acknowledged you didn't use? You intended to use it on Willy's head—"

"Wrong, Harry. Okay, I was able to lift the cover without the crowbar, but I didn't know that till I got there. I was nowhere near when Willy was pushed in—"

"Yes, you were." Glenda Ansen interrupted with sudden fervour. "I saw you. In among the trees."

"Where were you, Mrs. Ansen?" Bassett inquired.

"At my window."

"Your flat overlooks the Servants' Walk?"

"Yes." Eagerly.

"Therefore also some of the rough area—Dickie Debbs's Wood, so-called?"

"Yes. North Drive, Servants' Walk, woodland—" She tapped with a fist: one, two, three on the table-top.

"Where was Mr. Carter?"

"Among the trees."

"At what time?"

"He was there two-fortyish, and again around three."

"You saw him twice. In the same place?"

"Different places in the trees."

"What was he doing?"

"Bending down and standing up again."

"How can you be so precise about the times?"

"I was baking. Biscuits. They take fifteen minutes to cook. I looked out of the window when I'd put them in the oven, and again just after I took them out. I daren't sit down and settle to anything or I might have forgotten them. My oven timer is broken—"

"Understood. You put the biscuits in the oven, noted the time, measured off the requisite fifteen minutes, and mooched the fifteen minutes away." Bassett smiled, not unkindly. "In fact you don't like to say so, it smacks of nosey-parkering, but when you saw Mr. Carter you ducked back into the room to watch him. You could see him but he could not see you. Am I right?"

"Well, yes. I wondered what he was doing. I didn't watch him the whole time. I had to keep answering the phone—"

"But you did see Mr. Carter at least twice between two-forty and three o'clock?"

Glenda said yes. "Three or four times, in fact."

"They were short phone calls—"

"Oh yes. Seconds. Wrong numbers—"

"Did you see Mr. Carter go to the mound?"

"No, but he could have done. I didn't go back to the window after the biscuits were cooked."

"You can *see* the mound from your window?"

"Oh yes."

Bassett turned to William Brewerton. "Be very careful when

you answer this. At what time were you pushed into the ice-house?"

"Three o'clock, give or take a minute or two."

"You could swear to that?"

"I could."

Silence. Broken by Bassett: "Mrs. Ansen, how did you know the time of Reverend Brewerton's fall?"

She didn't like the question, but once more recovery was quick. "I didn't. I was just telling you the times I saw Jack Carter outside."

"Correct. You were. Miss Dalrymple?"

Dimple spread her hands. "I was only going to say it couldn't have been Jack at three o'clock. He was with me from about ten to—"

Andy Miller said, "Mr. Carter?"

Jack shrugged. "I told the truth about looking for tracks. The foliage on both sides of the Walk was bruised. By, say, the Scout cart we'd just left. I sent Bassett on ahead because I work better alone, no distractions. I scanned the triangle, by which I mean the North Drive to East Drive, the triangular stretch of woodland between them, then came back through Sir Marc's private garden to the service yard—"

"When I saw him," Dimple said, "I called him in to collect a box of fruit to lay down for Christmas. And insisted he stay for a sherry."

Jack addressed Bassett. "I'd seen the Rover leave, so I knew your interview with Fred was over. I assumed you'd be homeward bound, ergo—I let Dimple twist my arm. It was half past three when I finally went."

"Miss Dalrymple?"

"That's right. Absolutely."

"Thank you." Bassett gazed around the room as though counting heads. Andy Miller, notebook in hand. Sir Marcus leaning against the fridge. Jack. Dimple. William. Fred and Glenda. All silent, unmoving, suspended for a moment in time.

CHAPTER 20

"Mrs. Ansen—" Bassett fiddled with his pipe. "I'm going to put it to you that you were mistaken, that it was not Jack—Mr. Carter—you saw."

"I *did* see him." No hesitation. No second thought.

"The first time possibly," Jack conceded.

Bassett let that pass. "You work nights, Mrs. Ansen. Surely you sleep during the day?"

"I'm in bed by seven. Normally," she stressed, reminding everyone that today was an exception. "Six or seven hours do for me. Besides, I catch up on sleep on my nights off."

"Nevertheless, I suggest you were in bed at three o'clock yesterday afternoon, sleeping; that you saw nothing; that you are a romancer, a teller of fairy stories."

"Oh? Then how did I know *he* was in the woods?" She meant Jack, and her voice was savage.

"Because I just now told everybody in this room how we were in the Servants' Walk together, et cetera, et cetera. I don't believe you *can* see the Servants' Walk or the ice-house mound from your window."

"I tell you I can!" And oh! how she hated being contradicted. Eyes flashed hate, teeth grated, and she threw herself about on her chair feverishly. "If you don't believe me—go and see for yourself!"

Bassett surrendered. "I believe you." He closed his eyes, thought: You foolish woman! "Suppose you go and get those biscuits you baked." This time she did hesitate. Then, "I ate them," she said stonily. "Threw them to the birds. Anyway they've gone, what does it matter—!"

But her feet had begun describing agitated circles: her confidence was cracking.

"Don't look at me like that!" she flung at Fred. "They're lying. Making this up as they go along. It's a put-up job, all of it—that's why they brought us here. Just because they found out about the sheep they're going to put the lot on to you. You're the scapegoat, only you're too daft to see it! Liars! That's what they are."

"And liars invariably talk themselves into a corner, Mrs. Ansen," Bassett said levelly. "Jack!" he barked. "Where did you get the crowbar?"

"From the garage here."

"How did you know it was in the garage?"

"I've seen it many times, under the bench."

"Where was it when you fetched it last night?"

"I fetched it," Andy Miller said. "It was standing against the wall just inside the garage."

Fred darted a look in his wife's direction; as swiftly lowered his gaze; too late—all other eyes were now on her. She inferred accusation. "What are you all staring at? I didn't put it there!"

Which was true. Yet Fred's reaction had unsteadied her, that crack in her confidence was widening . . . Bassett wished he could feel sorry for her but he could not; not yet. It was Fred, his expression, more accurately lack of expression, that evoked his sympathy.

What was Fred thinking? Was he waiting for, dreading, the question he knew must come?

Bassett asked it: *"Whereabouts was Reverend Brewerton when you saw him, Mrs. Ansen?"*

"I—he—I—" She floundered wretchedly.

"Did you see Mr. Brewerton?"

She tossed her head angrily. "I don't know. I—yes—no—I don't know. I can't remember. I probably did, yes. But I can't remember—can't remember where—"

"Strange," Bassett murmured. He motioned. Sergeant Miller went and opened a cupboard door, drew out a cardboard box, stood it on the table. Bassett undid the flaps. "Mr. Brewerton's

milk jug . . . egg basket . . . and a parcel of burnt biscuits."
The items were produced one by one.

"In every lie there is an element of truth, Mrs. Ansen. You did
see Mr. Carter at the earlier time of two-forty. You did make
biscuits. You did look out of your window; in fact you looked
out several times while the biscuits were baking. You admitted
—no, you *forced home* the fact that you could see the Servants'
Walk and the mound from your window . . . But *not once* did
you mention seeing Mr. Brewerton. Yet you must have seen
him, the Walk is a long one.

"Would you like to say anything about that? No? Very well
. . . You omitted to mention Mr. Brewerton because, frankly,
you were concentrating on self-preservation. I pointed the finger of suspicion at Mr. Carter—you grasped at the chance. Yes!
Yes! he did it. The Poacher did it! He *was* there, I saw him! . . .
You convinced yourself: He did it! . . . Did what, Mrs. Ansen?
Pushed a man to his death—a certainty if Mr. Brewerton hadn't
been rescued when he was. But why? Why should Mr. Carter
push the vicar to his death? Mr. Brewerton was about to dis-
cover the sheepskins, but why should that bother Mr. Carter?
He wasn't involved with the sheep-stealing. So what motive
could he possibly have for harming Mr. Brewerton?

"You are a very foolish woman. By trying to incriminate Mr.
Carter and so get yourself off the hook, you merely pinned yourself more firmly on to it . . . Because if you *had* seen Mr.
Carter at three o'clock, as you claim to have done, you must also
have seen Mr. Brewerton. You'd have done better to keep quiet.

"The truth is that after that first glimpse of Jack at twenty to
three, it was Mr. Brewerton who held your attention. You saw
your husband at the mound, saw Mr. Brewerton stop and
watch what he was doing. You saw your husband leave. You
were called to the phone more than once, as you said, and each
time you returned to the window, William was that much
nearer to the mound . . . Then he was there. You watched him
find the manhole cover and start struggling to lift it off. When
he looked like succeeding you panicked, dashed down the steps
from your flat and round the back of the garages to creep up on
him from behind . . . He was puffing and panting from exer-

tion; that plus thumps and thuds he made hauling the cover deafened him . . . Your push took him completely by surprise . . . Quickly, with the strength of desperation, you hauled the cover back on. But—damn!—it wouldn't fit flush.

"You couldn't leave it standing proud, you had more than sheepskins to hide now. What to do? Panic rose again. You had seen the struggle Mr. Brewerton had with the cover, what hope had you, a woman, to raise and reposition it. Ah!—the very thing: the crowbar! You used the crowbar to manoeuvre the cover into place.

"The flush of success was shortlived. His milk jug and basket —he'd left them on the path. You took them to a dustbin, not your own, intending to bury them under refuse. There was no refuse, the bins were newly emptied. Panic, panic. Got it! Magazines! You raced up to your flat—gathered up a pile, raced down, packed them round the jug and basket . . . Done. Relief. You threw the crowbar back under the bench—"

"You liar!" Mrs. Ansen hurled abuse at Andy Miller. "I knew I hadn't left it standing up!"

"You did leave it dirty, however," Bassett said, his voice raised a fraction. "There is still damp soil and leaf mould on the floor where you chucked it. As for the biscuits, you forgot them, they burnt. Something that would not have happened if you hadn't left the flat—"

"*All right!*" Glenda Ansen put fingertips to both temples. "Don't go on and on. I did it. I did push you, Vicar. I'm sorry. I didn't think, I just did it—"

Bassett stifled a thankful sigh. He had begun to be tired of the sound of his own voice.

"I did it for him. For Fred. To protect him. I did it for Fred."

"No, Mrs. Ansen, you did it to protect yourself. You were terrified that the finding of the skins might lead to more intensive investigations—and that your alibi for the time of the murder might be brought into question . . . Fred didn't kill Derek Wilson, Mrs. Ansen—you did."

A small involuntary "Oh dear" from Dimple. A look of compassion from William Brewerton. A self-conscious expression on

Sir Marcus's face. And from Fred a moan, a start, a movement, a harrowing "What are you saying? Glenda couldn't have . . ."

"I'm sorry," Bassett said. "Your wife was seen."

"When Derek Wilson left the Prince William on Friday night," Bassett informed Fred, "he gave the Gullivers a message: 'Tell Fred I've gone on, I'll pick up a bucket and spade on the way.' Words to that effect. You never got to the Prince William, therefore you never received the message. But your wife did. She phoned the Prince William, was told Wilson had gone, received the message meant for you . . . You, Mrs. Ansen, understood the meaning of the message. You took the estate van, parked in a dark picnic lay-by, went to the churchyard on foot, and waited for Derek Wilson to turn up . . ."

"I didn't!" The cry was wrenched from Glenda.

"I think you did," Bassett said softly. He placed a hand, a gentle restrainer, on Fred's shoulder. "Isn't it true, Mrs. Ansen, that although Fred knew early in the week the sheep-stealing had come to an end he didn't tell you until Friday, shortly before he went out? Isn't it also true that when he told you the last handout would be small you became angry, thought he was being cheated? . . . After he'd left the flat you thought about it some more, getting angrier and angrier, until—well, we know what happened next, don't we?

"You may, afterwards, have told your husband you'd had it out with Derek, you may even have told him you had struck a blow, I don't know. That could explain why when Fred went to Wyndham and found no Derek, no instructions, he made no attempt to hunt out Davey—and subsequently lied about the weekend arrangements with Sir Marcus; the phone call he went home to wait for may have been one from or regarding Derek, his state of health . . . Perhaps Fred hoped you had only winded Derek—perhaps that was what you yourself hoped. Even came to believe when Saturday and a part of Sunday passed with no news . . .

"Which was why my telling you on Sunday afternoon that Derek had been found that morning was such a shock . . . If Fred was ignorant of your meeting with Derek, his shock may simply have resulted from fear of being found out about the sheep-stealing: My God! Derek dead in the churchyard! By the scout hut? The cart? Had he been seen? Did they *know* . . . ? You, Mrs. Ansen, said the first thing that entered your head: This morning?

"*This* morning. I heard the emphasis on *this*, but I confess that at the time the relevance failed to register. Why should it? No one knew on Sunday afternoon that Derek had died on *Friday*. Except you. If I'd said Derek had been found on Saturday morning, you wouldn't have been so astonished, and would have said something totally different, or nothing at all. Mrs. Ansen . . . ?"

She was sobbing. Quietly sobbing.

"I'm trying to help you now. Please believe me. Did you take the screwdriver with you deliberately?"

After a long time she answered, "No. No. I didn't mean to kill him . . . I thought Fred would be there, and I wanted to back him up, do his arguing for him if necessary, he'd be too weak to have a real go at Derek . . . I thought there'd be mud and boggy grass . . . and I wasn't going to spoil my nice clothes. I grabbed one of Fred's jackets on the way out . . . the screwdriver was in a pocket . . ." She laughed, tearfully, vaguely hysterically. "I'd no wellies either . . . would have had to borrow Fred's . . . but I wore my nursing flatties, .didn't mind ruining them." She looked at her husband, tears streaming down her cheeks. "I was so fed up, Fred. Our whole life down the drain, and you bring me here, to kowtow to *him*. It's so unfair . . .

"Lost his licence because he couldn't control his drinking," she sobbed round-eyed to Bassett. "Fred couldn't afford to drink till he found a friend here. Then even that friend conned him. Fred was going to let him get away with it . . . But not me. I've had enough of being walked on . . . I did do it. I did kill Derek. But I never meant to, honest . . ."

A moment, and Bassett relinquished his hold on Fred's shoulder. "Go to your wife, Fred."

Sir Marcus followed Bassett out. "Came to thank you, old man. Spared my feelings back there—"

"Thanks aren't necessary, Sir Marcus. I merely thought my 'You were seen, Mrs. Ansen' would suffice." Bassett was filling the pipe he had been playing with. He looked tired and drawn in the cold light of morning. "Ice was a bit thin in parts after that anyway."

"Shall I have to make a statement now to the police?" The prospect appeared to trouble Sir Marcus. It turned out that he was worried in case he was accused of withholding evidence.

"But you didn't," Bassett assured him. "The police were of the opinion—as was I—that they were looking at a man's crime. Their questioning on Monday was basically routine. Fred worked for Wilson, therefore Fred's movements on the night of the murder were of concern. Fred was in the clear, he was here with you and Miss Dalrymple. Fred's wife? Fred told them she worked nights and was sleeping. Was she working on Friday night? No, she was here, was Fred's reply. The police took that to mean she was on the premises and, like Fred, had two witnesses to the fact. They saw no necessity to question her personally or at that stage to query her whereabouts with anyone else."

"Yet you picked it up . . ."

"I had an advantage or two, Sir Marcus."

"You're much too modest, you did marvellously! Er—about a statement—"

Bassett smiled. "Doubt if they'll want one. Not unless Mrs. Ansen retracts, which is unlikely."

"Good." The smile was a boyish smile of relief. "Wouldn't like her to think I'd snitched. I'd best go back. I'll attend to a lawyer chappie for them, of course—"

Bassett lit his pipe and watched him go. "Wouldn't like her to think I'd snitched—" like a big schoolboy. And after she'd insulted him too. Bassett smiled to himself.

There was a faint cold drizzle in the air; he was in half a mind to return to the warm Aga-heated kitchen, but reason warned he could be in the way. Reason dictated. Instead he strolled the length of the service yard as far as the archway through which carriages once passed, and gazed upon the scene beyond the arch: chestnut trees and smooth green lawns and distant hazy panoramas. Pity Glenda Ansen hadn't been able to see the beauty all around her . . .

"You did marvellously," Sir Marcus had said. Not really, he thought. "Spared my feelings . . ." Spared hers as well. Hadn't wanted to spell everything out in front of other people. Hadn't wanted to say she had bothered him from the first, not as a participant in the sheep-rustling business—slaughtering wasn't woman's work—but as Meanness driving Fred to thieving and a Nag guiding the hand that struck the fatal blow. Hadn't wanted to explain why he thought it feasible in the end that she had done the murder . . . Hadn't wanted to pile on the agony by repeating what Sir Marcus had said when he asked him why he'd phoned Fred at the Pheasant . . .

Quote: "Matter of fact, I heard a ding-dong of a row going on earlier in the evening, old man. Thought when Fred went out in the middle of it he'd buzzed off to drown his sorrows. Worried me a bit. Already in trouble with the law, wasn't keen on Fred being hungover for our early morning drive. Cutting the tale short, I went ten or fifteen minutes later to have a chat with Glenda. Had a notion she'd be feeling miserable and I'd have an excuse to say come on, let's go and join Fred—keep an eye on him, in other words. I knew Fred disliked her working nights, so was going to ask her if she'd like me to sound out some of my friends for something more amenable . . . Didn't get as far as the door: she was banging about, carrying on the fight all on her lonesome, giving the flat a right old ear-bashing . . . Some time later I heard the van roar away. Glenda on the warpath. Oh hell! I thought, she's going after Fred, poor devil . . . Shortening the tale again, that was when I started phoning, got him back here pronto . . . Discussed his future, said I'd have words in ears, get him fixed up with work more suited to his talents. Tried to give him something hopeful to take home to his wife . . . After midnight when the van came back. Feared there'd be another barney, but no. The last I saw of them, they had their arms round each other."

And of course he had said Glenda was wearing one of Fred's

jackets . . . What had the row been about? "Money, old son, what else? Devil of a nuisance, money. Or lack of it, rather."

A row about money. Which tied in with Bassett's theory of feasibility. Take the dud consignment of sheep. Butcher Paul took possession of the carcases within hours of their being stolen. He wouldn't have waited any length of time before complaining to Derek about the quality, he would have phoned on Monday, Tuesday at the latest—the deal that went wrong. And Derek would not have waited till Friday to pass the bad news to Fred, he would have told him as soon as possible—the call he tried to make, witnessed by Susan. But Fred wouldn't have hurried to tell his wife, poor beggar knew there'd be hell to pay when he did . . .

Nor would Fred have remained angry from Monday to Friday. Truly, Bassett couldn't see Fred being angry at all, only disappointed . . . But Mrs. Ansen? Suppose Fred delayed telling her that this week's handout would be smaller than anticipated. Suppose he didn't tell her till the last moment, Friday evening. Bassett had imagined her chewing it over, getting hotter and hotter . . . "I'll show him! You might be daft enough to let him get away with it, Fred. Not me!"

And it was so. She killed Derek in a fit of temper. Kill once and it's easy to kill again; or at least not to care any more. To cover one murder she thought nothing of attempting another.

Jack appeared at his elbow. "Well done," he said simply. "Mystery solved."

"One mystery solved, Jack." Bassett sucked on a dead pipe, removed it from his mouth, stared at it with disgust, popped it back in, and struck a match; and gazed at his friend through a pitifully thin wisp of smoke. "Still the problem of Jessie's skeleton. Got to lay that ghost to rest."

CHAPTER 21

"Car in North Drive?" Bassett asked gruffly, giving the pipe up as a bad job and tapping it out on a wall. "Keep you company?"

A few paces walked, their strides evenly matched, then Bassett said, "Do you believe your friend Tom Bentley was a deserter, Jack?"

"I downed the first man who ever said it."

"Was that before or after you'd spoken to Winnie?"

"Tom wasn't the type to desert. He couldn't wait to get into uniform. He was keener than I was."

"He left camp with an embarkation leave pass and was never seen again. Could have got cold feet."

"Not Tom." Jack threw a glance. "Spit it out, Harry."

"It's a toughie."

"I'll help you out. What Jessie saw that morning on Wilson's property was wearing army uniform."

Bassett slowed to a stop. He took the envelope of photographs out of his coat and tipped the button out on to a palm. "I found that in Wilson's backyard. A composition button belonging, I think I'm right in saying, to the latter part of the war. They only used these buttons for a year or two."

"What you're really saying," Jack said levelly, "is that Jessie saw the body of Tom Bentley."

"I believe so. I also believe you're right—he was no deserter."

"Because of the uniform."

"Because of the uniform. A deserter usually shed his uniform as fast as he could. So Tom must either have just arrived, or he was on the point of leaving when he died."

"Go on," Jack encouraged.

Bassett continued carefully. "Tom never arrived home, they said. They being his wife, family, friends. I think he did arrive, having walked across the Malverns, hills he knew and loved, thanks to you. Nobody knew he was coming, his visit was to be a surprise for his new wife." His voice died on him. He cleared his throat but was slow to restart. Again Jack took the initiative.

"He found her with another man. Is that what you find hard to say, Harry?"

It had been; but now it was out. "He found her with another man," Bassett echoed Jack. "The two men fought. Tom was killed. They buried his body."

Walking resumed. "Go on," Jack encouraged again.

"The lover," said Bassett, "got the hell out of it, but not before some kind of pact had been made. They were in it together, they'd remain together, till death did them part. Credit to the lover, he could have done a bunk after the war. He didn't, he came back to honour his side of the bargain . . ."

"Keep talking," Jack said.

"In due course Molly Bentley moved in with her mother— the cottage which eventually became The Oaks. But she held on to the tenancy of Wyndham, ostensibly perhaps to have a home waiting should Tom return. Tom had been posted as a deserter, but as far as the village was concerned, he was missing in action —the tale Molly had spread. And scores of women hung on to the possibility that their 'Missing, believed killed' loved ones were still alive somewhere.

"The war ended. Life began returning to normal. In 1947 a young man knocked on Molly's mother's door. On the face of it he was a stranger seeking digs: bed and breakfast. He and Molly fell in love, and six months later were married."

Checking to see that the drizzle had ceased, Bassett brought out the *Gazette* photographs. "He was no stranger." He gave a photograph to Jack. "VE Day celebrations . . . Candid camera shot showing Molly and others dancing on the village green . . . Look at the man gazing at her from the sidelines. The man in uniform."

Jack studied the photograph. "Willoughby."

"Yes. Willoughby. Who was supposed to be a stranger to her

in 1947. It could be argued that she hadn't remembered him—
that on VE Day he was in uniform and most men look vastly
different in civilian dress, and that in any event memories of VE
Day centred more on jubilation than on faces . . . Which
could have applied where villagers were concerned, most
would probably have been hard pressed to recollect all the ser-
vicemen and women invited to join in the fun, but—look—"

He gave Jack another photograph. "In this one Molly has a
bag on her arm. It's distinctive. Looks tinselly. Flower decora-
tion, see? . . . Now—look again at the first photograph—the
bag on the table in front of the serviceman. Same bag. If Molly
wasn't actually with him, she was certainly sharing his table."

"You think he was the lover?"

"Don't you?"

"Just keep talking," said Jack.

"It could be that when Willoughby turned up in 1947 she
recognized him as a man she had met two years before, and
that sealed the new friendship. But then we'd have to ask why
the secrecy? Why not tell someone—Winnie—'Look who's
here? Remember he was at our Victory Party?' . . . I believe
he was the lover. On VE Day he could enjoy a degree of ano-
nymity, other meetings would have had to be clandestine. Until
—maybe his demob. Then he comes a-calling, courts her officially, they pretend to marry, all is cosy."

Bassett held the envelope open, Jack slipped the photographs
inside. "Cosy may not be the right word—" Bassett tapped the
envelope. "These may have had a bearing on their becoming
reclusive. Someone, somewhere, might have souvenir copies;
someone, sometime might take them out and study them too
closely."

"You said they buried Tom. Where?"

"I think Wyndham. By the back steps."

"That's why they stayed . . ."

Bassett nodded. "I think so. It's claimed criminals often return
to the scene of the crime. The Willoughbys daren't leave it.
Molly probably moved in with her mother as much for her own
sake as her mother's. I imagine meeting Tom, so to speak, every
time she stepped outside played on her nerves. But she held on

to the tenancy of Wyndham. It was still hers when the opportunity to buy one of the cottages arose. She chose her mother's, a far better proposition than Wyndham, obviously; and anyhow five years had passed, Tom's disappearance was old news, et cetera. Buy The Oaks—"

"Oaks Cottage it was called in those days."

"Buy Oaks Cottage, keep Wyndham in view, and trust to luck. Luck was on their side: Molly had finally to surrender the key to Wyndham, but subsequent tenants were short-stay, unlikely to do much more than tidy the garden. The Willoughbys may have known beforehand, of course, that this was to happen, making their decision to buy Oaks Cottage that much easier. Or they might always have planned to exhume Tom if necessary . . . Why didn't they move altogether when Molly's mother died? There's your answer—I don't think they dared. While they couldn't stomach living in Wyndham, neither could they bring themselves to move away and consequently live in daily fear of the law knocking on their door. Better to keep Tom in sight . . ." Bassett gestured: a kind of apology. "I'm speculating, Jack. I could have it all arsey-turvey."

Jack was pale under the beard. "Doubt if you're far out, or you wouldn't be saying it. Carry on."

"I repeat, then, luck was with them—until Wilson bought Wyndham. From their landing window they followed the progress of the building alterations—"

"And began sweating," Jack cut in to say, "when they remembered Tom's body had been buried in clay, and could therefore be partially preserved."

"Something like that. They'd be scared anyway, clay or not. When they twigged that an extension was to be added, it became a matter of urgency to move Tom's remains. To do this at a weekend was chancy, but they learnt that Wilson's neighbours were going away. Mr. and Mrs. Glass were the only ones who might have seen them, none of the other cottages overlooked. They'd have kept vigil to make sure Wilson didn't stay the night, waited for the small hours . . ."

"And Jess delivered the milk and nearly caught them."

"Yes. I imagine they were so engrossed they didn't hear the

Land-Rover. Or if they did they didn't anticipate her delivering round the back. They just had time to duck out of sight, daren't even stop to extinguish the lamp. They'd have been as shaken as Jess was. After she fled they finished what they were doing, tidied up, chucking rubble and left-over sub-soil down the well, and in their haste tossed the scaffolding ties away too—they'd had to shift the scaffolding to get at Tom. It was the loose scaffolding that had me gnawing away after Jessie told her story. Why was it loose? Why had the earth underneath been disturbed? At one stage I wondered if Tom had been brought down from Smelly's for re-burial under concrete—" Bassett waved that to the wind with a taut hand. "Jessie related the tale of her fright only to Jan and me. It was the Willoughbys—Molly Willoughby—who started the Hallowe'en joke idea, to ensure that Jess wouldn't be taken too seriously.

"And to be honest it would probably have worked if they hadn't been careless with the scaffolding. And if Derek Wilson hadn't been killed."

Both men came to a standstill. "Did you ever have me tabbed as the lover?" Jack asked.

"Once. Briefly." Their eyes met. "You used to be fond of her."

"Winnie told you."

"She told me about three children: two boys and a girl—"

"Winnie's a romantic."

"Aren't we all, deep down?"

Jack the Poacher peered beyond—far beyond—Bassett's shoulder; and back at Bassett. "What happens to kids, Harry?"

"The cliché—they grow into people."

They smiled at each other; walked on. "You've made some sense of things that made less sense to me as I grew older," Jack said. "Why Molly stayed here for one, when she seemed at variance with everybody. I thought: Perhaps her parents' graves . . . That was a long time ago, though. I stopped thinking about it."

"Did you never suspect . . . ?"

"In retrospect maybe I did suspect something, though I couldn't have told you what. At the time? We are very naïve when young. Some of us. When I came home after the war I thought she was a widow and, in plain English, I knew she had always preferred me even though it was Tom she married. I let her know how I felt about her, no more than that, I was as cut up about Tom as I thought she was . . . When she told me to get lost I was hurt, don't mind admitting it. Then Winnie explained how Tom was a possible deserter and, well, I understood. You see, Molly knew I'd never move in without a wedding ring. Laughable nowadays, but then—?" Jack shrugged off a small grin. "Again, it hurt that she hadn't taken me into her confidence; but that also I understood: she wanted to prevent me from learning of Tom's disgrace, was how I saw it. It amounted to the same: if I was told Tom was alive, I would do the honourable thing. Molly knew that, so she said nothing. I got the short sharp shock treatment—and admired her for it. I did try to see her again, naturally, but having the door slammed in your face can happen once too often . . ." Another shrug. "I also admired her and cursed myself for being an old-fashioned fool when she set up house with Willoughby. I knew they couldn't be married."

"Not then at any rate."

"You asked if I suspected," Jack said then. "Suspected what?" There was a hint of bitterness and sorrow in the question. "Yes, I heard, and in the end was forced to accept as true, that she'd started playing around the minute Tom's back was turned. If I'm honest, it was that—not the door slammed in my face—that finally stopped me going to her. Know why?" The bearded chin thrust outwards: a touch of pride, a touch of shyness. "My ma and pa . . . Yep. My ma had a hell of a life one way and another with my pa, yet she was faithful to him till the day she died; and he to her. Those were the principles on which I was brought up. Good old-fashioned love and loyalty."

"It's still around, Jack," Bassett murmured.

"I'm sure it is." And in a different voice: "Did I ever consider the other—murder? No. What did cross my mind was that if Tom did desert it wasn't from cowardice, it was because of Molly. Yes . . . that did cross my mind. And I wouldn't have been surprised to look up one day to see Tom standing there. In the early days, that is. Anyhow, thanks for telling me . . ."

"Don't thank me yet," Bassett said. "I want your advice. I've just told you what I intend telling them . . . Correction. What I *did* intend telling them. Afterwards—what they did about it would be up to them. Now I'm not sure I want to say anything. They've spent forty years in a prison of their own making; a very beautiful prison physically but a prison nevertheless. They are old now, and they have only their home and each other . . . a strange sort of love, but real, I think. They are together in their solitariness. Do I have the right, Jack—does anybody have the right to try them all over again?"

They both fell silent. "That well in Wilson's yard," Jack said suddenly. "Christ!" He came to an abrupt halt, running a hand over his face, disfiguring it. "You found a button—!"

"Nowhere near the well," Bassett replied to Jack's pained eyes.

"Where is Tom now, then?"

"I think . . ." Bassett began. Yes, yes; it had to be. "The Willoughbys have a bed of newly planted roses, Jack. One of the roses, I noticed, is called Peace . . ."

Their cars were in sight. Neither man spoke as feet scuffed gravel for the last few paces. Then they both spoke together: "Sun's coming out!" and laughed.

"Come for a meal on Sunday," Jack said.

Bassett: "I'd like that."

"One o'clock?"

Bassett said he'd be there. "Only one problem." He rubbed his nose with a knuckle. "Don't know where you live."

"You don't!" Jack exploded softly. "And you call yourself a detective!"

Bassett flicked an eyebrow. "Retired," he said with a grin.

Grin returned. "The Oast House—"

"The one with the lake? The bird sanctuary? Good grief!"

"If you could see your face!" Jack said mirthfully. "You had me living in something like Smelly's only roofed, and having to chip ice off a water-butt for a wash in the winter—"

"Just never heard you talk about your home."

"Never heard you talk about yours either. Coppers don't. Nor do Intelligence. Yep. That used to be my game." They grinned at each other. "There's another reason . . . Keep a secret? I earned the Poacher tag all those years ago. Now it earns me jam to put on my pension bread. Yep again! It's my pen name. I write. Country stuff. But keep it quiet. Don't want my old pals here to know, it'd spoil everything. They'd stop behaving naturally in my presence, conversations would lose spontaneity, and my country tales would soon lack—dare I say it?—innocence."

Bassett was, as they say, tickled pink. "None of them's guessed?"

"I've got away with it so far . . . Be on time on Sunday," Jack said, unlocking his car door.

"Jack—? Are you married? Do I bring flowers for your wife?"

Jack winked. "May give it a try one day soon. Helen Geeson. You know her. If she'll have me."

"Oh, she'll have you," Bassett mused aloud as he watched Jack drive away . . . It wasn't Bassett Helen had been interested in . . . those visits . . . it was Jack. More accurately perhaps, what Bassett might have been finding out about Jack.

Never mind, he'd enjoyed the flattery. He raised his eyes heavenwards. "I was only window-shopping anyway, Mary."

If she heard she'd laugh, remembering a private joke.

About the Author

Pat Burden was born in Birmingham, England, the eldest of seven children. She has been a nurse, a dental nurse, and a secretary, has worked in public relations, and for British Rail, and a national bus company. She loves to travel, and in the sixties took off with her husband, Land-Rover, and tent overland to Australia, where among other adventures she cleared virgin bush with ax, machete, and rope, and sweated in a laundry in subtropical Queensland.

She now lives in an isolated cottage in Herefordshire, England, with her husband and their Labrador. When not writing she enjoys reading, cooking, embroidery, and walking. *Screaming Bones* is her first novel.